CW01163097

AZALEA AND I
ON THE ROAD

RM HOWE

Copyright © 2024 by RM Howe

Paperback: 978-1-964744-75-9
Hardcover: 978-1-965632-70-3
eBook: 978-1-964744-76-6
Library of Congress Control Number: 2024915901

All rights reserved. No part of this publication may be reproduced, distributed, or transmitted in any form or by any electronic or mechanical means, without the prior written permission of the publisher, except in the case of brief quotations embodied in critical reviews and certain other noncommercial uses permitted by copyright law.

This Book is a work of fiction. Names, characters, places, and incidents either are the product of the author's imagination or are used fictitiously. Any resemblance to actual persons, living or dead, events, or locales is entirely coincidental.

Ordering Information:

Prime Seven Media
518 Landmann St.
Tomah City, WI 54660

Printed in the United States of America

TABLE OF CONTENTS

Chapter 1:   LONDON 1
                     In which Barbara is invited to become a
                     Responsible Young Professional 1

Chapter 2:   BELGIUM & BEYOND 13
                     In which Babs gathers first impressions
                     and Azalea's charm works magic 13

Chapter 3:   HEIDELBERG 39
                     Introducing Angelique ~ the plot thickens 39

Chapter 4:   SALZBURG 71
                     In which Hyena Face makes an appearance
                     and Reverend Burnett faces a crisis 71

Chapter 5:   THE ALPS 105
                     A Dreadful Accident! 105

Chapter 6:   SLOVENIA 117
                     A Romance in the making 117

Chapter 7:   STILL IN SLOVENIA 141
                     Cliffhanger! 141

Chapter 8:	SPLIT, CROATIA 165
	Sparkling Seas and Dreadful Danger 165
Chapter 9:	MORE CROATIA.. 177
	A murder is discovered and Gareth faces arrest..... 177
Chapter 10:	FAREWELL TO CROATIA................................... 192
	In which Uncle Charles joins the team 192
Chapter 11:	VENICE... 224
	In which Barbara proves herself and Gareth saves the day 224
EPILOGUE	*Future Bound* 262

CHAPTER ONE

LONDON

In which Barbara is invited to become a Responsible Young Professional

'You'll fly across the channel to Brussels where you join the coach for Heidelberg and Salzburg. Then across Austria to Croatia, where you travel south as far as Split. You return through Venice, Paris – and so on. It's very good value for money. I just want a tourist's eye view.'

At this point in my life the trip was an inconvenience, but things don't always turn out as you think they will.

Uncle Charles smiled craftily and added, 'I'll throw spending money in too, as well as all expenses. Will £1000 do?'

That got my attention – a small fortune for the starving, newly-qualified student.

'Surely you'll have a job to spend all that much in two weeks? All food and excursions are covered. There'd only be coffee and so on, unless you've acquired a taste for something stronger at uni?'

'No,' I answered his last question first. 'Well, except for a good bottle of plonk. Sometimes a brandy after a meal, or ...' I stopped as I caught Uncle Charles looking at me quizzically. 'Er ... I would treat the spending money with respect. I'd rather bring most of it home and put it into my savings account.'

He looked pleased. 'Yes, and as you are joining the firm soon, Barbara ... there'll be a good salary. This is an extra.' The fact that Uncle Charles had directed me specifically to come to his flat and not the office had intrigued me. I'd even dressed up for the occasion, aiming for the Responsible Young Professional look as he'd handed over some autonomy in the business. And the promised money that went with it. I had spent most holidays from uni learning the ropes of Uncle Charles's travel business.

'Sooo, Europe in Springtime,' I said wryly. This wasn't exactly what I had expected. My mother's brother, Charles Madden, had raised me after my parents separated in an uncomfortable divorce. A confirmed bachelor with severe commitment phobia, Uncle Charles is married to his business, Madden's Magic Carpet Tours, which he built himself, from the ground up. You would never guess that a reserved child, small and too quiet for her age, would take his notice, but he became my refuge, providing relief from my parents' fighting. He got me out of the house whenever he could, to ride along when he took out his sightseeing tours, or if he had time, to take me to the zoo or cinema. It was heaven. But there came a point when, still upset by my parents' constant squabbling, I began to booby trap things around the house, a form of childish retribution to make them stop. The child psychologist announced these antics as the catch-all Cry for Attention. In any event, the only sorts of booby traps I could organise only added further aggravation to the situation. In the end I was temporarily placed with Uncle Charles until home life settled down once more. He knew I needed someone to consider my feelings, and do what was best for a little girl in my situation. After my parents separated and my mother was busily auditioning for Husband No 2 it subtly became understood that I was better off with him. A fact that Charles made very plain to my mother. She gave no resistance and I was happily settled, safe in Charles Madden's secure, luxurious world in London. I did have to change schools, and an au pair named Becky was hired immediately to oversee the basic motherly duties, starting with fitting me out in new school clothes and practically a whole new wardrobe. What should have been a fun afternoon on our first day together shopping turned into a very frightening experience that still makes me shiver to think of it. Nervous in her new duties and barely more than a girl herself, Becky failed to notice that I was not keeping up as well as I should. Honestly, I was dragging my nine- year-old feet a bit. It was just as we rose to the second level on the escalator that I noticed an enormous freight lift, doors standing wide open. I slipped off to investigate, leaving Becky chattering away to herself, never realising I had disappeared. Until she heard my screams.

I had been taken by surprise to see the lift filled with mannequins, standing on pedestals like so many life-sized Barbie dolls, or even – to my child's mind – like zombies. They would keep coming back to haunt me over the years with their gleaming, evil smiles.

I had gone on screaming until Becky came running . She held my hand very tightly after that.

But then, the worst was over. I worked very hard to excel at school and go to university early. I was the youngest student in my undergraduate course of Travel Management and Tourism combined with Languages. My compulsory one year abroad had been in Spain, which had been a wonderful cultural experience. Being based in Barcelona had opened up a whole new 'language' for me, being so different from what I had studied as 'perfect Spanish' Castellano.

Uncle Charles made our home life fun. I suspect his rare dips into the world of motherly females were for my benefit, attempts at providing the requisite female. Women were easily drawn to his charm and his suave, good looks. He was fifty-two but still had the ability to turn female heads, which always amused me to watch. Aside from school, my life with Charles was really a very happy and glamorous one. He combined child-rearing with his workaholic philosophy, and ended up raising a niece with a taste for exotic travel, who showed a flair for languages like her linguist father and who longed to join Uncle Charles's specialist coach holiday firm, for foreign travel only – no such thing as mundane UK travel for him.

'Will they all be old?' I hadn't yet been on one of Uncle's tours …

Not exactly the type of responsibility I had hoped for but maybe it was a test or something.

'A mixed bag in the main. These days most people want to fly, but there's a new breed who want coach trips again. Before you come into the firm and get known, I want you to be a passenger on as many tours as possible: the Near and Far East, the Med, South America … you name it. It's no use my going. Everything would be laid on for me and I wouldn't be able to judge what the clients were getting. Your name is different from mine, and you've been away at uni for three years. We'll be able to use you until you're spotted – as you will be sooner or later.'

I wavered. 'Isn't it a bit undignified to snoop?'

Uncle Charles's eyes shone very blue in his sunburned face (he sometimes went on his own tours for fun). 'I don't look at it that way. I'm protecting my clients. I love my clients. They've put me where I am today.'

'They and you together.' I added, thinking of his business acumen. I had a hunch there was something more behind this apparently innocent jaunt. It merited a probe.

'With your languages,' he said persuasively, 'you're the right one for the job.'

I had an idea. 'Just a minute. Could I have Azalea? Azalea Dunbar. You know her as Lea. I think I could get her to come.'

'That'll be nice for you,' he said dryly. 'I can see you are going to be a cool-headed business type – an asset to the firm. OK, Lea is on the books – for this first trip at least.'

Then I pounced and looking him straight in the eye, I said, 'Come on. There's something more to it than a simple vetting of the arrangements.'

A look of bafflement crossed his strong features. 'I'm not sure what you mean.'

'There must be something. Why this tour? Why not the Far East or Asian ones? They're relatively new. Across Europe to Croatia must be tried and tested, surely? It was almost one of the first you ever set up.'

'It was.' He grinned happily before his face faded into a frown. 'No, it's got to be this one first.' When he saw the 'why' framing on my lips he added hurriedly, 'Just a feeling.'

'You never do anything without a good reason.'

'All right. It's nothing more than this. At the promotional cocktail party we had last month I asked one of my best clients if she had enjoyed the tour she had been on. This tour. She's been just about everywhere and is starting all over again since she became a widow. Anyway, she didn't reply straight away – and then the oddest look crossed her face. Terribly afraid, as if she had seen a ghost. Only for an instant but I caught it.'

'Was she mugged or something? Not that it would be your fault and certainly no reason not to talk about it. In fact, just the kind of thing you would mention.'

'I asked her that. The obvious, and she said no, but I still got the impression that something had happened to her. I could see her shuddering inwardly at some picture in her mind. And then she said she'd had a wonderful time and would be coming in to the office to book to Australia any day soon. '

'At least she hasn't gone over to some other firm.'

'No.' He stared at me, troubled. 'It may be nothing to do with the tour. It might have been a private matter. I know other travel firms have had trouble with thieving and things of that nature but she just wouldn't say anything. Annoying and worrying. I don't know what it is, but I've got this bee in my bonnet. '

'And you'd rather it made honey than gave you a sting!

I understand. Europe it is then. Tell me again where we are going.'

He leafed through the latest brochure and placed it where I could follow his pointing finger. 'You fly across the channel to Brussels where you join the coach for Heidelberg and Salzburg. Then across Austria through the former Yugoslavia, where you travel south as far as Split. You return through Venice, Paris etc. It's very good value for my clients. I just want a tourist's eye view.'

'A tourist eye view with a difference. Are the couriers and drivers your own staff?'

'No. We use local tour and coach drivers, depending on circumstances and deals negotiated. They join the tour at Brussels. This is where your degree in languages will come in useful. You can listen to private conversations and people will assume you don't understand.'

I had studied Spanish, but had added Italian, German, and French in my own time. It all came so easily to me.

'You can keep your eyes and ears open. Under our contract we have to accept what is offered from my European partners. This usually works well, but there's no harm in doing an extra check and keeping an open mind. Any suggestions for improvement gratefully accepted.'

'Suppose the tour is perfect? I mean, suppose I have no criticisms?'

'Then that'll be fine. You'll have had a good holiday at least.'

'Shall I keep a log?'

'Good idea but don't make it obvious. There are always people working little price scams, and they might not like it if they think you are on to them.'

' How do you want me to get in touch with you in a hurry if I have to? '

'Try the office landline first. I won't be at home much but will always have my mobile and I'll be looking out for messages. So, yes – certainly keep me posted as you go along.'

'All right. How do I get my tickets?'

'Through any travel agent. Not our main office.' He tapped the brochure. 'Tour No. 78E. 'E' for Europe. Don't draw attention to yourself at any time. It could be embarrassing to everyone concerned. I'm not even sure you should tell your friend what you're up to.'

'Azalea? She'll think I've lost my mind, going on a coach trip round Europe. I'll have to explain something to her.'

He looked so hurt that I kissed his cheek out of guilt. 'We'll love it once we've got used to it. It's a marvellous way to start my job in your firm. Madden's Magic Carpet Tours encompasses the globe. Something to suit all tastes.' I sounded like one of his adverts. 'To be honest, I could never see myself sitting for long at a desk. This end of the business will suit me fine.' I looked him squarely in the eye and said, 'Could we maybe do the Far East next time, eh?' 'All right, my little jet setter. I'll see what I can do! Then there's the new one in South America I've just negotiated. Unless I keep that for myself – even if I do get the preferential treatment.' His eyes gleamed. 'So what's with the new tan?'

'Nothing the junior partner need worry about. Only a fun holiday with a passing acquaintance. Now – let's get going.'

It was enjoyable listening to him talk, and my pulse quickened. Even on a routine run like this there would be possibilities for excitement and, I hoped, adventure. There'd also be the chance to practise the languages I had studied, mainly on his recommendation.

For the next few minutes Charles did all he could to put me in the picture, gave me a cheque, and showed me to the door with a touch of the Olde Worlde courtesy I appreciated after four years of the casual manners at uni.

What would Azalea think? We had just agreed that a short spell in Paris was indicated to get us into the mood for tackling our careers. Anyway, Tour 78E touched Paris.

Only briefly, it's true, but not an opportunity to be passed over!

When I rang her up Azalea was in, which made a nice change.

'Lea, it's me, Barbara.'

'Of course.' She sounded as abstract as some of her paintings.

'How would you like to go to Croatia Friday next?'

'Mm? Just give me time to phone my fairy godmother for funds.'

'Azalea, it's all expenses paid.'

'What's the catch?' She was suddenly paying attention.

'My uncle Charles is going to treat us. All expenses paid.'

'Did you say all expenses?'

'I did. Plus a bonus.' I wondered if I should give her some of the thousand pounds.

I decided I might. There again, I might not.

'How old is Uncle Charles?'

'How ...? Oh, he isn't going with us. He wants us to go in his place.'

'I see.' She didn't sound as if she did.

'He's Charles Madden, of Madden's Magic Carpet Tours. His tours go all over the globe. You know, the firm I hope to join. Am joining!' I giggled. I could imagine the looked of dawning awareness to accompany the soft groan she stifled.

'That Uncle Charles!' she said politely. 'Can I take my sketching book?'

'Naturally. I'll take my camera too. It might come in useful when you want to fill in some of the detail.'

'Do you mind? Actually I shall be glad to leave this country for a week or two. It's getting a bit hot for me. I was just being my usual, kind self, but he seems to have misinterpreted my interest.'

I grinned. It had always been a mystery to me why Azalea was so constantly besieged by men. Men of all ages, shapes and sizes. No one could call her beautiful, for none of her features matched, though the whole effect was endearing. Her front teeth were dazzling white and her smile had a radiance devastating in its effect. Her figure was almost none existent but willowy, and she was always throwing on clothes which did little for her except keep her warm. She also had a facility for standing as if every bone were out of its socket. Rarely visiting a hairdresser, she chose to chop off her soft, thick, blonde curly tresses, when necessary, in the bathroom, with nail scissors. The result was as interesting, and as beautifully stunning, as one of her paintings.

'Azalea, one word. Don't mention to anyone about my being related to the head of the firm.'

'Not if you say so. I was told in my horoscope this week that I was in for a surprise,' she confided, apropos of nothing. 'When shall I see you?'

'I'll let you know. I have to apply for the tickets now. That's why I rang. I had to know if I was to book for you too.'

'Please. And thank you.' She still sounded surprised. Guessing she was about to ring off, I said hastily, 'What about clothes?'

'Does it matter?' She sounded even more surprised, so I let her go, making a mental note to pack a couple of dresses for her. We were much the same size and height veering towards tall, if not exactly the same shape (Azalea doesn't get all the attention) . She was even more hard-up for cash than I was, spending most of her spare money on painting materials. We had been at uni together but she had got further and further away from her first subject, concentrating on the art course instead. Finally, a commission from a publisher to illustrate a children's book had decided her that henceforth she would dedicate herself to Art. So it looked as if she would continue to be poor.

My first move was to get the tickets. After depositing Uncle Charles's cheque in the bank, I backtracked to a travel agency and leafed through a few brochures as though I had not made up my mind. After about five minutes of sales talk I let the agent think he had persuaded me to book Magic Carpet Tours, trip No.78 HOE. I idly wondered when the 'HO' had been added to the 'E' but didn't pursue it, and let the agent make two reservations on the spot.

I saw Azalea only briefly before we met at the airport for the late flight over the channel: she had been down to Devon to see her godparents in the hope of scraping up a little cash. The coast air was fresh and clean in the spring air.

I watched her from the car park through the huge, glass wall of the terminal. Three men escorted her from a sports car in which they had all been squashed. They were carrying between them what appeared to be her luggage, a shoulder bag on which the strap was already broken, a hold-all which bulged so much the zip would not close at one end, and a sketching block strapped to the back of a leather briefcase.

Azalea herself looked enchanting, despite unmanageable hair and suspiciously smudged lipstick. I saw her before she saw me and, able to enjoy her royal (if very late) progress down the road from Visitor Parking to the airport entrance, was treated to a downward, pungent sniff that arrived slightly ahead of her approach.

'Sorry about the smell, Babs,' she called as soon as she saw me. 'My strap broke and the bottle smashed. I'm absolutely stinking.'

'What bottle?' I asked, eying the young men who were looking at her as fondly as if they had invented her.

'Brandy. I thought we might celebrate. Isn't it a shame? Actually it was a gift.' She introduced the men to me, following it up with, 'Don't try to remember their names. They gave me a lift. Just ships that pass in the night.'

'Good sailing,' I told them as the 'meet and greet' tour guide hurried us through to the departure lounge to board the plane, having to explain to the staff that we were not drunk. We were too late for the VIP departure lounge where we could have met some of our fellow travellers. Luckily our seats were at the rear, so we hadn't got to pass too many people from the back steps, but even so, they sniffed the air in startled wonderment. One man passed the remark that it must have been quite a party.

'Cherry brandy,' beamed Lea. 'I haven't drunk it. Just bathed in it.'

I made the acquaintance of several of our fellow passengers bound for the tour. An elderly couple close by us – the Reverend and Mrs Adam Burnett – they smiled sympathetically. I gave them a good mark.

'Accident?' he asked above the toning-up hum of the plane.

'A cheap bag.' Azalea showed him the strap which had broken and then turned to wave frantically at her three young men through the porthole as the plane began to taxi down the runway. The airport was a very small-time affair, the viewing window so close to the tarmac you could almost hear one of them sighing as we taxied past. They looked after her with expressions ranging from the sadly fond to the plain exasperated. I had the feeling the trip was going to be entertaining. Reverend Burnett showed a practical sympathy, producing some treasury tags. With several of these he made a temporary repair of the shoulder bag.

'Actually, most of the brandy went on my legs,' Azalea explained. 'If I could wash them ...' The atmosphere in the confined space of the plane became less oppressive as she disappeared into the toilet as soon as was allowed. It was astonishing the amount of information she obtained on the way there and back; she seemed to have exchanged notes with three people and was on nodding terms with three more. Expressions relaxed and smiles dawned when faces were turned in her direction. I could see Azalea was going to be invaluable to me; her artless friendliness would disarm anyone, surely!

As I examined this thought, my heart jolted, and began to race. Perhaps I was letting myself in for more than I had bargained. If there happened to be any persons engaged in practices harmful to Magic Carpet Tours and gainful to themselves, they wouldn't take kindly to anyone curtailing their activities.

CHAPTER TWO
BELGIUM & BEYOND

In which Babs gathers first impressions and Azalea's charm works magic

Outside a very foggy Brussels Airport ('Welcome to Europe') at an unspeakable hour, we waited for the coach which was be ours for the next fourteen days. There were quite a few people milling around by the entrance, and I wondered if they were also on Tour 78 HOE ('Highlights of Europe'). There were crowds of people pushing past, through, and around us, going in and out of the terminal as briskly as if it were midday. Buses and taxis disgorged their passengers and sped off from the kerb where we waited. We were just about to duck back inside the terminal to get out of the choking exhaust fumes and the damp, when a clump of early travellers – or late, depending on how you looked at it – suddenly scuttled out of the way, and our coach pushed through the fog, a knight in shining, chrome armour. The Madden's Magic Carpet Tours banner sent a wave of relief over both of us.

'Yes! We're saved,' Azalea said as we queued to climb aboard, many of our fellows falling in quickly, ahead and behind us. The driver had a decidedly smarmy smile for everyone, but let his eyes linger a little too long on a shapely, well-dressed woman just ahead of me. She paused on the step to draw her coat closed, stumbling as she tried to keep from dropping hand luggage and various items. I nearly went sprawling into her. Startled by the commotion, her husband took in the situation immediately and gave the driver a warning look as he helped us regain our footing.

The coach was much more luxurious than I had expected, and I felt a pang of guilt for whining at my uncle about taking the tour. It was in continental style with a door at either side, though at opposite ends of the vehicle. The seats could be altered to accommodate various positions and were thick and wide. Very comfortable. There were toilet facilities, and a tiny pantry for the Tour Manager. Everything looked gleaming and new. A small red-haired person, in a smart uniform which looked as if it had been stitched on her, was charming and eager to please. As she helped to put my small case on a rack over the seat about halfway down the coach (larger pieces went in a hold at the side) she said, 'Welcome to Europe. My name is Mimi. If I can help you in any way, don't hesitate to ask me.'

'What good English you speak!' Azalea said, wide-eyed. Her own linguistic accomplishments included school French and even less German.

Mimi grinned charmingly. 'It's not surprising. I am English. '

'Are you going to be with us the whole tour?' I asked.

'No. Only as far as Salzburg. This is my first run on this route. Someone fell ill. I've been on the Swiss tours mostly.'

'Mimi?' queried Azalea. 'La Boheme?''

'Well, actually it's Monica. I thought 'Mimi' sounded more romantic.'

'We'll keep the secret,' I said, deciding I could cross Mimi off the list of fiddlers. Of course, first impressions could be deceiving but I didn't think so in this case.

The coach was filling up now.

'Have you all got your passports handy? You'll need them to change money and at the hotels, of course.'

Seating myself rather hurriedly – for Azalea, had let her holdall fall on my head – I watched the sleepy holiday makers file into the seats allocated to them by the courier as she consulted her list. The driver, who was busy putting luggage in the hold, was not yet with us. When there were still ten seats vacant, I caught Mimi as she flashed by.

'Are there others joining us later?'

'No, we're all here. It's early in the season. Nice not to be filled right up, I always think.'

I counted heads: twenty of us. Perhaps it would not be too difficult to sort them out presently. Azalea was talking over her shoulder to someone behind, who answered languidly, 'I'm glad there's no night travel. It's so tiring, even with these recliner seats.'

Azalea agreed enthusiastically, though I doubt if she had ever sat up all night in a coach in her life. When I was able, I swivelled my head round at the two women in the seat behind us. Azalea made the introductions.

'I met them on the plane.' They'd obviously been charmed by Azalea's friendly air. The elder of the two volunteered, 'I'm Pansy Watford – and this is my sister, Marguerite.'

'Call me Daisy,' the younger one said ingenuously. With her red hair, she was a more highly-coloured version of her sister, who had faded to pepper-and-salt, but she was not as self-assured in her manner. There might have been ten years between them. What intrigued us was that Pansy treated the younger Daisy as if she were very young and vulnerable – yet she looked all of forty and therefore capable of taking care of herself. Maybe she enjoyed feeling young, and found it less stressful to defer to her sister all the time!

I was so busy watching everyone that I suppose Azalea noticed, for she said presently, 'What's eating you? Do you suspect there's a foreign spy on board? Or have you secret plans to deliver to the Prime Minister, holidaying incognito in Switzerland?'

Alarmed at being discovered, I turned back to her, eyes darting to the other passengers. 'Does it show? I don't think we're going to Switzerland.' Did she really think there was a spy on board? Then I realised she was joking but still inquisitive.

'Is Uncle Charles expecting you to work at it all the way across Europe? You're going to be exhausted.'

'I'll tell you later.' Though Charles had advised me not to reveal the reason for my trip, Azalea had been more perceptive than I'd realised. Besides, she might be more use to me if she knew my difficulties.

Then she relaxed and I saw the reason: a young man further along the coach had stood up to get some object from his bag and was glancing in our direction. In a leisurely way he looked us over, his grey eyes steady, and for a moment I felt a stab of envy. He would be sure to devote himself to Azalea for the rest of the holiday. All the unattached, and some of the attached, would follow suit, unless they were on different wavelengths. I decided to start the log in my new, fat notebook to take my mind off it. 'Did I tell you about your horoscope?' Azalea said sighing as the young man seated himself so that we could see only his neat, shining brown hair. 'You are to meet someone shortly.'

'I'm going to meet about thirty people – if you count the driver and courier.'

'So you have been counting heads!'

We watched the driver approach the coach. He was a man of about 40, solid-looking, clean-shaven and with a bullet head.

'No, I mean you are to meet someone special,' Azalea sang out, just as a hush fell over the coach.

Irritated, I said, 'Is every Aquarian in the world going to meet someone special this week?'

'Why not? We're all affected by the spheres. I was born under Pisces – I'm influenced by Jupiter and Neptune.'

She broke off to smile radiantly at the driver, who blinked long lashes from unexpectedly beautiful eyes as he bowed to us all, and said with a thick accent, 'My name is Mihajlo Radnin. Call me Mike. I am your driver all the way. Please pass any messages through Mimi. I will try to please.' Of this I had no doubt.

There was a clapping of hands as Mike subsided behind the wheel but not before he'd sent a penetrating glance in Lea's and my direction. As the clapping ceased, we heard him singing 'Land of Hope and Glory' just to show that he appreciated we were British. The coach started its long journey on a burst of laughter; we were all friends from the start. At least we seemed to be friends.

Almost immediately Lea fell asleep, no doubt tired by her partying in Devon. After I had had enough of looking at the flat, mist-shrouded countryside which was becoming clearer with every minute, I took the list of useful phone numbers and suggestions Uncle Charles had given me, and started keying the numbers into my mobile to keep a second copy. We were just slowing to a stop for our first coffee stop when Azalea stirred.

'This is how the money goes,' Azalea said, awakened and grumbling as she followed the others out. 'I managed to raise a hundred pounds. My godparents are lambs.' Her own parents had died in a car crash when she was a child so we had had a lot in common.

'You can save it. I told you, I'll pay all expenses,' I said grandly. 'I've got enough cash for each place we pass through.'

'My, my! Aren't you the efficient one.' Her yawn threatened to dislocate her jaw.

'Not entirely. I read the hints and tips to travellers. And I'm compiling my own list – the one in the brochure will probably be longer next year. Black or white?'

'White. Oh no, it isn't done, is it? When in Rome.'

'This not being Rome, you might as well have what you fancy.'

We had followed the others from the warm coach, finding the cold outside air sharply refreshing. We were wide-awake and soon ready for that small – very small – coffee. The coach had pulled up alongside an inn where there were tables and chairs beneath a veranda. Some flowering shrub was in full bloom, rioting along the length of the veranda rail – a most attractive spectacle. Later, we suspected the flowering shrub was on the bill. Many had ordered second coffees to make up for the first disappointing one.

'Anyway, it was good coffee,' Azalea comforted when the coach was off again, the tyres singing on the highway. 'Yes, but we've been done.' I made a note for Uncle Charles. 'Do you get it? Mike suddenly appears and shouts, 'Time to be off,' and we rush to pay the waiter who, knowing we shan't meet him again, charges us far too much.'

I was busy working out the euro rate.

'Do you know what each cup of coffee cost? £6. Outrageous.'

'Perhaps that shrub outside was a rare shrub,' Lea suggested. 'Look, you aren't going to calculate every mouthful I swallow, are you, because if ...'

I gave her a nudge with my elbow. 'I'll explain later.' Discreetly I compared notes with the Reverend Burnett and his wife across the aisle. They had been charged the same excessively high price for the coffee, as had probably everyone else in the party. At twenty passengers, that came to £100. Not bad for quarter of an hour's work and a few coffee beans.

I considered. Mimi had said she was new on this tour, so it looked as if Mike, for all his beautiful blue eyes and willingness to please, might be an accessory to a small con: when Azalea and I had gone to what we laughingly referred to as the powder room, a door nearby had flown open and we couldn't help seeing that Mike had appeared very much at home in the kitchen, a large glass of something at his elbow.

Mimi told us that short stops were made every two hours, not necessarily for people to have sustenance but mainly to let them stretch their legs. Unless we were running late that is. Our next lengthy stop was for lunch, but here there was no opportunity for anyone to make an easy touch as the cost of the excellent meal was covered by a voucher. If I could persuade Uncle Charles to have vouchers to cover unlimited coffees this might foil the fortune-hunters. A glance at the itinerary told me we were to stay the night, and some of the following day, at Heidelberg.

Because I had been keeping my eyes open, I had noticed earlier that whenever we left the coach, a man of about 45, sporting a shaggy mop of brown hair and seated three seats away on the opposite side of the aisle, always took his case from the rack. Even when he had strolled out at a short stop before we rolled into Germany his eyes had rarely shifted from this case. All the borders were deserted, of course – ahead of Brexit.

Lea, who had an uncanny knack of reading my mind, said softly, 'It's an artist's case. The sort you can open. It means you can start painting anywhere.'

'Then you'll have things in common with him,' I joked.

She considered. 'I doubt it. All that hair. It's like a theatrical wig. He joined the tour at Brussels. He wasn't on the plane coming over.' Azalea lost interest but I continued to watch the man. Feeling my eyes on him, he turned instinctively to catch me at it. I ducked down as fast as I could, remembering Charles's admonition not to embarrass anyone. Presumably not even myself. But I continued to speculate about the hairy one. Why should he seem so on edge? Surely on a holiday like this he should be relaxed?

Azalea touched me and I saw that the Reverend Burnett was holding out a bag of boiled mints. 'My mother told me never to accept sweets from strange men,' I said, taking one. 'But I feel we're already old acquaintances. Thank you.'

We were soon all sucking contentedly. On a minty sigh, Azalea said, 'You get into a dreamlike state on these coach tours. I can well understand how couples could meet, fall in love, and get engaged before the end of the journey.'

I answered, 'You have a facility for imagining how couples could meet, fall in love and become engaged anywhere on earth.' I leaned across her to speak to Mrs Burnett. 'Your husband is quite safe from us.'

'I know.' She put her hand in his and squeezed it and they exchanged smiles. His seemed a little quick, and a little forced. Easily embarrassed I thought. Perhaps it was an age thing – shouldn't be seen canoodling! Sweet when you do see it, though.

'You're lucky,' Lea said wistfully, as though wolf whistles had never ever rung in her ears. Then, as though following a line of thought, 'What is Heidelberg like? Have you ever been there?'

'Yes, briefly, years ago,' Reverend Burnett said. 'It's like most university towns, full of students and bicycles and nightclubs. There are some wonderful historic buildings. And there's the river Neckar.' He smiled reminiscently. 'Everything in life, I suppose.'

'Except The Student Prince.' Azalea was still in her wistful mood.

'He may still be there in disguise,' he comforted.

'If he is, Azalea will find him,' I declared. 'Or rather, he will find her.'

'He'll have to be quick,' commented Mrs Burnett. 'We leave after lunch for Salzburg that day.' Blushing a little she added, 'Where we had our honeymoon.'

'Fifty years ago exactly,' added the Reverend Burnett proudly.

Azalea and I exchanged glances – so it was a Golden Wedding Anniversary tour!

Interest revived as we came in sight of the Rhine, and we were pleased to find we had a lengthy break at Cologne whose skyline, with its twin spires piercing the sky, we had been admiring for some time.

'The cathedral or shops?' asked Azalea as we scrambled out, ignoring the others who were being led like sheep into an inn where tea was being served. It was an agonizing decision. Overhearing, Mimi settled it for us.

'Do both. I'll not let Mike leave you behind. We've made good time so he has no excuse to gripe.'

Blessing her, we ran like hares in the direction of the cathedral and I felt virtuous that we had decided to add to our artistic knowledge instead of stuffing ourselves with cakes. I had a guilty pang when I remembered Uncle Charles and his £1000, but surely I couldn't be expected to devote every minute to his work? As we wandered down the dreaming aisles of the glorious building we saw the Reverend Burnett and his wife but did not disturb them.

Pausing only to take a few photographs, we next rushed off in the direction of the shops to gloat over the goods displayed. After mentally converting a few prices into English pounds we decided we could only look and not buy. Some of the joy went out of it. But I did pick up a copy of the Stadt Revue, a magazine detailing the local attractions and events to see what my uncle may like to mention in our brochures. In addition to the twin spires of the Cologne Cathedral, that is. Saunas also appeared to be very big here (what kind I wondered!) as did attractions for children. There was even a theme park with a roller coaster, sponsored by a celebrity.

We were sauntering along when I saw the artist we had christened the Hairy One coming towards us and I stopped dead, causing Lea to bump into me. In exasperation she said, 'Really, Babs, you simply aren't yourself.'

I pulled her towards a pair of lederhosen in a shop window and made her look at them.

'Lea, do you promise not to reveal to the others what I'm going to tell you?'

She gazed at me in fascination. 'I don't have a bible on me, but I can cross my heart and spit.'

When I had finished telling her about my commission from Uncle Charles, she replied thoughtfully, 'Yes, I can see why he couldn't do the tour.'

'And you'll be a great help, with your trained artist's eye.'

'But what has Mr Paul Wemys to do with it?'

'Who? Oh, the Hairy One. Is that his name? How did you find out?'

She giggled endearingly. 'I thought he might be famous. I just read the label on his case as we passed down the coach.'

'Oh. Right. Is he famous?'

'I've never heard of him. Have you noticed he walks just like a stage comedian – as if one leg were shorter than the other?'

'So he does. He caught me staring at him. I mustn't draw attention to myself!'

She gave me an appraising look. 'That'll be hard. Most men notice you anyway.'

I would have pursued this interesting point, feeling my dark looks were boring in comparison to Lea's, but she looked at her watch. 'We'd better make it back to the coach quickly or Mike will be furious. He looks a short-tempered fellow. We're overdue, unless Mimi gave us a margin.'

We returned by the route we had come, but on the opposite side of the road, and presently fell in behind Wemys again. Sauntering a long way behind him was the good-looking young man who had stared at us earlier. They were headed in the direction of the coach too so we relaxed and caught up with Reverend and Mrs Burnett, who looked very contented.

Out of the corner of my eye I saw the good-looking man, who was now ahead of us, not glancing our way but, I was convinced, fully aware of us. I might try Azalea's trick and read the name on his suitcase label. But perhaps that wouldn't be necessary; I had a feeling we would become better acquainted without any effort on my part. We boarded the coach and took our seats.

The journey, which had mostly been in sunshine, now became clouded over, the coach being cooler in consequence. Less than an hour later, our coach entered Bonn, and inevitably, coach conversations with neighbours turned quietly to politics and the fall of the Berlin Wall. One or two discussed Beethoven, Bonn's favourite son – the man who was rumoured to hate his home town.

As the sun came out again, we languished into our previous torpid state, managing to express interest as we turned south to follow the Rhine, which rolled through green hills thickly planted with vines. Strings of narrow barges slid by, hooting as they passed through the villages. The sight of castles perched dramatically on crags sent everyone into ecstasies, making Mike look so gratified that one could only suppose he was a German – even with a name like Radnin, which sounded more Slavic. Mixed parentage perhaps?

'I have a picture just like that in a book I read as a child,' commented Lea contentedly, nodding at the ramparts of a stony citadel.

'You're enjoying yourself!'

'Yes. It would be such a waste otherwise. Aren't you?'

'In a way.' I replied thinking of my mission.

The lush and rolling green of the countryside gave way inevitably to the first signs of urbanization. Farms and a few homes became suburbs, replete with shops and petrol stations plastered with ads for fast food and cheap fuel. The mountains rose yet higher into view then dropped, unveiling the city of Heidelberg and its castle, nestled against a long glistening sliver of the Neckar River.

We held our breath as the coach took a dangerous curve rather fast. Azalea shut her eyes; perhaps she was praying. Mike was a driver who evidently evoked much prayer. We had discovered that he liked to speed on the autobahns and provide himself – and us – with lengthy stops. We were not sorry when we pulled up at our inn in Heidelberg, a small, pale yellow, stucco-fronted building on a cobbled street barely wide enough for the coach. But what struck me was that everything was so fresh and clean, and that flowers were everywhere. Baskets hung from windows, over doors, and in glazed pots on the pavement.

The windows had green-painted shutters, there were baskets of flowers above either side of the door, and all looked peaceful and quiet; we were travel-stained and weary, grateful for the promised haven. It was nearly seven o'clock, plenty of time to bathe and dress before dinner. We were told our room was Number 7 on the first floor and found we were overlooking a back courtyard. The twin beds had spotlessly clean linen and a simply enormous continental quilt. Azalea held on to a bed post and shook with laughter as she pointed to the bloated object.

'How do you balance that on the bed at night?

'You don't. It always slides off. I suppose that's why the beds are so close together. To catch one or the other. I speak from experience.' The 'Travel Germany!' brochures we had at the office had boasted full, glossy, colour photos of fabulous hotels, sporting luxurious bathrooms and spacious bedrooms. I wondered how long it had been since Uncle Charles had been on this tour. I made a note to check if the inn was on the contract. This dinky, eighteenth- century jewel must have been great in its day, but modern travellers were not going to be happy about such simple accommodation, no matter how rich in authentic charm.

We were looking around and opening the window when we became aware of an altercation out in the hallway. Azalea opened the door slightly and through the gap we saw the stout man (the proprietor, we presumed) who had greeted us courteously downstairs. He was listening to one of the members of the coach party, a youth of about nineteen – slim, pale and shy, and trying to hold his own in the conversation. He seemed very young to us – nineteen or twenty, going on fifty! Perhaps our uni stint had given us a more sophisticated edge at twenty-three and twenty-four. 'I ordered a single room. I paid extra for a single room, which was ordered in advance.'

The man shrugged. 'A mistake. No single room. All taken.'

'But I can't sleep in a double bed with a man I've never seen in my life. Any man in fact. I refuse to. A single bed in a double room might not be so bad, but not a double bed... 'The youth's colour and temper were rising about equally. The proprietor pretended he did not fully understand. 'You complain when you get home, eh?' He twiddled the jewelled drop on the double-guard watch chain spread across his handsome frontage. 'What good will that do me now?'

'It is only one night. I am sorry. You go down and have good dinner and you feel better.'

'Can't you shuffle the rooms round a bit?' There was a desperate note in the youth's voice.

'What is this 'shuffle'?'

'Can't you swap me a room – oh hell.' This last was a response to the proprietor's real or feigned puzzlement.

'I told you, the rooms are occupied. You are being difficult.' The proprietor dug his heels in.

'I am only demanding my rights.' The youth dug his heels in too.

The proprietor seemed to ponder the situation. 'I tell you what we do. I give you my room. My wife and I will find a place downstairs.' He looked resentful.

'I couldn't let you do that ...' the young man responded automatically and exasperatedly – as the proprietor had no doubt hoped he would.

Azalea and I exchanged a glance. We both had the same idea and stepped into the corridor. The double had to be more comfortable than the singles with oversized quilts crammed together in our room. 'We can offer a solution,' Azalea said, smiling at the younger man. 'You must take our room, which has twin beds. We will take your room. We can put up with sharing a bed for one night under the circumstances. Hopefully it is a very large bed.'

She peeked around the equally large proprietor who eagerly stepped aside to let her see the huge expanse of double bed that would, no doubt, please.

'Yes. Yes, it is,' the proprietor beamed suddenly, all trace of irritation gone.

'This really is very good of you,' our fellow traveller said, sighing with relief. 'Thank you so much.'

'Perhaps you could tell the person you are sharing with, and bring your things across.'

'It's a front room,' he warned. 'Probably noisier.'

'That's all right. Azalea's snores will drown anything out.' I threw a conspiratorial wink in her direction.

'I'm Colin Barnes,' he said, offering his right hand in gratitude. Colin seemed to have forgotten the proprietor, but I was watching him and I saw a look of fury come over his face. It was gone instantly once he was aware I was looking at him. How odd, I thought.

'You are most kind,' the proprietor said, hurriedly. 'Then if this little matter is settled to your liking I will attend to my business, yes?'

Colin Barnes glanced at him long enough to say vaguely, 'Yes, thank you,' before he continued to look deeply into Azalea's eyes. She blinked a little and so I started my Operation Rescue, grown smooth with much practice.

'Well, that's settled them. I'm Barbara Wills. This is Azalea Dunbar.'

'I'm Colin Barnes,' he murmured.

'Yes, you just told us. Come in and help us move the beds for you. They're jammed together at the moment.'

He wandered in after us but was little help, so Azalea and I tugged the beds apart. 'There you are. Who's your room mate for the night?' she asked.

'A Mr Wemys.'

'Do you think he'll mind moving? He might have unpacked by now.'

'I'll see. He doesn't look to have much stuff with him and he didn't want to share the bed either. Just didn't want to make a fuss. He was leaving it to me.'

When we went across to Number 14, Mr Wemys looked rather startled, but he accepted the situation instantly and gratefully, confirming he hadn't been happy about sharing the double bed. He received the full voltage of Azalea's smile (I was always more conservative with mine). Had he not responded, I would have considered him sub-human. We had almost to push Colin Barnes from our new room.

'It's most likely we shall meet again,' I told him kindly. 'Considering we're to be together for the next two weeks.' 'Oh yes, yes of course.' He got himself to the door. 'I'm terribly grateful. I wonder how often this sort of thing happens on these tours! It could spoil a holiday.'

'Yes, I wonder,' I said, thinking of the strange look – almost of malevolence – I had surprised on the proprietor's face. When Azalea and I were alone, I sat on the bed and made a few more notes in my diary.

'More perks?' she enquired, stripping off her shapeless outfit and going to the washbasin where she switched on the light. I was mildly surprised to see she wore only panties under her dress.

'Not worried about gravity taking hold prematurely?' I asked.

'Hmm?' she answered, not paying attention.

As I stared out through the window I became aware that the rooms across the road were afforded an excellent view of our situation. Hastily I drew the curtains shut.

'You'd better get a move on,' Azalea said. 'We haven't time for baths now. I don't propose to queue up there. This is an old-fashioned place isn't it?'

'Must be in the old part of the town. Anyway the bed seems comfortable enough.' As Azalea appeared to have finished with the washbasin, I got busy and emerged just as she was about to dive back into the strange garment she had thrown off earlier.

'You're not going down to dinner in that?'

'Why not? It'll save unpacking.' I had noticed a ham sandwich in one of her bags that had accompanied us from England and wished she would unpack. I made a mental note to remind her to throw it out. The last thing we needed was food poisoning.

'That's no trouble.' I snapped open my case and shook out a simple blue dress which would have made a bean pole look sexy. 'Try this for size.'

She put it on, not even glancing in the mirror. 'Thank you. I love the colour.'

After swallowing, I said conservatively, 'You've never looked better.'

I wriggled into a black sheath and Azalea zipped me up. We were soon ready, and upon exchanging notes, discovered were both ravenously hungry. It was now a quarter to eight and as we emerged into the corridor, we were startled to find it in semi-darkness, a faint glimmer of light coming from a bulb that must surely have been filched from a child's nursery. We groped our way down the steep stairs.

'Would you say he was overdoing the economy?' I asked as my heel caught and would have plunged me down, head first, but for Azalea's quick action in righting me. 'These steps are hard.' I rubbed an ankle.

'So long as they don't economise on the food,' she answered.

There was no one in the hall to direct us so we just followed the delicious smell to a pair of swinging doors, entering a panelled room bursting at the seams with people. After the semi-darkness of the stairs, the room appeared to blaze with light, and we stood dazzled until we saw someone stand up and beckon to us. As we approached the table, a second man stood up; he was the tall, dark young man we had noticed earlier in the coach.

'This seems to be the only place for two left vacant,' the older man said, pulling out a chair for Azalea, who was nearest to him. I slipped into a seat which was built into the panelling of the wall and smiled at them collectively.

'We're rather late,' Azalea murmured.

'But worth waiting for.' The older man's blue eyes gleamed behind horn rims. 'I'm George Lonsties. I'm travelling on my own.'

'A happy bachelor,' concluded Azalea, who never lost any time getting to the heart of things.

'Not really. A widower. My wife died three years ago.'

'Ah. What were you born under?'

He looked startled. 'What ...? Oh, you mean my horoscope? Let me think. August Ist.'

'Leo,' she said promptly. 'Leo the lionhearted, that's you. You are influenced by the sun. Diamonds are lucky for you.'

'Aren't they lucky for everybody?' he asked, teasing her indulgently.

'Sunflowers and marigolds are your flowers. There are some marigolds in the baskets over the door of the inn. You will meet your fate on this trip.'

Mr Lonsties threw back his head and roared with laughter, so that other diners looked in our direction. I saw the Watford sisters glancing up in surprise; 'Call-Me-Daisy' looked wistful, as if she would have liked to enjoy the fun.

I turned to my companion, who hadn't said a word so far. I had noticed him earlier. His thick, dark hair and wide, grey eyes gave him a striking look and his build was strong and lean. But it was his capable air that attracted me. It made those deep grey eyes all the more mysterious. 'They seem to be getting on very well,' I said. 'I'm Barbara Wills, by the way. It's been an interesting day hasn't it?'

'Very. I was glad you came to our table. Actually we defended it for some time.' His gaze was flatteringly significant. I was right. He had noticed us and had contrived an introduction of sorts.

'I wanted to meet you,' he continued, offering his hand in a most genteel manner. His hands were strong but well- manicured. 'I'm Gareth Findlatter.' Something seemed to be amusing him and I became very watchful. He had the ability to listen but be aware of everything about him. You suspected him of never missing a trick.

'Nice to meet you. Will they be long with our food? We're starving. We didn't have any tea.'

'No, I didn't either. I saw you in the town – where was it, Cologne? If it's Tuesday it must be – ? One of those types of tour. Pity we hadn't time to see more of it.'

'I suppose that's the drawback of tours – they're always sweeping you on. Still, you can always come back and have a proper holiday later.'

'Mm. Have a roll.' He offered a basket of assorted breads. I selected one and began to eat. A bowl of heartening soup was suddenly placed before me and I devoted some minutes to the inner woman. With the soup came a wine waiter and I was persuaded to join my table companions in sharing a bottle. It wasn't bad, but as I was coming to expect, overpriced, though the amount was not much felt when it was divided into four. We insisted on paying our share, explaining that the friendship would last longer that way. The food was very good: veal under a creamed sauce with cabbage and potatoes. We ate heartily, noticing when our appetites were satisfied that diners at other tables had been offered other dishes. We had been given no choice but had been brought what we were to eat. The sweet dessert was poor so I declined it and took cheese which was offered without biscuits. This latter was to irritate Azalea for some time to come. She loved her cheese and biscuits. Coffee was an extra, one in which we did not indulge. So much for 'all expenses'. Another note for Uncle Charles.

'I'm dying for a cup of tea,' Azalea sighed.

'Easily done,' George Lonsties declared and asked the writer to bring us cups and a jug of boiling water. When these arrived, he took an envelope of tea bags from his pocket and dropped a couple in the water, giving them a stir. Though he had received a tip, the waiter stayed to watch these antics with an air of profound pity on his dark face. But we didn't care. The tea was nectar though we drank it without milk. Too much effort to explain that tea is much better with milk! The men helped themselves from the sugar bowl.

Somewhat befuddled by the food, and by the warmth of the dining room, I found myself becoming sleepy, and was suddenly glad that my companion was not talkative. I saw Azalea shake her head, and in a moment Mr Lonsties leaned across the table and declared, 'I have offered to adopt her and she has refused. As soon as I heard she didn't have any parents, I made my honest offer and...'

He was grinning all over his flushed face. With his well-covered figure, one could imagine him as an ideal Father Christmas.

'Are you quite sure your feelings are those of a parent?' I asked abstractedly. I studied Gareth Findlatter, finding him even more attractive close to than I had imagined. His skin was smooth and his pulse – as revealed by his open collar – gentle and unhurried. Just a whiff of cologne wafted from his skin and I found myself drawing nearer to place it. He was probably in his early thirties and it was his steady gaze and his easy smile that were attractive, inviting a taste of a handsome, well-shaped mouth. I detected the trace of a faint Scottish accent held under control as well. There was an air of abstraction that might be natural to him, though I doubted this, sensing that part of his mind was occupied with something vital, making him all the more attractive to me. What girl can ignore an enigma? Especially one that looked and smelled so enticing. He paid scant attention to Lonsties and I became aware presently that he was anxious to be out of the dining room, which was rapidly emptying.

The hallway was cold, with the night air flowing through the open doorway. After glancing up and down the narrow street, we went back to read the notices placed over the radiator. George Lonsties pushed open a door which led to a stuffy lounge. At one end, our driver and courier were seated smoking, having just finished a meal, for a tray was stacked with empty dishes. A foursome played a card game; two others were busily writing postcards at a table. Mimi came across. 'Everything all right? Are you going out?'

'Everything's fine.' I said. I checked with Azalea who shook her head at the second question. 'No, I think we'll have an early night. We'll just get the news on TV.'

'I'd be glad to escort you,' Mr Lonsties offered. 'I know Heidelberg. There is quite a night life here for students. Lots of live music and cheap beer.'

'Not tonight, thank you,' I became aware that Gareth Findlatter was standing in the doorway, not paying any attention to us, but watching the turn of the stairs. I couldn't help but feel a little dejected.

'If you'll excuse me,' he said suddenly. The door closed after him.

'How are you getting on with your fellow travellers?' asked Mimi. 'They seem a pleasant bunch except for...' She broke off, realising her lack of tact.

'Those we've met seem very nice,' agreed Azalea. 'The Burnetts are sweet. We think they're on a trip for their Golden Wedding. They said they'd had their honeymoon in Salzburg.'

'Really?' Mimi looked intrigued. 'I'll find out for sure.'

Our driver, Mike, moved his thickset body across to the piano. 'We could make it memorable for them at Salzburg, eh? I will play some music and we have a drink to them.'

'Good show,' Lonsties approved.

Azalea looked doubtful. 'If you think they'll like a fuss? The Reverend seems to want to keep things quiet.'

'No,' Mike insisted. 'It will be a happy memory.' He chuckled as he dropped his cigarette end on the piano lid, missing the ash tray and the fact he should not have been smoking at all. He must have been very familiar with his surroundings and the people in it, to get away with such behaviour.

Lea winced but made herself lean on the piano in a friendly way, brushing off the offending ash and cigarette end. 'What are you going to play now?'

'I don't know until my fingers tell me.' He rattled off into some catchy folk tunes, and what he lacked in style he made up for in volume. When he was well launched be gave Azalea a calculating look which gradually dissolved into an engaging grin. As she was saying something over her shoulder to George Lonsties, she missed some of it. Mike was quite the ladies' man. He bounced into the melodies of The Blue Danube and it occurred to me that Mike's casualness was not genuine. He knew very well what his fingers were about. Probably he played a selection from The Blue Danube each tour through Heidelberg, cashing in at the end.

Other people had entered through a door at the far end of the room, from the bar, we surmised, for most of them carried glasses in their hands. They joined lustily in the drinking song and ordered a drink for the pianist who said, 'Why aren't we all drinking? Come along folks.' Was he on commission? I wondered. He belted out a repeat of the famous drinking song. I took a shot of the happy scene, thinking it would look good in a brochure. I also decided I would send Mike's photo to Uncle Charles, to see if he could find anything out about him, as well as giving him my ideas so far.

Lea's vast yawn caught me unawares and I became infected by it when I received a half wink. A few minutes later we were cautiously feeling our way up the dimly lighted stairs to our room, checking that it was indeed Number 14 once we had switched on the room light. Almost immediately Azalea went along to the bathroom and was surprised on her return not to find me ready for bed.

'Mike must be a godsend wherever he goes. He certainly works at it. Are you disappointed that we didn't go out?'

'No, it's not that. I've been making discoveries. This key doesn't lock the door from the inside.'

'That's interesting.'

'Also, that other door seems to be locked on the other side, with no bolt on this side.' I nodded in the direction of the small door which probably opened up to form a suite with our room.

'Even more interesting,' said Lea, staring solemnly at me. 'Now you've got me going. You don't suppose something was planned for Colin Barnes?'

'I've been wondering.' I told Azalea of the look of fury I had surprised on the face of the proprietor when we had suggested swapping rooms. 'You don't suppose we're making too much of it?'

'He offered his room to Mr Barnes. What reason could he have?'

'He probably knew it wouldn't be accepted.' Our brains were working overtime.

'Why not put Colin Barnes in a single room in the first place?' Azalea asked

'Whether it was a mistake or done deliberately, he was put to share a double bed with a total stranger. Not surprising he objected! Do you think they wanted to blackmail him?'

Azalea giggled. 'You've been watching too much TV. The proprietor would hardly risk his licence for the amount a lad could carry on holiday.'

'At the beginning of a tour? It could be worthwhile if they do it often enough – perhaps every night a new victim.' I shrugged. 'Perhaps I'm imagining the whole thing because of what Uncle Charles said about that client. Anyway, we might as well do something on our own account about both doors.'

With no little effort we pulled the bedhead against the inner door and wedged a chair back under the handle of the door opening on the corridor. We also laid a few booby traps in case of an intruder. We looked under pictures and examined every fitment in the room. They all appeared innocent.

'Plenty of dust under the bed,' muttered Azalea, rising to her feet. 'Get along to the bathroom or we'll never get any sleep tonight.'

I enjoyed a quick bath which decided me on making another quick note to Uncle Charles about the low standard of the plumbing as well as everything else, and was returning to our room when I saw someone standing in the gloom of the corridor. My nerves jumped and I switched on the torch with which I had armed myself. It shone on Gareth Findlatter who appeared to have paused merely to light an illegal cigarette. Where were the smoke alarms? The list was growing. Anyway, this was one thing I didn't like about Gareth. Surprising how many people smoked – and quite heavily – outside the UK. Cheap cigarettes help. He was outside Number 14 and made no move to let me enter.

'Do you mind? I want to go in.'

A strange look crossed his face. 'In here?' 'Why not?'

He stood aside and I went in thoughtfully. Of course, he'd seen the previous occupants enter. I opened the door to see him moving slowly down the corridor.

'Mr Findlatter.' He swung round, waiting. 'It's not what you think. Mr Barnes was upset so we decided to swap rooms. I don't mind sleeping with anyone if it's not for long.'

'I see.'

I went hot as I realised what I had said – and his interpretation of it. 'I meant Lea and I have exchanged rooms. We've exchanged our twin-bedded room for this double-bedded one. Mr Barnes had ordered a single room and ...'

He was smiling now as he came a step or two nearer. 'You don't have to explain.'

'I wanted to make it clear,' I persisted, feeling angry and rather prim. I turned the beam of light on the floor. 'As a matter of fact we're worried because our door won't lock.'

'Try putting a chair under the handle.'

'Yes, we'd thought of that.'

He was quite close now. 'I'm in Number 20. If you're scared in the night, just give me a shout. I'll hear you. I'm a light sleeper.'

'Thank you. I don't suppose it'll be necessary. Good night, Mr Findlatter.'

'Good night, Miss Wills. Sweet dreams.'

Over his shoulder I saw the elder Miss Watford peering along the corridor. When she realised I had seen her she scuttled round the corner, disapproval in every line of her narrow shoulders. I bet the younger Miss Watford would have enjoyed seeing the 'fun'.

I had a thought, and turned back to Mr Findlatter, who was still lingering. 'Mr Barnes is in with Mr Wemys,' I said. 'I gather they are not very happy about the mistake. Even having to share a twin – though it's better than a double. You see, I've already learned several names.' I don't know why I added the last bit.

'Yes, these tours break down all barriers.' He looked thoughtful.

'Well, not quite all, do they?' I let myself in and closed the door. Phew, I was glad to get out of that one! From the wide bed, Azalea enquired sleepily, 'Who was that?' She was almost invisible beneath the giant quilt – we still had one, even in this room.

'Mr Findlatter. I don't think he is altogether what he seems.' I stretched a damp towel over the radiator.

'What? Why?'

'Number 20 is that way, beyond the bathroom. He had no reason to come this way unless...'

'Unless what?'

'Unless he was watching Mr Wemys,' I muttered, and jammed the chair under the door handle, re-laying my booby traps en route. The nylon cord we would use to drip dry our clothes did double duty as a trip wire tied between dressing table and washbasin legs. And our cases and shoes were strewn about to cause a fall that would hopefully alert us before we could be killed in our sleep.

No doubt we would feel very foolish in the morning.

CHAPTER THREE
HEIDELBERG

Introducing Angelique ~ the plot thickens

Perhaps it was not surprising that we felt jaded when we were roused in the morning by the sound of the vacuum cleaner in the corridor.

'I refuse to get up at six o'clock,' grumbled Azalea after consulting her watch.

'Heidelberg is calling you,' I yawned.

'Heidelberg can scream its head off, but I'm having another hour – or two,' she added after consideration, 'I hold the world's record for quick dressing.'

'I don't wonder.'

'What?'

'I said I shouldn't wonder if it's going to be a hot day.'

As I felt the warmth of a sunbeam crossing the bed, I snuggled down blissfully as Azalea had done, covering my ears against the crashes from the corridor. From the racket, the cleaners seemed to be throwing heavy pans at each other, chattering with joy when they scored a hit. Real sleep was impossible, particularly as at seven o'clock a stout young Fraulein knocked on our door, and after some preliminary skirmishing and ineffectual rearrangement of the furniture on our part, brought in a large watering can, threw up the window and leaned alarmingly far out, giving us a splendid view of red, woollen-clad legs. She proceeded to water the two hanging plants above the front entrance. We watched her as she reared up, crowing with laughter and shouting at some passerby. We gathered she had made a direct hit.

Flushed with success, she turned toward us, beaming. 'That vas Rudi. He is a student. I hate him.' Quite an announcement for seven o'clock in the morning.

From Rudi's answering remark, I gathered the feeling 'vas' mutual but she waved him away fondly. So nice to be in this room where love-hate bloomed each morning. Knowing I should put this and the crack–of–dawn cleaning cacophony in my report made me feel a little guilty.

'You moved your bed,' she exclaimed. 'All English spinsters do that. It is an English custom, yes?' Well, perhaps not that guilty. Not waiting for a reply she went on: 'You do not get up? Breakfast is being served. Today we have croissants.' This last was said proudly, as with a flourish from her watering can she departed, not in the least dismayed that we had not exchanged a single word with her. Azalea and I looked at each other.

'It's true,' Azalea observed thoughtfully. 'Travel does broaden your mind.'

We both paused to smell the wonderful aroma of freshly- made, baked goods wafting in from the bakers' shops down the cobbled street. I opened the little window to get the lie of the land. 'If we don't go down soon, the croissants will have gone. I see Call-Me-Daisy is already on the hoof,' I said, referring to Marguerite Watford climbing ever so primly into the coach, Lonsties gallantly to her aid.

Abby Fraser, the curvaceous beauty who had caught the eye of Mike the driver, ground out a cigarette and stepped back into the hotel as her husband, Ted, spoke to her. He looked in a huff. The coach was in front of the little hotel, glittering in the morning sun. Mike stood in the quiet, cobbled street jabbering ferociously on his mobile, punctuating his conversation with his cigarette. Our view wasn't very wide, but it was enlightening. Ted stepped into the coach as Lonsties and Call-Me-Daisy stepped out and walked back in, arm in arm. Mike met him as he stepped out of the coach, and said something to Ted, all traces of a smarmy smile gone. Apparently Ted didn't care for his topic of conversation because in an instant he had Mike cornered, up against the back of the opened coach door. His hands went up in a 'No, it's all been a big misunderstanding' gesture, and Ted stepped back quickly into the hotel with one final, warning finger jab to Mike's chest. Mike must have been after Abby Fraser again. Why would she want his smarmy attentions? Holidays do strange things to people.

Just then a couple I didn't recognise climbed into the coach rather quickly.

'Who are they?'

'Who?' Azalea was flinging herself into the garment she called her dress. I noted that again she wasn't worried about gravity taking hold. Lucky her.

'I don't recognise that couple over there. They look all 'first day of school and sweaty palms'.'

'The Turners? Well, they're married, but not to each other.' Azalea already had them sorted out. 'I saw she'd forgotten he didn't take sugar. I thought they might be on their honeymoon but not now.'

'Yes,' I responded. 'You can spot the honeymoon couple. Everything they have, including their luggage, is brand new. She's even forgotten to take out the card of matching mending-wool from the back of her jumper. Actually, I'd have had a hard time describing them. You simply never see them, they keep that much to themselves.'

'The Lyons you mean?' Azalea caught on immediately. Pretty and blonde with nice clothes – cheap, but she's so petite they look great. He's small, but really lean and muscled! Both of them no more than our sort of age, I would say. Or a bit older – mid twenties?'

'You'd be invaluable on the investigation side of things,' I said admiringly. 'I couldn't help seeing the wool when I followed her down the coach. I debated whether I should tell her and then decided it might be kinder not to.'

Azalea must have approved. 'I forgot to say: Mimi would like to know if we'd like to join a coach tour of the town. You know – all the places of interest.'

I let my face drop. 'Let's just potter about and come back and 'do' Heidelberg some other time.'

'Suits me. I want to buy one of those gorgeous trilby hats with a feather in the band for my godfather.'

'They're expensive, and you'll have to carry it everywhere.' I knew I was beaten from the start. 'Salzburg will be full of them too.'

'All right, I'll get one in Salzburg. And I shan't carry it. I shall wear it whenever we have to move our things.'

'It'll certainly add a touch of authenticity to the legend,' I murmured.

'What legend?'

'That the English are mad.'

Breakfast was good, and as we came back along the corridor we almost bumped into Colin Barnes. We looked at him somewhat anxiously, but were reassured to see that he appeared easy in mind, if a little sleepy.

'You've probably missed the croissants,' Azalea told him pleasantly. He obviously hadn't gathered his wits yet because he stared at her blankly.

'But the cheese is still on, you'll be glad to hear. No biscuits though.' Evidently this oversight still rankled with her.

'I never eat much breakfast,' he said, and smiled, showing his nice teeth.

'You should. You're too thin,' Azalea began in a motherly tone which utterly charmed him. He would have detained her to enlarge on a fascinating discussion about diet, but I took her firmly by the arm and propelled her to our room. We found the beds had been made up with fresh linen, and our few possessions stacked near the washbasin. We took the hint and packed.

'Makes you feel so dispossessed,' Azalea muttered, echoing my own feelings. I made a note in my log, feeling a proper Cassandra, but recalling the maid's remark about being an English spinster got me through it. 'W-a-t-e-r-i- n-g c-a-n,' I keyed in on my mobile under: 'Rude Help.' I would be ready the next time. Now, where had I put my paper notebook? Mustn't leave that behind.

Even though we did not 'do' everything, we loved Heidelberg, and at every turn, met our fellow passengers – none of whom looked upset in any way, I was glad to see. In the broad light of day and in the storybook atmosphere of the Old Town, we felt our imaginations had been working overtime last night. Rows of two and three-storey buildings huddled together over twisting, narrow lanes, like grand old ladies in stucco dresses of yellow, blue, and pink, each one adorned with baskets of flowers trailing pea vines, geranium and petunias. Up they went to the castle's twin towers flanking the old bridge that had spanned the Neckar River to Heidelberg castle, stopping abruptly as their cobbled streets went on before them, swirling together to create the broad approach to the bridge. Only pedestrians were allowed in this area, which lent an authentic air to the medieval style of the original old town. The wealth of Heidelberg's history touched me, the beauty – the very texture of it coming to life around me in the morning sunlight.

We discovered too that Mr George Lonsties had deserted us in favour of the Misses Watford. Glancing after them idly, Azalea queried, 'I wonder if he will offer to adopt Call-Me-Daisy?'

'Miss Pansy will protect her, have no fear. Besides didn't you think he was after someone wealthy?'

'Daisy is wealthy. Hadn't you noticed?'

'On a modest tour like this?' I responded, forgetting it was all paid for.

'That's nothing to go by, and besides this tour isn't that cheap. Those two have been everywhere. If you see a cobbler's shop, let me know and I'll get my broken strap mended. Besides, everything they wear – all their possessions – are just about the best you can buy.'

Always mentally alert when with Azalea, I followed her conversational agility with ease. 'Yes, but have you noticed – if you've got money, you ain't got youth – bit of a snag!'

'That's what makes it so fascinating. There's a cobbler's shop over there.' A picture of a shoe on a sign hung over a door in a row of interesting shops, two of them bakeries, and each building painted a different colour. Rather than looking cheap, it conveyed the beautiful and relaxed charm of another time. An older gentleman stepped out onto the pavement wiping his brow with the tail of his apron, then stepped back inside. 'Will you ask him nicely?'

'No, you just do it. You won't need words.' I callously prepared to enjoy myself. I could be like that sometimes. Undaunted by my lack of co-operation Azalea crossed the narrow street to find the old man working at his bench, which caught the light through the window. She smiled at the blue eyes which examined her shyly before they looked at the bag she was holding out. Sweetly Azalea mumbled something that sounded like, 'Bitte, willst du mein bagstrap menden?'

A gleam of amusement lit up the leathery, old face. 'Aber naturlich, gnadiges Fraulein. Für Sie wurde ich mögliches tun.' He gave a couple of twirls on his machine and handed back the bag with a bow.

'Danke. How much do I owe you?'

'Nichts.'

'You are so kind,' Azalea said, 'I shall think of you every time I use this bag. Thank you.'

'Danke. Ich habe für Sie etwas.' He shuffled to the back of the shop and Azalea was turning away when I said, 'Wait. He has something for you.' Azalea's natural and ingenuous charm was why she hadn't needed to concentrate on her languages at school – or indeed on anything much that didn't take her fancy. I was eternally amazed she had got through uni with flying colours. Her art degree was impressive. I might have known she would sail through this small episode, without granting me the vanity of displaying my own linguistic ability.

The cobbler carried a glass tumbler in which was a single pink rosebud. He took out the bloom and handed it to Azalea, who went as pink as the rosebud with pleasure.

'For me? How beautiful.'

One might have expected her to pin it to her dress. Azalea tucked it behind her ear, pleasing the old man even further. He bowed again and watched her progress down the street. Every five seconds she waved and he waved back. It had been love at first sight.

'If only he had been fifty years younger,' I observed.

'No, no, no,' Azalea cried. 'That doesn't matter. I'll never forget Heidelberg because of the dear old man and the rose.'

She walked down the street with its overhanging buildings and artistic signs, perfectly happy in the moment. I followed, rather enviously, though becoming aware that the rose over her ear was attracting attention. It was over the left ear.

I tried to recall what I had read about flower lore in such places as Hawaii or Fiji. The flower worn over the left ear meant you were seeking a husband? Worn over the right ear it meant you were engaged? Presumably if you wore it on the top of your head, you were open to all reasonable offers.

A small boy in lederhosen piped, 'Ist Sie verrückt?'

I did not translate but pulled a frightful face at the boy, and off we went down cobbled streets and up toward the castle, nestled in stately elegance into the hillside. We stopped to see the statue of a brass monkey holding a mirror perched on Karl Theodore Brücke (bridge) leading to the castle. The plaque beside it explained:

Why are you looking at me?
Haven't you seen the monkey in Heidelberg?
Look around and you will probably see
More monkeys like me.

A good thought to keep in mind in a city frequented by an international tourist trade. Live and let live, I say. But apparently they've had incarnations of the monkey statue since the 1500's. Just then a mob of Japanese tourists crowded in taking pictures and it was then we realised you could stick your head up inside the head, making the plaque all that much funnier. Once the Orient Express had swarmed on to other sights, Azalea and I took pictures of each other, first with my mobile, then with my camera to download onto the company web site.

The morning went by quickly, and I reminded Azalea that we had better return to the inn before too long as we had to leave straight after lunch, 'What was the name of it?' I added.

Azalea looked at me guiltily. 'I can't remember. It's near a cake shop.'

'The place is full of cake shops. How could we have been so stupid? We didn't even check the name of the street.' We had been walking about all morning and the thought of our being lost made us realise how tired we were. As it was already turned twelve o'clock we decided to skip the meal at the inn, especially as we couldn't find it, and bought ourselves various yummy morsels, retiring to eat them in a churchyard nearby. Had we not been vaguely worried, we would have enjoyed even more the alfresco meal and the sun on our heads.

'What's that,' asked Azalea. 'That noise?'

I stopped munching to listen and then we both stared toward a whimpering sound, as a tiny animal, not much bigger than a kitten, limped round the corner of the church and approached us cautiously. When it was about three yards away, it sank onto its haunches and whimpered, watching us out of eyes that were like wet blackcurrants. Though its coat was thick it shivered, despite the warm sunshine. Uneasy about our interest, it was turning away when Azalea said, 'It's starving. It scarcely has the strength to walk. Poor little dog,'

'Dog?'

'Yes, it looks like a cross between a griffin and ...' she hesitated.

'A lavatory brush?' I hazarded.

She ignored me, all her attention taken by the small creature. 'Nice dog,' she said, coaxing it with a piece of pie. At first it backed away, but the smell of the food was too much and it snatched it up and ate ravenously, having difficulty in swallowing. With food came courage and a small wave of a plumy tail.

'I didn't know griffins had plumy tails. Of course it might be the other side of the family. If you give it any more pie it'll be sick.'

Azalea had her hands on it now. 'I can feel every rib. The poor darling.'

'Let's leave it the rest of the food,' I said. 'And just hope it won't eat it all at once.'

'We can't leave it here,' she said indignantly.

'We can't take it with us. Besides, we're late as it is.'

'It said in my horoscope that I was to meet someone this week who would need a lot of care and attention.'

'That's me. I am looking after you and you are doing the same for me – I hope.'

Her expression was solemn. 'Don't you see? I was led to this churchyard. We can't abandon this poor creature now. I wouldn't enjoy another minute of the holiday if I did.'

This poor creature looked at Azalea hopefully, recognising a friend. I knew the look so well. For better or for worse, Azalea was committed. I could see she was revelling in this second affaire de coeur. If ever I got her safely back to England ... !'

'We must call at the nearest police station and report that we've found him,' she decided.

'Do you think they'll care very much?'

'We can leave our name and address. I mean, where we are going. Then, if someone claims it...'

I stared at her. 'Are you suggesting we take this creature with us? On our tour? Isn't it supposed to be registered? Look for the tattoo or microchip or whatever,' I urged her referring to my vague memory of EU regulations for pet travel.

'Not if it's a baby,' Azalea was starting to whine. 'That's only for grown-up ones. I think.'

Oh, oh, the pouting had started! I forged on: 'I don't care, Azalea. We can get into a lot of trouble. We best leave it.'

'I can't. What if something happened to it? And besides I can't feel a chip -'

'Too teeny.'

'Or see a tattoo.' Azalea peered madly into the tangled mass of filth and fur.

'How could you!'

'We can say it's ours and get it registered.'

'We really haven't the time for a vet's appointment. Plus we'd have to prove ownership,' I explained.

But Azalea wasn't giving in.

Then there was the matter of a pet passport and proof of vaccination, wasn't there?

Her lower lip started to tremble, but the upper one stiffened defiantly.

'Oh, Azalea. I know how you feel, but we could get in trouble. And what about the reason Uncle sent us on this mission in the first place? How are we going to catch criminals if we're sneaking around ourselves?'

Azalea's head dipped ever so slightly, allowing one small tiny tear to drop gently from her right eye. To add to that, a pair of blackcurrant eyes seemed to be searching my cold-hearted heart plaintively, through a mass of dull brown grunge. Damn.

'Well, we might try as far as Salzburg,' I conceded. 'By then the police might have traced its owners.'

And hope the police confiscate the little beggar, I thought desperately. Uncle Charles was going to love this. 'I have a strong feeling the owners don't want to be traced if it has any at all. Anyway, while we're at the police station, we might enquire where our hotel is. We're going to feel silly describing the two hanging baskets over the doorway.'

Azalea fed the dog a last piece of pie and let it lick her fingers. 'I believe in signs,' she said. 'If it follows us we'll regard it as a sign we are to look after it. If it leaves us at the churchyard gate, we'll take it as a sign that ...'

'It hasn't got any sense,' I said bitterly. 'Judging by its cute look, it's got plenty of that though.' The blackcurrant eyes suddenly seemed to take on a decidedly worldly look of satisfaction. This was borne out as I opened the gate, for the dog nearly tripped us up in its anxiety not to be left.

'Isn't he sweet?' Azalea sighed. 'I shall call him Hans.'

'Gretel, might be better,' I suggested.

'You mean ...?'

I nodded. 'I watched the technique behind the bush. She's one of us.'

'She's a darling. Look how she's watching us and wondering which way we shall go.'

'She's not the only one who's wondering.'

'This way,' Azalea said firmly. 'East, towards Mecca.'

Whatever her methods of reasoning, they brought us presently to a police station without having to ask directions and where the very masculine stereotype of Teutonic pride in uniform happily repeated my speech to Azalea. 'So, you see, Miss – ah?'

'Azalea,' Azalea answered demurely, casting her spell on her prey.

'Miss Azalea. You must have a pet passport to move about the EU. And in order to do that you must prove ownership and vaccination, and that all the proper fees have been paid.'

'Sir?' Another officer called over, managing to look like Michelangelo's David as he paged through reports neatly attached to a clip board. 'I remember a couple called in about a lost dog last week.'

Hope glowed in the Teutonic one's eyes. 'Yes? Is it the same?'

'Yes. It is. I took the report myself.' The David handed a snap of the Gretel, blackcurrant eyes peering out from under a large pink bow tied into tawny fur. I looked at the wanted posters on the walls to get through this little drama. 'The couple that made the report state here,' he said manfully referring to a carefully written report, 'that they were travelling and could not wait to find the dog when it wandered away. If found, the report says, 'Please try to place it in a good home.' Aside from the colour, Herr Hartmann, I'd say we have a match.' I was willing to argue that without DNA there was no way to be sure, but I could see I was outgunned.

'Very good,' the very Teutonic Officer Hartmann answered enthusiastically.

'And,' the David continued from across the room, pulling a large manila envelope from a shiny black cabinet, 'the paperwork is all here. Everything is in order.' He produced another clipboard with the paperwork to put the dog into Azalea's name.

'Oh joy, it's official,' I said blandly. Herr Hartmann's sheepish grin told all. Then he let his hand rest gently on Azalea's shoulder. 'I'm so happy for you, Miss Azalea. We animal lovers must stick together, no?"

'Oh just Azalea, please, Herr Hartmann! And yes, we do,' she added breathlessly.

I flashed as beatific a smile as I could muster and thought to myself: Oh, sister! You can turn it off now. They're going to let you keep your dog.

In a short time we were being sped back to our inn in a car driven by yet another muscular youth in uniform, and aside from the fact that he seemed to think he was sharing in the biggest joke of the season, I was seriously pondering the ratio of Heidelberg Polizei to the female population, and weighing the pros and cons of moving here permanently.

As we stepped from the car, Azalea carrying the dog on her arm, the policeman put out his hand to help her, withdrawing it hurriedly as sharp, needle-like teeth showed in a business-like way. There was a curious sound coming from the dog, rather like the whirring of an old clock before it strikes the hour.

'A good watchdog, nein,' the man said admiringly, and then, as his face convulsed with laughter, stepped back into the car to the chorus of our profuse thanks. We rushed into the hallway to be met by Mimi, who, in relief at the sight of us, did not notice what Azalea was carrying.

'I've put your bags on board,' she said, and not letting us catch breath, hurried us out to the coach park where Mike had the coach waiting with its engine running. Mike started off with a jerk that unseated nearly everyone in the coach, keeping them well occupied so that they did not notice Gretel. If anyone noticed the strong smell of dog, there were no complaints and we were able to go to our new seats across the aisle. Only Gareth Findlatter seemed to see us.

Feeling his stare on us I glanced up, to find him looking anxious before he had time to compose his expression. Nice of him to worry about us, I thought. There were smiles at Azalea, who still wore the rose, all along the coach. As she dropped into her seat, she propped the shoulder bag so that it blocked the view from the seat across the aisle. 'We'll give her a bath tonight. Poor darling, she's worn out.'

Almost immediately after a hopeless attempt at some sort of toilet, the dog fell asleep on Azalea's knee, twitching and groaning and sometimes – to our horror – snoring. To cover the sound, Lea was smitten with sudden coughing fits. When Mimi came round we covered the sleeper with a scarf.

'Would you like a cup of coffee?' Mimi asked with a friendly grin. 'You'll have to drink it with me at the back, or they'll all want it.'

'That would be lovely,' I said, just as the scarf heaved, and the dog sat up and sneezed.

'What's that?' asked Mimi, round-eyed in fascination. We got up and moved toward the back and the kitchenette.

'A good question,' I muttered. 'Just a souvenir of Heidelberg. That and the rose.'

'Dogs are not allowed on the coaches,' Mimi said automatically.

'We're not sure it is a dog.' Azalea said, trying to cover it up. Gretel refused to be covered up, thinking Lea was playing a lovely game. And all the while, the creature looked at her with love shining out of its blackcurrant eyes.

'Any pets,' amended Mimi, visibly weakening. 'I would say it was some sort of dog. You have to have it registered, papers and so forth,' she trailed on distracted by Gretel's grubby charm.

'The owners reported it lost to the police in Heidelberg. We checked,' I added quickly.

'Yes, and the owners didn't want the little darling. So we get to keep her.' Azalea cooed. Lucky us, I added mentally.

'All her papers were there, left with the police. She must have gone missing very near where we found her.'

'A miracle,' Mimi said reverently. A miracle the owners got rid of Gretel so easily I thought cynically. 'Just amazing,' Mimi mused. 'Goes to show you, doesn't it?'

'That's what I said,' Azalea replied wistfully, aiming at me. 'It was a sign I was to find her and care for her.' I refused to feel guilty for my lack of faith. Or love for Gretel. Frankly I had other fish to fry. A worried uncle, my future in his company, and the fate of our clients. The mobile buzzed: Uncle Charles right on cue. Silencing the ring I looked about hopelessly for a more private place to talk. On a coach, options were slim or none at all. I stepped into the small toilet area and answered.

'Babs! Checked those snaps on Interpol web site. Made a few calls.' Uncle Charles must have been worked up: he chopped off his articles of speech when he was upset. 'Watch him. Involved in burglaries and other petty thefts. Picked up two years ago on blackmail charge. Never proved.'

'How did he get himself in this situation then?' Thorough background checks were required for coach drivers.

'Good question. Checking on that too.'

'What about the other matter? The double bed episode. Any thoughts?'

'Not yet. Just be careful. Otherwise, everything all right?'

'Yes, fine. I'll send an email with any developments from Salzburg.'

'Good enough. We'll stay in touch. Watch yourself.'

And he was gone. I'd have to call him back later when we got to Salzburg and explain about the dog. I had chickened out this time.

'How long till we get to Salzburg,' I asked, ignored as Mimi and Lea contemplated the mysteries of the Universe and Divine Intervention.

'It would be kind of cute, if it was clean,' Mimi considered, petting at Gretel's grunge-coloured fur disdainfully. Apparently the spiritual view did have its limit.

'We thought of giving it a bath.'

This launched a deep discussion of how to go about sneaking a small dog past a concierge and the best method of hotel dog-bathing. Mimi dipped down into a small refrigerator for a small packet wrapped in white butcher's paper. 'I bought some lamb chops to save me time in Salzburg. That's where I live. I married an Austrian. Do you think he will eat raw meat?' Her husband? I wondered. Shouldn't she know?

This question was superfluous. They had settled both dog and meat packet on the counter, where Gretel quickly attacked the parcel. Azalea moved them both into the small sink while Mimi made coffee.

Misty-eyed, Azalea said, 'It's so good of you. Please let us pay for them. I think we'd better save some of the chops for later.'

Gretel soon disposed of the meat of the first chop and was attacking the bone, which was almost as long as herself, while we repaired to the pantry. We enjoyed our cups of coffee with Mimi, who scarcely ever glanced at the passing scenery except to check where we were. I was worried about Mike and what he was up to. We would have to keep a close eye on him when we made our stops.

My expression must have belied my fears for Mimi smiled at me inquisitively.

'I suppose the scenery palls on you in time?' I asked.

'Not in Austria, it's so fabulously beautiful.' Ah, German Alps weren't quite so appealing. Dramatic but they could seem stark.

'We shall miss you when you leave the coach at Salzburg,' Azalea said wistfully.

Mimi's deep breath threatened the seams of her uniform. 'I've been thinking about that. Carl – my husband – was taking some time off but couldn't get much, so I might as well stay on this tour. I'd have to get permission, of course from HQ. Actually I don't speak Croatian but my German is useful. Carl gets in from the Swiss run tomorrow and I'll speak to him about it, but he can't really object.'

'You mean ... you might come with us all the way?' Azalea looked flatteringly ecstatic.

'Yes.' Mimi nodded in the direction of the sink where the pup was getting angry because it couldn't make much impression on the chop bone. 'Remember, if anyone complains, I'll have to do something about it.'

'We'll keep her quiet,' Azalea promised. At the moment there seemed no difficulty as Gretel slept heavily when we were back in our seats. The problem might become more acute later, for with good food might come high spirits and the need for a dog toilet. She had already given a sample of her playfulness.

We tried to relax and watched the scenery flashing by, Mike evidently determined to make up for lost time. Mimi thought he was overdoing it, for even her practised undulations to the motion of the coach were becoming difficult. Her remonstration was greeted with a dark scowl., 'English,' hissed Mike, forgetting the intercom was switched on.

'Men!' Mimi signalled to us with her eyes as she switched off the microphone. After a thorough glance round the coach she subsided in her seat at the front and we all sank into the torpor which was becoming familiar to us now. Only something sensational in the way of scenery roused us and this was provided in Bavaria where Mike allowed us a brief tea stop at an inn outside Munich.

Azalea carried Gretel in her shoulder bag where she settled down happily with a second chop. We arranged to go in separately for tea and I won the toss to enter first. The cream cakes were glorious and I would have liked to linger over them but I gulped down some tea while Azalea dashed off in search of a grass plot. When we met, she said, 'Successful, so that's one worry over.'

We sighed with relief. I took the shoulder bag which was jerking about and rushed into the coach, releasing the pup who immediately became playful, making nips at my fingers with her rice-like teeth. I passed the time by watching our driver Mike chatting up Abby, Mrs Fraser, who was in fine form today. She looked the high-maintenance type who invested heavily to make sure she didn't look it. She smiled back openly. My, my ! Curious, I tucked the pup under my baggy T-shirt and trotted back out, over to their little scene. They were really getting on well when Mr Fraser joined them. I only reached them by that point and didn't really hear anything until the end when Mike shook his hand and, looking back toward the coach, explained he really did have work to do. For my benefit no doubt, as well as Ted Fraser's. But there was no mistaking that momentary 'caught-out' look that blew across his face like a passing thunderstorm on a spring day, before it flashed back again into his obsequious smile. Mike tipped his driver's hat at me and turned, ambling back to the coach.

Ted and Abby had their heads bent together in some serious conversation as I headed for them. Spotting me, Ted smiled nervously, and guided Abby directly back to the coach without even a hello. Abby must be quite a handful to keep in check. It seemed Mike made the most of his position as driver for the firm, chatting up whoever took his fancy – assuming that's what it was – and also in general, as he spotted Wemys and made a move to corner him.

Wemys up right behind me into the coach carrying that art case as always, but Mike stopped him as he boarded, his German accent unmistakable. 'Mr Veemus, would you like me to lock that case up for you? Then you could move about freely without being concerned for its safety.' Wemys declined of course, and nearly ran me down as he went back to his favourite seat. Maybe Mike was just goading him about the mysterious way he dragged that case around everywhere he went, like a nervous little squirrel with an acorn, or maybe he was intent on finding out why Wemys was so attached to it. Potential for theft or blackmail on Mike's part?

Gradually the coach filled up and I was becoming anxious when Mimi finally went to round up Azalea. They emerged from the inn, followed by a stout gentleman who handed Azalea a parcel with a courtly bow. Mimi jumped aboard after Azalea, who stayed at the door, waving until we were round a bend. Mike was making his usual time. In a hurry to meet a girl at the next stop? Hard to imagine that women fell for his smarmy charm.

'He was so sweet,' she said contentedly as she seated herself. The pup made a dive for her, discovered that the bag smelled interesting and pawed it experimentally.

Azalea opened the bag. 'Oh lovely. Some scones and cakes – those wonderful marzipan things – my favourites. I just complimented him on the cakes and he told a girl to fetch some more. He's a widower with nine children. They sound such an interesting family!'

'He'll probably remain a widower if he has nine children,' I concluded.

We all three ate in blissful contemplation of our good fortune until I realised the pup was eating equally as much as we were. Considering her size, it was likely that trouble lay ahead.

'I don't suppose she can deny herself,' Azalea said sympathetically. 'Well then, someone ought to deny it on her behalf!' I snapped. Azalea looked pained.

We found when we looked around the coach that some of the passengers had rearranged themselves in the previously empty seats and the seat opposite to ours was luckily empty. But not for long. Mr

Findlatter came and talked to us, and inevitably got round to asking us what the whirring note was coming from under the scarf. Lea and I exchanged glances, and then she lifted the covering and revealed the now stout creature who already seemed one of the family.

He chuckled at Gretel's tough pose. 'That's quite a growl you have there, if you can call it that.' He tickled gently around her ears and chucked under her chin, giving Gretel a chance to nip at so close a target with her tiny teeth. He laughed good-naturedly and softly closed her muzzle between his thumb and forefinger. I thought it was funny, but Azalea did not.

'You're hurting her feelings,' Lea said. 'She's not all that funny.'

'I'm sorry. It was so unexpected. What are you going to do with her?'

'Give her a bath for a start. Get her back to England. Whatever we can do. You'll keep our dark secret, then.'

'You mean ... they don't know about her?'

'Mimi knows.'

We explained the circumstances to date and he said he would help all he could. 'Though it might not amount to much as …'

Here his voice trailed away and I finished for him, before I could check myself, 'You have to watch Wemys.'

There was an appalling silence. I wished I hadn't said it. Other than observing him watch Wemys and that I was a little suspicious of the man myself, I had no cause to comment on Gareth Findlatter's activities. I had made a few notes about him for Charles on my mobile. I felt my face grow hot. His gray eyes met mine and they looked very cold indeed, all the laughter lines gone.

'What made you say that?'

Feeling foolish I blurted, 'Things add up to a hunch. I do apologise. It's no affair of mine.'

His expression relaxed as he watched my face. 'Don't worry about it. It'll soon be over.'

'At Salzburg?' Azalea asked. As he nodded she went on, 'We only noticed because we have trained eyes. I am an artist and Barbara is doing a little job for someone.' She winced as I kicked her ankle.

The smile was back in his eyes again. 'I'll keep your secret if you'll keep mine.'

'Agreed. Are you a policeman,' I asked.

'No. Are you?' His direct and level look said one thing, while the curl at the edges of his very intriguing mouth said quite another. Retired and doing private investigations perhaps?

I made a denial and he laughed companionably. By now the pup had accepted Mr Findlatter and graciously allowed him to scratch behind her ears, before she drifted off to sleep, overcome by the warmth of her surroundings. We estimated that she was almost as tall lying down as she was standing up. If anyone saw her lying there limply, they might think her to be a bit of coarse fur thrown down. It was only when the shining eyes were opened that she looked so alive. We called her a pup because of her size but she was a fully-grown toilet brush.

'You might not be continuing with us after Salzburg?' I asked, feeling unaccountably bereft.

He hesitated. 'I really don't know. Something should resolve itself – or show the way forward.'

Perhaps thinking we might question him further, he moved on and we relapsed into our thoughts, not exchanging notes until a scene of grandeur amid the mountains made Azalea break out lyrically. Roused too, the dog sat up and barked, which precipitated a further fit of coughing on Azalea's part. Obviously anxious, the nice young man, Colin Barnes, came to the back of the coach and seated himself opposite.

'You're not getting a cold?' he asked. 'I've had my window open. Are you in a draught? I know the air con was not on and it seemed a bit stuffy.'

'No draught.' She gave him a lovely smile and tried in vain not to look mysterious.

'We might as well tell him,' I said, whisking the scarf from the pup and watching his reaction. A slow, engaging smile widened his face. He and the pup stared at each other unwillingly until the animal made a playful sortie towards him in the same instant that Colin put out a tentative hand.

'That beats all,' he said and awaited our explanations.

'So you see,' Azalea wound up softly, 'we couldn't do anything else.'

He looked deep into her eyes. 'No, you couldn't. You certainly couldn't.'

I broke it up by saying, 'Don't press too hard on her stomach. It's stretched to its limit.'

'Oh, sorry.' Colin moved his hand away hastily and came back to present surroundings. 'What are you going to do with him?'

'Her. We don't know yet. Take her back with us. We shall live a minute at a time.' Azalea sounded more confident than she probably felt. 'You won't talk about this to anyone? We particularly don't want Mike to know.'

'I'll not say a word.' He gave her an eager look. 'Just let me know if there is anything I can do.'

'Thank you. I knew I could rely on you. You and Mimi and Mr Findlatter are the only ones who know yet.' The secret band was growing by the minute.

'Welcome to the club,' I said. A spasm of amusement crossing his face surprised me; there was more to Colin Barnes than met the eye.

'I think we're arriving somewhere,' Lea said, and almost immediately Mimi confirmed this by rushing down the coach with such meaningful grimaces in the direction of the pup that it must have intrigued some of the passengers. I was hoping it was Salzburg and sneaked a look at the caller ID as I turned my mobile on. Heads were turned in our direction but we gave reassuring smiles all round. A surreptitious glance at the screen showed Uncle Charles had called back three times, leaving a message the first two times. He was getting frustrated and probably worried. I'd have to find a way to phone him discreetly.

Under his breath Colin breathed, 'I'm going to enjoy this trip. I had my doubts at first but now I'm glad I came.' I smiled back anxiously, in a panic: the mobile display glowed and the screen flashed Magic Carpet Tours. I couldn't answer.

'So am I,' enthused Azalea. His face glowed in response until she added, 'If I hadn't, I'd never have found this darling.' She dropped her darling inside the shoulder bag where the toilet brush disappeared with a startled look but an air of acceptance. Anything must be better than the churchyard existence.

We felt we ought to enter Salzburg to the sound of music, as in the film, but all was quiet, the streets fairly empty, the workers gone home and the shops closed for the day. We went below the castle on its hill, across a swiftly flowing river by a wide bridge into the old part of the town. The street was narrow and the buildings four or five storeys high, their dark facades relieved by gaily painted shutters and quaint signs over doors. Mike drove us into a quiet courtyard where, across the cobbles, was our inn, looking like an illustration in a fairy tale. The few people in the streets had appeared cosmopolitan because of their plain clothes and rolled umbrellas, but here a man appeared from the recesses of the inn clad in short lederhosen, bright green socks, plaid jacket and with a cock feather in his hat. I snapped him against the background of the inn on my mobile though the man scowled when he saw me doing it, then sent it to Charles's mobile with a text that we had just arrived in Salzburg, everything was fine, and I would call ASAP as promised. I was hoping the mood of the photo would convey that we were safe and had just been unable to phone.

'Perfect,' I sighed with relief. Now maybe my uncle would calm down. My phone was down to one meagre bar, nearly dead. Sending the snap must have done it. As I turned to go in at the doorway to our inn, Mike and I nearly collided. 'Oh, so sorry,' I stammered. Catching me, he put me straight, with the usual nominal concern for safety. As I looked up to thank him, I was startled to see a snarling look that matched the scowl of the man in lederhosen. Was Mike angry with him on my account? Not like him to be as concerned as all that!

'Oh, don't worry about me,' I assured Mike. 'That guy's probably just having a bad day at the salt mines or something.'

'Hmm?' Taking no notice of me, Mike's eyes never faltered from the man across the street as he distractedly and somewhat rudely pushed past me in the narrow doorway. The man's gaze shifted from Mike and back to me, questioning, as if he were fitting together pieces of a puzzle. He had paused in the shadow of an outbuilding, openly and rudely studying me. He had a slightly hyena-ish look about him to start with: a broad, toothsome face drawn back into a scowl now deeply etched into his long, angular face.

Mike followed his gaze over his head to find me peeking from the door. 'Best get in and get yourself sorted out,' Mike said, abruptly.

One more look back at the local in lederhosen sent me scuttling into the pump room. What was he so mad about anyway? You dress up in costume in a tourist town and tourists are going to take your picture. It should be as simple as that, but then I couldn't shake off the feeling there was something more going on – that he was a threatening predator, like the hyena he resembled. Mike stepped back into the door, his face in profile, and I was prompted to text a short message to Uncle Charles that Mike and the man in the previous text might be involved in a blackmail scheme.

I was relieved to blend into the sea of my fellow passengers where they overflowed in the hall, waves surging into the public rooms until they were controlled by one Heinrich Junior. All of 70, Heinrich Junior was as expert at guiding clients into the rooms allotted to them as a skilled billiard player is in getting balls into the pockets. Within minutes, where there had been chaos, calm reigned. Nevertheless, I kept an eye on the door for the Hyena in traditional clothing.

I didn't mention it to Azalea when we got to our room. No sense in both of us feeling jittery. The habits of dogs provided distraction enough. 'And no one spotted the pup,' Azalea said with satisfaction, releasing her, at which the puppy promptly made a pool on the cold floor covering.

'It's your dog,' I pointed out as I plugged in my mobile to charge while I called Uncle to see if he had got my messages yet and to tell him about the dog, 'so you'll have to clean up after her. Also, it would appear, you'll have to house train her – or is she just short of walks? Either way, it's your responsibility'

Looking thoughtful, Azalea mopped up with a shoe-cleaning cloth, wrung out at the hand basin. 'We might bathe her now,' she said and then exploded as the dinner gong sounded. 'There's no time to do anything on these tours. It's hell.' The voicemail greeting droned in my ear. I dialled the number of Uncle Charles's apartment and left him a quick, superfluous message to check his mobile to let me know when he learned anything – as if he wouldn't. Turning to Azalea I said, 'Well, it isn't everyone who wants to bathe a dog. Ask if it was our fault that we were late in starting out.' I tried not to sound too stuffy but Azalea muttered to herself as she made preparations to go down to dinner. These consisted mainly in placing the cobbler's rosebud tenderly in water and settling the pup, with the last chop, under the bed. We guessed she might go out like a light once she was fed. As silently as we could we stole from the room and locked the door, hoping she would not notice our going. On the corridor we waited for an outcry but all was quiet from within. We tiptoed down the passage.

In the dining room, those who were fortunate enough to be seated by the window could look out onto the cobbled yard and get a glimpse over the roofs at the castle. We, being latecomers, had to content ourselves with a table in the corner near the kitchen. This we shared with a middle- aged couple who, we soon learned, were a bank proprietor and his wife, Mr and Mrs Gordon. The talk gradually veered to their hobbies, horse riding (hers) and stomachs (mostly his). He was a chronic dyspeptic for whom Azalea had promised a cure after the first five minutes, giving him the address of a firm specialising in herbal remedies.

'That and sharing your wife's hobby would be perfect for you,' Azalea told him with all the confidence of a complete amateur. 'Horse riding would shake up your liver and take your mind off your worries. I am sure it must be nerve- wracking working in a bank and being responsible for people's money.' Her face was alight with compassion for his problem and he was completely captivated. So was his wife who did not seem to mind when he patted Azalea's hand. This was a brief caress, for the waiter slapped down plates of hors d'oeuvres whose mysteries we were soon unravelling in some enjoyment mixed with apprehension.

'Did you bring those pills?' Azalea hissed at me and then dissolved into smiles as Mr Gordon gave a yelp of laughter. 'This is a case of physician heal thyself, isn't it?' she said. 'I was referring to those anti-upset pills. They're invaluable when you go abroad.'

'Yes, I packed them,' I assured her.

We ate rapidly, anxious to get back to the bedroom to check on the pup. When we were having cheese and biscuits (yes, biscuits) Mimi came up to us, followed by Mike. They had been doing the round of the tables and ours was the last, with Mike's scant patience wearing thin. Mimi sang out,' I'm off now.'

'This is where you live,' said Azalea, remembering.

'Yes. I'm going off duty. Mike will be able to help you with any problems. Are you doing anything this evening? Some of the others plan a tour of the town. It was Mike's suggestion.' Yet more commission going his way, I wondered ?

'Only an idea,' said Mike easily, staring hard at Azalea whose smile was becoming fixed. She gave a swift glance at me and we had no need for speech.

'Thank you but we don't plan to go out anywhere special tonight. We might go out later to get some fresh air.'

'Room all right?' queried Mimi with a directness we could not misinterpret.

'Rather. Peaceful and quiet,' we said in unison. I noticed she had her fingers crossed.

'Well, I'll say au revoir then until nine o'clock the day after tomorrow.'

Mike turned to her in aggressive surprise. 'I thought there was a switch made here?'

'There was going to be.' Mimi smiled. 'I rang through and they said I could continue.'

'I see.' Mike looked thoughtful – almost put out. He bowed suddenly and with a muttered Excuse me, turned on his heel and left us. Hmm. Something else to report. I wondered if it had anything to do with working cons with specific couriers.

Mimi shrugged. 'Odd fellow, but a good, safe driver. Ah well, it takes all sorts.'

'You've been splendid,' Azalea began. 'We're terribly grateful to you for not splitting on us.'

'And break up the team? Never. Well, good luck – and be careful.' Azalea's converts had instant, deep and lasting loyalty.

Of course, when Mimi had gone, we had to explain to the Gordons about Gretel and they said they were thrilled to be admitted to the club.

As we went upstairs, Azalea said, 'They're nice. We are lucky, Babs.' When she put the key in the door a whirring noise came from under the bed, followed by a shrill, furious bark.

'It's only us,' hissed Azalea, putting on the light. The pup wriggled forward, showing her pleasure, her tail going frantically in a curious, circular motion. When she had washed us both with a rasping pink tongue she calmed down slightly, but followed every movement, occasionally getting herself trodden on.

The sympathy extended to her by Azalea made her groan with ecstasy, only curtailed by the piece of cheese I had taken from the dinner table. As the pup ate (against my better judgement – my fault this time – why had I done it?) Azalea ran warm water into the hand basin, testing it with her elbow in a professional manner that made me stare.

'Could I borrow your shampoo,' she asked, not looking at me.

'My shampoo? Why mine.'

'I didn't bring any. And we can't use soap.'

'Why not? Would her hair drop out? Would it matter? She seems to have plenty.' Subdued by Azalea's 'we are not amused' look, I handed over the shampoo bottle and watched her prowess with the pup, who after the first shock seemed rather to enjoy the warmth and attention. As Azalea dried the now much more solid creature, she said in delight, 'She's a blonde. She's going to be beautiful when she's dry and we've combed her.'

'With my comb?' I asked suspiciously. 'She is going to look enormous when she's combed out and dried.' She didn't deign to answer but brought the dog a saucer of water and watched it lap with as fond an air as if she were its mother. I swear there were tears in her eyes. When and if the separation came, no doubt Azalea would go into mourning. I would have to lend her my black dress. I was not prepared for her next words which just go to show you cannot ever fully understand another person.

'I wonder what Mr Wemys carries in that case that is so valuable?'

My mouth opened but I couldn't reply.

'Well, if he is an artist, he must consider his work to be so good he can't bear the thought of losing it, or he's carrying something precious and ...'

I interrupted her. 'If it were valuable he wouldn't get it through the customs without an export licence. He could be trying to smuggle it instead.'

Seeing she was suitably impressed, I handed her my second-best comb and watched her groom the pup, who wasn't too keen on this part of the operation. 'And considering Mr Findlatter is always just one step behind him ...' I trailed off, for Azalea obviously wasn't with me. 'Isn't she adorable?' Azalea stood back to admire the creature, who looked up with an almost sickeningly romantic, adoring manner.

The tail, curled like a chrysanthemum over her back, was revolving more madly than ever.

'She is rather angelic,' I admitted weakly, feeling the creature's eyes expectantly on me. I liked really big dogs but Azalea loved every creature imaginable.

'That's it. Angelique. We shall call her Angelique.'

'I've got used to thinking of her as Gretel but she does look like an angel,' I agreed.

Azalea gave me an 'I told you so' look which I deflected by turning the conversation back to our mystery: 'So tomorrow we try to find out what Mr Wemys is up to?'

'Yes, why not?'

'It was odd that Mike should look put out about Mimi continuing the tour.'

'Mm. I never thought I would develop into the sort of person who watches behind lace curtains.' Azalea picked up Angelique and kissed her, switched on the electric fire and put the pup down again in front of it to dry off. Her former bedraggled coat was taking a more sensible shape, with a leg at each corner!

As the knock came on the door, we stared at each other in dismay. After some pantomime between us, Azalea opened the door an inch. 'Oh, it's you. Come in.'

Looking shy, Colin Barnes slid in and for a moment did not notice Angelique as he was so taken up with Azalea. When he did spy the pup he stopped dead in his tracks. 'That's not...'

'It is. Let me introduce you again to Angelique.'

'My word, she's a, a, er – pure bred something. Hairy, wide muzzle. I didn't spot it before because she was all matted up.' He stooped to stroke her ears with a long finger. 'I just called in to see how you ladies were settling in with Angelique here.'

'Everything's just fine. No trouble at all.' Azalea let her charm rest on the unsuspecting Colin. 'I don't suppose you would like to take a stroll with us before we turn in?'

He looked deep into her eyes. 'Oh. Why – I'd love to.' His Adam's apple bobbed convulsively. Watching him, I recognised that there would be several aching hearts before this trip was over – for one reason or another.

We were glad of Colin's company when we gave Angelique a last airing. As we went down through the hall, I found I was rather hoping Gareth Findlatter would be in sight, but he was not. But then, neither was the Hyena – thankfully.

CHAPTER FOUR
SALZBURG

***In which Hyena Face makes an appearance
and Reverend Burnett faces a crisis***

At breakfast Azalea said, 'I don't want to rush round all day. Would you mind if I painted? I'd like to climb somewhere above the river and have a go at the castle.' I couldn't blame her.

If Heidelberg looked like a tale from a storybook, then Salzburg was the real thing. I wouldn't have been surprised to see seven dwarves trailing Snow White through the racks of goods on the pavements in front of the shops. Again there were flowers everywhere. The castle was in view wherever we went, even from outside the tiny hotel window. Perched and looming above the town, tucked into the alpine mountains, snow-covered peaks at higher elevations peaked out behind it, glistening white and pink as the sun's rays climbed their slopes, illuminating the rich, dark shades of black and green alpine forest so famous in this region. Where Heidelberg Castle had been rebuilt in stolid eighteenth-century stateliness, the creamy walls of Salzburg castle were pure baroque elegance, sporting towers and crenelated curtain walls. Like any castle, it had been added to and repaired throughout the years. But this one still retained the look and feel of its original purpose as a fortress when it was built in 1077, and was known as Festung Hohensalzburg, or simply Salzburg Fortress. It rose sharply above the town, hovering like a protective Aunt. Or Uncle.

Being inside the edge of the alpine forest gave the air a crisp tang, and at this elevation the sun seemed that much brighter than in our hardworking Manchester. No, I couldn't blame Lea for wanting to forego the usual tourist gawping, and to spend the day capturing the feel of this magical place. But mysteries seemed to be my thing on this tour, whether or not I wanted it that way. I had missed out on taking the tour of Heidelberg castle – I really didn't want to miss out on Salzburg too. The original fortress town still existed inside the high walls, where the streets were filled with commerce as they have been for centuries. 'You spend the day painting and I'll keep my eye on Angelique. But perhaps I ought to circulate among the guests a bit for Uncle Charles's sake. I'd like to take the castle tour.'

Azalea looked guilty. 'Should we have gone out last night with the others? To see what Heidelberg offered in the way of night life?'

'I don't think we missed much. The tour was very interesting – at least I heard so from the Burnetts – but they were a bit taken aback when they had to go into a nightclub. I gathered they wished they hadn't gone – it was rather expensive. But Mike insisted, and they didn't want to seem spoilsports.'

A local Heidelberg travel guide claimed over 300 clubs, bars, and restaurants, all promising a fabulous nightlife for the younger set, and brimming with excitement. Hard to imagine the Reverend and Mrs Burnett in loud, smoky bars rocking out to the latest in German punk. They should have waited to visit urbane, genteel Salzburg's more sophisticated fare.

As we exchanged glances, she voiced my thought. 'Another little graft? He's a busy bee, isn't he? Perhaps he was afraid Mimi might spoil his chances, his schemes, if she continued on this run.'

'I would like to know what he's up to.'

'Well,' said Lea, throwing her all-purpose bag over her shoulder, 'I want to know what your Mr Findlatter is up to. There's more there than meets the eye.' I certainly hoped so.

'One of us must go on his next suggested outing,' I decided. We set aside detecting for the moment as we stepped out onto the pavement of Salzburg to face the day. It was breathtakingly beautiful and sparkling. Feeling our spirits rise with our surroundings, we laughed as I helped Azalea transport her painting materials to the perfect spot inside the public grounds of the castle. Crowds milled about, enjoying the period costumes and playful shouts of the vendors, watching street acts swallow fire and juggle apples. The sparkling city of Salzburg opened dizzyingly below us; red and ochre roof tops were arranged narrowly between rows of thick, dark tree tops. The copper-patinaed domes of Salzburg Cathedral poked stridently up into the cityscape, reminding me to visit them and see the frescoes inside.

All was heaven for the first time on this trip. That is, until Azalea became chagrined to see someone had forestalled her. The very mysterious Paul Wemys had already set up his easel case and was contentedly painting the view – not of the castle scene, to which he had his back turned, but of the roofs of the town. Behind his back Azalea silently mouthed the question on both our minds: Casing the joint for some reason? We had got the hang of all the jargon by now.

Wemys's painting was good too; even I could see that. But where I had only appreciated the morning light on the colourful town, Wemys had captured it. He was a genuine artist. We had scarcely recognised him at first for he had had a much-needed haircut. Had he been in too much of a hurry before leaving home to have a trim? Today, the case he had guarded so jealously was wide open to the crisp sunshine and the gaze of passers-by. I caught Azalea glancing in there and wondered if her curiosity might get the better of her, given the opportunity.

My mobile buzzed in my back pocket, startling me into answering it before I took a good look at the caller ID.

Finally it was my uncle.

'Oh, hell-ooo,' I answered, sprinting out of earshot.

'So, anything else?'

'Seems this driver is very interested in Abby Fraser. Ted, her husband, keeps warning him off, though. And then our driver seems to be getting something back from the proprietors of the places we stop at for coffee and drinks in bars at night. Nightclubs the same.'

'Well, not nice. But hardly a crime.'

'I get the feeling there's something other than unbridled lust for Abby Fraser.'

'It's up to you if you want to follow something potentially purely personal between passengers – and driver. Just watch yourself.'

'And there may be a scheme with the Heidelberg accommodations. Seems like a lot of money for so antiquated a place.'

'No, that's the right place. Clients like to have an authentic stay occasionally.' Complete with authentically rude chamber maids. 'Going to try and join you. Few loose ends. All alone. The weekend you know. Be careful, won't you?'

He was trying to keep the worry out of his voice. But there it was: poor little Babs, always in need of rescue. Help was on the way. I wanted to solve this before he got here, to prove I could take care of myself. Maybe not just to him, either.

I ambled back over to join Azalea. Wemys studied the sky as he put down his palette (he was painting in oils) and said, 'That's enough of that. The light's changing too fast for my comfort."

Azalea (who had been painting in water colours) smiled sweetly at him. 'I'll look after it for you if you want to go for a stroll.'

'It's very kind of you. I think I'll have a look in the castle. It's years since I was in there.' He tidied up his case but left it open before he strolled off, remarking, 'There's a little dog that seems to have taken a fancy to you.'

'Really?' She gave Angelique a wink. 'Perhaps it's an art lover."

Wemys laughed and went off. He had scarcely disappeared through the castle archway before Azalea was rummaging through his case.

'Quick!' I crowded nearer, trying to block the view from the others. Angelique moved nearer too.

'I thought there might be a false bottom and he was smuggling drugs or something,' she said, disappointed, when her search revealed nothing except that Wemys' artist's case was exactly that.

'You would think they were the crown jewels the way he drags it around.'

A laugh immediately behind us made us whirl round guiltily and, though distressed, we were relieved to see Gareth Findlatter, who no doubt had been watching our antics.

'He's probably got rid of what he was carrying,' Mr Findlatter said, and we couldn't be sure if he was pleased or sorry.

'So you are watching him. I knew it.'

'Aren't you?'

'No, of course not,' I began indignantly, before floundering as I realised we had been caught with our hand in the till, so to speak. I looked to Azalea to back me up.

'We have a reason,' she said gently, licking her brush clean. It has always been a wonder to me that she hasn't died from chemical poisoning.

'I'm sure you have.' He waited, but Azalea shook her head.

'We can't explain.' There was a resigned, almost noble air about her concern. It was very well done – she would be invaluable in amateur dramatics.

'No, it's always hard to explain,' he admitted blandly. 'That's why I didn't try.'

'He's smuggling something?' Azalea persisted.

'Didn't you know?' He tried to read our expressions. It must have been easy, for my mouth had fallen open and Azalea looked as jubilant as if she had completed a crossword puzzle.

'How exciting. A real live smuggler. I wondered if it was drugs. I was examining the case to see if it had a false bottom.'

A strange, almost bewildered expression crossed his face. 'You're joking. No one would smuggle drugs from England into Europe.'

'Oh. That's obvious.' She made a helpless gesture and I saw his gorgeous gray eyes narrow and the muscles in his jaw jerk. For a moment he did not look at all the pleasant person he had seemed – he seemed dangerous. He stepped back into the shade of the trees: I followed his glance to where Wemys had emerged on the ramparts of the castle. When he realised we had seen him he waved. We waved back, but when I turned, Mr Findlatter had gone.

'A strange young man,' Lea said thoughtfully. 'I don't think he believed us.'

'Who would,' I said bitterly. 'He probably thinks we're a rival gang detailed to get the loot – whatever it is.'

She burst out laughing. 'I never knew coach tours were like this. You've only got to tell him you are merely vetting the arrangements for your Uncle Charles and …'

'And I might as well take the next bus back home. Besides, Mr Findlatter never tells us anything about his affairs. No, I want to find out what Mike is up to for one. I just hope Mr Findlatter won't talk about us to the others.'

'Why should he,' comforted Lea. 'He's up to something himself. Another one to observe.' She looked content at the prospect so I took heart. After all, my business was to look after Uncle Charles's affairs, and there my responsibility ended. It was not up to me to hold the hand of every member of the tour party. But an art thief was pretty exciting.

As Wemys came back, Azalea closed her portfolio, the water colour having dried almost instantly in the rising heat. 'Yours is still tacky,' she told him, and though her look had been casual, I felt it had been thorough.

'I'll finish it later,' he said. 'A few of these will pay for my trip and a bit over.'

'You're a successful artist,' she said admiringly. 'I'm just an amateur. Can you give me any tips?'

Hardly able to believe my ears, I had to look away hastily to cover my surprise. So often I had had to listen to her protestations that art was a personal thing, and that one must not be influenced by anyone else. Azalea was on to something.

His pale eyes flickered, and for a moment it looked as if he were going to respond to Azalea's charm, but he contented himself by saying, 'I've made a bit of money by copying Old Masters from time to time.' He grinned suddenly and we found ourselves warming to him. 'I can paint a better Mona Lisa than the original,' he boasted. 'In fact, I might have another go if we're in Paris long enough.'

'Fantastic.' Azalea was laying it on a bit thick. Of course, it was inevitable that he should accompany us back to the hotel for lunch. Angelique followed so closely that when we paused, her nose pushed against our ankles.

As we came in sight of the post office, Wemys excused himself. 'I've got a little bit of business to attend to.'

'And we've got to get stamps.' I nudged Azalea. 'For our postcards.'

'A weakness of ours,' she said. We joined a group at the counter and presently became aware of a policeman and a man in plain clothes who emerged from an inner room. I had stepped behind Wemys and I saw a pulse begin to beat in his temple. He was very pale as he moved towards Poste Restante and showed his passport. In a few moments he was handed a large, flat package – perhaps measuring two feet by one foot, for which he paid out a small sum of money.

It was then that the policeman and his plain clothes companion stepped forward, one on each side of Wemys. 'If you would allow us to see the contents of the parcel?' they said politely. They were joined by a small man, and the three of them formed a half-ring round Wemys, urging him along the counter.

'What's all this?' Wemys began but he did not appear angry. It was almost as if he had expected the encounter. 'It's only a painting.'

'Then you will not mind letting us see,' said the man in civilian clothes.

'Open it,' snapped Wemys and stepped to one side, as if in bewilderment or disgust. The small man of the trio untied the parcel with elaborate care, scrutinising the wrappings when his companions moved impatiently and then, rather as an anti-climax, lifted out an oil painting – a view of London from Waterloo Bridge.

"Well?' enquired Wemys sarcastically. 'I have an export licence for it.'

'We find that strange,' the policeman said. 'Such a painting, not being valuable, could be exported without a licence.'

'Yes, if you would permit me?' The rotund little man brought out a bottle of fluid and a rag. Weyms laughed.

'You think I've painted over a valuable masterpiece? I assure you I haven't. But go ahead – take off some of the paint. X-ray it if you like. It will amuse my client – perhaps even add to the value of the picture.'

Pursing his lips, the little man bent to his task, watched in fascination by his colleagues. There followed a low-voiced conversation, after which all three men bowed to Wemys and gave their apologies. One of them attempted to restore the package to its former neatness.

'Don't bother,' said Wemys roughly. 'Here, give it to me.' He stowed it under his arm, glared at them, muttered something uncomplimentary, and stalked out of the building.

Azalea and I stepped hastily to one side, and it was then we saw Mr Findlatter, who had also witnessed the scene. Perhaps had even engineered it?

I gave him a long look but he did not glance away. It was not possible to tell what he was thinking; his face was expressionless. My heart thumping, I followed Azalea to where he stood, not even glancing in the direction of the three men, who were retiring to an inner room.

'A valuable painting is missing,' Azalea pronounced. 'You think Mr Wemys has it. Why don't they search his things?'

A smile started in his eyes. 'I feel sure they have.'

'Really?' I had a feeling Mr Findlatter had too, but now was not the time to say it.

He looked at me. 'You won't mention to Wemys – about me? It will be better not to. And I'll not mention about you going through his effects. Then too, there was all that hanky-panky about changing rooms.'

I glared back, speechless. Azalea recovered her breath first. 'We won't say a word. Why should we? It will spoil the happy party feeling. We're all getting on so well together.'

'Yes, aren't we?' His expression was bland. 'Shall we all be having a splendid time at Hellbrunn this afternoon? I see a party is arranged.'

Before Azalea could reply, I snapped. 'We're going. Why not?'

'Why not, indeed?' He moved to the door and we followed, not intending to let him out of our sight, but he didn't seem disposed to leave us. It was embarrassing to have him point out that Angelique was about to follow us openly into the inn. In the excitement we had overlooked her. Hastily, Azalea scooped up the obliging little creature and dropped her into the shoulder bag. A muffled wuff came from Angelique before she accepted the inevitable and was silent.

At that moment the Burnetts came in, looking radiant after their morning's walk, and paused to exchange pleasantries with us. The man at the desk handed the Reverend a sealed envelope which he accepted in mild surprise. Obviously having something on her mind, Mrs Burnett ran upstairs and her husband opened the envelope. As he glanced at the contents, which appeared to be a slip of paper round a snapshot, the change in him was grotesque. He looked as if he had had the shock of his life.

'Bad news?' I asked.

'No. No, it's nothing.' He hastily stuffed the envelope into his breast pocket. The greyness was leaving his skin; he took a deep breath and was able to command himself again. 'Will you excuse me?' He went upstairs slowly, looking years older than when he had entered the hotel so happily minutes before.

We glanced at each other. Even Mr Findlatter looked concerned. 'That's too bad,' he murmured.

All during lunch (which incidentally was delicious, being ham, egg, tomato and mushroom cooked in the oven on individual platters) we could not help watching the Burnetts, who had elected to dine a deux in a corner. It was obvious he was toying with his food, and that his wife was worried to death about him. And all this on their silver wedding tour when they should have continued to be happy and contented. His abstracted air lasted until we were aboard the coach bound for Hellbrunn when he relaxed with a visible effort – mainly for his wife's sake, we imagined. It was pitiful to see her anxious little side glances when she thought he was not aware; but whatever it was that was worrying the Reverend, he was not going to share it with his wife. At least not yet. Salzburg must remain a happy memory for her. Even Mike had said we must make it memorable for them; that he would play some appropriate melodies.

Lea and I were distracted somewhat by our immediate neighbours, the Frasers. Mr Fraser appeared depressed, as if he wished he had not come on this holiday but she looked satisfied and was full of talk. She was another who had been everywhere and seen everything, and now, apparently, was on the second or third time round.

'You'll enjoy Hellbrunn. Won't they, Ted?' She said, pushing up the waves of her bronzed hair. There was a grunt from Ted, but his eyes brightened when Azalea leaned forward and said, 'Do tell us about it.'

Mrs Fraser was somewhat at a loss about the historical background of the palace we were to visit, though she remembered vividly enough to warn us about the gadgets and water traps in the grounds which were likely to catch out the unwary.

'I was soaked last time. They won't catch me again, I can tell you,' she said and we got the impression she was returning to the palace purely for the purpose of letting the attendants know she was on to them and their schemes.

About every place we mentioned – whether on the tour or off it – she usually replied, 'Oh, we've been there. We've seen it, haven't we Ted?' But she did make me think about keeping my lifeline high and dry. I slipped my mobile down inside Azalea's all-purpose bag where I knew it would be safe with Angelique guarding it, and Lea guarding Angelique.

Reading from the pamphlet we had picked up in a travel agent's, I learned that Hellbrunn Palace (Schloss Hellbrun,) had been built in the seventeenth century as a summer palace for an archbishop, whose sense of humour had been so acute that he had devised his extensive and beautifully laid-out pleasure grounds as traps for his friends and visitors. Reminded of my own tries at booby-trapping my parents, I reasoned it was probable that he ended up without many friends. We found the place full of damp grottoes where mechanical toys moved by means of water power. It was no place for the jittery: streams of water were apt to fly at you from any angle. When the archbishop had chosen to dine out of doors, his guests were still not immune: the fountains could play on them at a touch.

It was near the palace steps that Angelique caused a minor sensation. Once free of the palace, Azalea had let the pup have her freedom on the grounds of the surrounding park. We never glanced in her direction, and if people wondered why Azalea had a small dog's nose pressed close to her heels, they did not ask. The palace grounds were also home to a stone theatre, and a small zoo. The animals were fascinated by Angelique, watching her as long as she was in sight. When I later saw a black cat seated on a handsome balustrade

– watching the rabble with a disdainful air – I suspected there might be some action, but was not quick enough to prevent it. At sight of Angelique, who had not as yet seen him, the cat appeared to lose his nerve and wish to absent himself from the scene. He poured himself silently down the steps and disappeared amid the bushes. It was too much for Angelique, who hurled herself after the retreating creature with shrieks of joy. Her cries grew fainter as she headed up the hillside for the Monatschlosschen, a building erected simply because a guest commented that to do so would improve the view. Built in a single month, it had been dubbed the Little Month Palace – a folly that now housed an interesting collection of peasant furniture and costumes. Clearly they don't make archbishops the way they used to.

Azalea and I split up amid the paths but could see no sign of the pup. I was searching among the undergrowth when I became aware that someone was watching me. It was quiet amid the trees; I could not hear Azalea calling, and even the birds were silent. There was that familiar, haunted feeling, fearing attack around every corner, and suddenly I was back in the freight lift with those zombie-like mannequins falling in on me …

On that day so many years ago, I had watched secretly from behind a rack of women's coats as the assistants carefully settled the mannequins together. One of them called for help with a stand and I crept quietly up to them, thinking how wonderful it would be to dress the mannequins in some of the glamorous things I had seen that day. Slipping on a piece of tissue as I stepped onto the hard floor-covering of the lift, I accidentally knocked into a gracefully extended hand that rocked its owner, which rocked into the mannequins beside it, and in domino fashion, they each rocked in turn, one wobbling harder over here and another catching the wrist of another over there – and so on until the mannequins were all a-wobble. I had stood transfixed, unable to move, unable to shout, and certainly unable to get out of the way when they all fell on me – hard, dead fingers and limbs poking into me as their wide, evil smiles gleamed. Trapped on the floor of the lift under the weight of so many dead plaster bodies crushing me was bad enough. Lying there until the floor proprietor and his assistants returned a few minutes later was worse. It wasn't until they lifted away the last of the viciously smiling dummies that I finally had enough air in my lungs to scream …

So here I was, over twelve years later, my heart thumping, forcing myself to turn and look at the man standing behind the bush. He was grotesquely ugly; I was paralysed with horror until I realised he was wearing a mask. He spoke but the lips did not move; only the eyes glittered behind blackened sockets.

'Little girls like you should mind their own business.' The words were in German and I pretended I didn't understand, willing myself to run. As he loomed closer I stepped back, then caught myself. I wasn't nine years old anymore. And this was a real threat, not a plaster one.

I answered him in German. 'Go away! Or I shall call the police.' He laughed behind that hard, shiny, grotesque face, and though I couldn't really see his eyes, I knew that if I could have, I would have seen him laughing at me. Stabbed by the impotence of my words and flooded with the shame of the vulnerable, my mind went blank. My feet felt pinned to the floor.

I should have run. I should have screamed. But I couldn't. I was trapped by my own fear. Deserted by my good intentions. Suddenly this ugly, masked thing was on me, pushing me to the ground. His thumbs dug into my arms, his knee between my legs. Oh no! I cried, but no sound came from my panic-dry throat. I tried to fight, but my arms were frozen. It was like being trapped in a dream. I could see his delight at my fear through the eye-holes of his mask. I could smell the sour stench of wine and cheese on his breath. I wished I had the courage to snatch the mask from his face. I forced my hands up against him, scratching at him, but my finger nails only scraped the sides of the mask. My feet and hip pushed me up and away from him, my legs just getting free, when suddenly he was lifting me, lessening my leverage against the ground, my only defence. The next thing I knew was that his knee was in my back and a cord was twisting round my neck; my head nearly jerked off my shoulders. He landed between my shoulder blades, sending my arms flailing to my sides. I tried to wrench the cord away but I couldn't get my fingers between it and my throat. His knee was in the small of my back, holding me down while he pulled my throat to him, twisting the cord so that I couldn't breathe. Lights shot before my vision; faintness crept over me. I felt his hands on my jeans, going through my pockets, just before I blacked out. He was looking for something. I couldn't scream, couldn't do anything but struggle feebly against the enveloping blackness.

In the whirling void I heard shouts and suddenly was staggering free, falling to my knees as I took in great draughts of air. I felt sick, my neck throbbing. My head was one bursting ache. And I was filled with shame. And fear. It was the Hyena – he had followed me.

Some children ran past, not seeing me – I could not have shouted if I had wanted to. The man had disappeared. Hearing quick, neat steps along the path, I crawled and stumbled in the direction of the blessed sound to find Azalea approaching.

'Not a sign of her,' she began in a vexed voice, then noting my shocked appearance she asked, 'Babs! What's happened? You look awful.'

My face and throat were red with struggle, and there was evidence of my near suffocation – my clothes were dirty and covered with the leaves and twigs from the forest path. I was sorry my appearance frightened her, because seeing her made me feel better than I ever had in my life. I tried to take a step toward her but I was shaking violently. Azalea eased me back down, gently onto the cool, soft turf. Her touch was slight, tender. She drew me to her comfortingly, showing that fiercely protective side of Azalea. 'Oh, Barbara…'

I wept for a minute or so, and, trying to regain myself as I became aware someone else may come along any minute, tried for normality once more.

'A man …' I started, then stopped, not wanting to frighten her. 'I was blacking out. He had something around my throat. He must have heard you coming and took off.'

'You might have been ….' Thankfully she stopped there. 'Well, you look quite ill. We'd better notify the police so they can look for him before he hurts someone else.' Clearly she had misunderstood the reason for the attack. She helped me to my feet, which was made difficult by the pounding my spine had just taken. 'We'll have to tell the police, Babs.'

'We can't. I bet it's got something to do with Mike and his blackmail scheme. I wouldn't be safe in either event. Mike's our driver. I don't think he'd stick around if he thought we were on to him. That makes it even more crucial that he doesn't find out. So we can't say anything.'

Lea was trying hard to do the right thing, bless her.

'I have to figure this thing out by myself, otherwise …' It was my own shame at being a helpless victim that I didn't want Mike to know about. 'Otherwise. I'll look helpless.'

'You will not, Babs. No one thinks that but you. You know that.' Sighing, she gently plopped me down on a nearby bench. 'Okay, explain. What's this to do with Mike?'

'He and this Hyena Face guy in lederhosen exchanged some pretty serious threatening looks as I was trying to get into the hotel. The look on the other guy's face made me afraid that he had got the wrong impression, and thought I was either in Mike's camp or a threat to both of them – if they are working together. I sent both snaps to Uncle Charles and he checked them on Interpol's web site. Mike had some prior convictions for burglaries and a charge for blackmail. But that was never proved.'

'Let's get you cleaned up,' Lea comforted me. 'Come on.' I had regained some of my composure by the time I had explained in more detail about the little drama on the pavement outside our inn the night before, though little attacks of involuntary shudders did keep coming and going; I was still in shock. Azalea made me sip from her water bottle.

'I'm all right now. Let me talk it over with Findlatter first.'

Azalea agreed that was good advice. It bought me time too. I really didn't want to involve the police for all manner of reasons. My pride at being able to cope on my own was one of them.

'He acts like he knows what he's doing. But be careful. And we mustn't split up anymore.'

'Definitely not. You're my hero, Azalea. Let's find Angelique and have a real drink.'

'I'm sure you've earned one. But your neck is all red. He must have been a beast. Hadn't we better see to it?' she said gesturing toward the public rest rooms.

'In a minute.' I was eager to get back into the safety of the crowd, but as we re-entered the throng outside the shops I sought my attacker in every face.

I pulled my collar up as high as it would go and buttoned the top button as I went inside a shop. I was out again almost at once.

Glad to distract myself and Azalea from the whole event I said, 'No one has seen a cat or dog, but look who's over there. Mr Wemys and quite a few of the others: Call- Me-Daisy, you know, and her sister, with George Lonsties.' We hung round for a few minutes and saw Wemys emerge from the same shop. He came straight across to us in the most friendly way. 'Some interesting masks in there. I wouldn't mind painting some of them. Could be amusing.'

'Each to their own. I've seen some strange masks,' I said, pulling my collar ever tighter around my throat. My head had started to thrum terribly in the sun.

'You've been in? I didn't see you there.' Was Wemys being coy, or was he really as innocent as he seemed?

'No, out here. A man wearing a mask nearly frightened me to death.'

I heard Azalea's indrawn breath. Wemys looked at me with what seemed like genuine compassion. 'How extraordinary. Let's see if we can find a drink somewhere. You look all done in.'

'My thoughts exactly,' I answered coolly, settling for outrage in place of courage at the moment. What is that old Italian proverb? Keep your friends close and enemies closer? 'Yes, let's.'

Had Mike's blackmail scheme expanded to netting Wemys? Was the improbable Hyena Face threatening Mike on Wemys' behalf – and I simply got in the way? Who knows? My head whirled with ideas and pain.

We found a cafe near the entrance and ordered three stiff gin and tonics. We watched a flock of ducks as they splashed about, enjoying themselves in the water. That distraction and the good English gin quickly calmed my involuntary shudders. Even my head ceased to ache, and I held the cold glass to ease the burns on my throat. I could tell Azalea was worrying about the loss of Angelique only secondary to myself. Or was I flattering myself there?

As the cheque was brought to Wemys, Lea murmured, 'In my horoscope it said trouble was imminent. I didn't mention it in case it depressed you.'

I couldn't prevent a wry grin. I wondered if I were to be paid another visit by the man behind the hideous mask. Obviously I was treading on someone's toes. In whose business was I interfering? Was Mike already onto me? Did Wemys feel we were too interested in his career? Or did I just fancy Gareth Findlatter so much that I was taking his side against Wemys, who had so gallantly bought us drinks. Was the hotel proprietor in Heidelberg annoyed with our interference? Or had we stumbled on something we did not recognise yet? Into my mental vision floated the Reverend 's look of sheer, transfixed horror before he got hold of himself. I was sure he was being blackmailed. But what could this really nice man have done?

So many questions. I concentrated on my drink.

'You're both very quiet,' Mr Wemys said, stubbing out a third blue Gauloise.

We didn't tell him about the attack, or Angelique, who seemed to have gone from our lives as dramatically as she had entered. Azalea tried to rouse herself but looked as if she had just come from the funeral of her grandmother. My shock was wearing off, leaving me suddenly very tired. It was a relief to have George Lonsties approach our table with Pansy and her sister, Call-Me-Daisy. They were obviously charmed with their escort, who had risen considerably in their esteem. Lonsties' money and sophistication showed, despite his age and size. He was a charmer, that much was certain. I was comforted by his sudden presence.

'This is nice,' he boomed, pulling out chairs for them. 'What'll you have, girls? It's on me. We've got fifteen minutes, Mike says. So make the most of it.'

Yes, by all means, I thought, exhausted.

The 'girls' chose happily and if we were quiet, they didn't notice, for Call-me-Daisy and Pansy were full of their experiences in the grottoes. Both had been caught in the mechanical showers, but were now dried out. The fun of booby traps was very far away to me just now, and I found myself forcing a sympathetic response. Lonsties laughed indulgently – he had been before and knew when to dodge the fountains. Both women were acting a little coy, I thought, as if they had something on their minds – some scheme in which Lonsties was involved. All three were larger than life, exaggerating their responses to everything that was said or done. But perhaps my nerves were still on edge, and the girls and Lonsties only a little self-conscious. Seated slightly apart from the group, I watched George Lonsties give the younger Daisy a shrewd appraising look, and I wondered just how often he had visited Hellbrunn. Then as Daisy turned to him, laughing, he assumed the Father Christmas expression which seemed natural to him. As we climbed back into the coach we saw the Burnetts were already seated. Mrs Burnett gave us a bright smile but it had a brittle look around the edges; her husband looked frankly washed-out. 'An interesting place,' he agreed politely and stared through the window as if the antics of the ducks attracted him.

As we passed to the back of the coach Azalea sighed, 'That's that, I suppose. No more Angelique.'

'I don't think so. Colin Barnes is looking very mysterious.' I pointed to where the young man was making violent signs to us from a nearby doorway. He was holding the front of his jacket as if he had a bad case of heartburn. Beaming, Lea waved to him, grabbed her shoulder bag and slipped from the coach right under the nose of Mike who frowned and looked pointedly at his watch. Feeling tense, I waited, and I knew as soon as Lea returned, that Angelique was with us again.

Colin grinned at us under cover of the high seat backs and whispered, 'Found her barking at a cat up a tree. It was twice her size. Knew you'd be worried. Lucky thing she took to me from the first or she might not have let me pick her up.' He took her out of hiding, and she licked every available inch of Azalea and myself before falling into an exhausted sleep. Much to my chagrin.

'Oh you darling,' said Azalea all dewy-eyed and Colin Barnes beamed. He had taken the compliment to himself.

'I was just lucky.'

Yes, so lucky. And, of course, my mobile rang as if on cue. I sent the call into voicemail without bothering to look at the ID and slipped it back into Azalea's bag. I'd have to call Uncle Charles back when I was alone to give him the update. Instead of being an asset to the firm and to him, it seemed to me that I was still a child in need of his protection. That was a bit of an over-simplification, I suppose. Azalea agreed. The aftermath of terror, the dazzling sun, and the gin were taking their toll. All I wanted was a bath and bed. Gareth Findlatter glanced back at me but I returned his gaze coolly, not wishing to give anything away until I had a chance to talk to him at length about the assault, half wanting to gauge whether or not I felt he could be involved. I felt not. But I had other pressing worries on my mind. I leaned my head back against the soft seat and closed my eyes to all. Someone had thought that strangulation fitted my case. Also Reverend Burnett was in a daze of unhappiness and I had the womanly intuition that it was concerned with something pertaining to this coach tour. Something he could not even share with his wife, therefore too horrifying. Her concern was for him, not the subject which was making him so miserable. Something had gone sour for Reverend Burnett when he opened that envelope, and saw the slip of paper and snapshot. At least it had looked like a snapshot, but he had thrust it so hurriedly into his pocket that one could not be sure. Was it news of his sons? Surely he would have shared even bad news with his wife – unless he didn't wish to spoil her holiday. But her holiday was already spoiled. Any wife could tell when her husband was worried. How to help him in my Uncle's absence? If that were possible. My mind whirled. I was still in shock.

Uncle Charles had told me to record all my reactions concerning the trip. I reached into Azalea's all-purpose bag for my mobile, where I had put it just before we entered the palace. And that's when hit me. The attacker who had nearly garrotted me to death in the Schloss Park had to be the Hyena in lederhosen, and he was after the photo I'd taken of him. He was looking for the mobile. I was sure of it. But what about the mystery surrounding Wemys and Gareth Findlatter? I must confess my Nancy Drew and Miss Marple instincts flagged if only briefly when I thought of Findlatter. I glanced over at him and caught him looking at me, worried. I smiled nervously, checking that my collar covered my throat, and retreated once more to my inner sanctum to reason things out.

I debated calling Charles about my attack and all the rest of it when we got back to the hotel but realised that I wanted to prove who did it before I called. No point in having him fretting and fuming while I could just be more careful and solve the case. And not be a victim in need of rescue for a change. I still felt very wobbly but I was determined.

As we were decanted near the hotel, I kept close to the Burnetts, and heard him say, 'I'll go to the bank and get some money changed. I hate being kept short of small change.'

'Won't they change it for you at the hotel?*' she asked.

'I prefer the bank. You go in, dear. I'd like the walk.'

'I'll come with you.'

'No, dear. You have a rest – get ready for dinner.'

'But it's ages to dinner.' She stared at him, perplexed, before giving a resigned 'Oh very well.' She followed the crocodile which was slowly disintegrating and which suddenly lost its tail end as Azalea and I fell out to follow Reverend Burnett at a discreet distance.

'You need to get some money,' I hissed.

'Why do I need to?'

'To buy your godparent's hat.'

'I have enough cash for that.' She smiled. 'You really mean we have to find out what dear Reverend Burnett is up to. I'd better let poor Angelique out. She'll suffocate soon.'

It turned out that it was not suffocation that was worrying the pup. Panting and grateful she rushed to the nearest gutter and performed ecstatically, rolling her eyes until the whites showed.

'A near thing,' Azalea muttered. 'This coach tour is going to have its problems anyway, apart from your adopting half the travellers and suffering their tribulations.'

'If Reverend Burnett is miserable because of something that has happened on this tour, then it is my duty to find out what it is and report back to my Uncle Charles.' When she still looked dubious I added, 'You do see?'

She smiled at me with affection. 'I can see Uncle Charles has a treasure in you. I just hope he appreciates what you are doing on his behalf.' A second later she was flying up a side street in pursuit of Angelique who had spied yet another cat. I waited, fuming, trying to keep our quarry in sight. The pup must have a thing about cats. This one got away easily and I watched with approval as Azalea brought

Angelique back and spanked her. Angelique stared up at her as if she could not believe her senses, and scarcely took her attention off Azalea for the rest of the walk to the bank. Reverend Burnett was at the far end of the counter, at the place marked for Exchange, as we pretended to wait our turn. He was some time for he got a lot out on credit cards. If the clerk was surprised, it did not disturb his look of indifference. As the Reverend came away from the counter, I turned and studied a leaflet on the wall. I doubt if he saw me for he was so preoccupied.

I joined Azalea outside where she had elected to stay with the pup and we followed the Reverend, who was walking quickly now, as if he had some definite purpose in mind. Once, he stopped to buy a paper but did not do more than glance at it. Could he read German? Also, were we following too closely? We dropped back a bit, to be detained by the traffic lights when Angelique nearly committed suicide under a bus. After that Azalea carried her as we went hot foot in the direction we had seen Reverend Burnett heading. Crossing the river by the Statdbrücke, we nearly lost him again when he speeded up, and we only found him again when he paused to study a map of the city. 'At least we know he isn't sightseeing,' Azalea muttered as we passed many famous buildings at which he did not give more than a glance. We hadn't much time to look either, though I recognised the Rathaus from a brochure at our office. This city hall was situated in a stately if not rather dilapidated neighbourhood of four and five-storey residences of former burghers, dating back to medieval times.

We were soon approaching a main street of the newer part of the city, the Mirabellplatz. Reverend Burnett seemed surer of himself now for he approached the opulent Mirabell Palace (originally a love gift to an archbishop's courtesan) and went inside the entrance, coming out quickly and going through the wide gates into the gardens. We nearly bumped into him but I was just in time to snatch at Azalea's wrist and drag her round the corner of the entrance pillars. The pup gave a grunt of protest as her ribs were nearly stove in, wagging her tail in relief when Azalea put her down.

We watched the Reverend slacken speed; he appeared to examine the flower beds and admire the fountains before choosing to seat himself on a bench – the third from the gates. It was unoccupied except for himself: the gardens were almost deserted as the time for the evening meal approached. He kept glancing at his watch, and suddenly rose to his feet and walked away, paying little attention to his surroundings.

'He's forgotten his newspaper,' I said and had to repeat myself for the Reverend had spotted us and raised his hat.

'You've left your newspaper on the seat,' I pointed out, feeling foolish.

A tic started in his cheek. 'I've finished it but, of course – mustn't leave litter lying around!' He went back to the seat, picked up the folded paper and strode off, this time round the fountains. A woman in a smart dress over which she wore a green, peasant apron reproved us, 'You should not allow your dog to walk on the grass.' These fastidious Austrians were just too much.

I smiled at her. 'It isn't our dog. It's just following us about.'

Her expression became tender. 'Poor little thing. I will take it to the police.'

'Oh no,' squealed Azalea. 'We were just about to go ourselves. Really, don't bother – we're going that way'. I translated. When she had gone Azalea picked up the pup and put her in the shoulder bag.

'I'm not taking any chances. Look, there goes Reverend Burnett – back to the same seat again. How odd!'

We watched from across the gardens, seeing him seat himself and glance at his watch, after which he stood up and walked rapidly to the entrance, leaving the newspaper in its former place.

Azalea was for following the Reverend but I said, 'Wait.' A group of people passed the seat but did not even glance at the paper, and then a small child in a red jersey ran along, scooped up the newspaper without examining it and ran through the gates. We followed. The traffic caused the child to pause before swooping across the Mirabellplatz and down a side street. Here he shoved the newspaper under his jersey and ran on, intent on his destination, and allowing us to sprint after him. After a while he started to flag (much to our relief as I was still unsteady and tired easily) and was soon down to a dogtrot, and finally a sluggish crawl, stopping in front of an imposing building. Here he showed signs of nervousness, wiping his hands on the seat of his pants and even scraping his boots on the foot scraper at the top of the steps. After pressing the bell push, he waited, but not for long. A man came out, took the newspaper from him and handed him a coin. It was Hyena Face. Grinning, the lad ran from the place as the man went inside, the paper held casually under his arm.

'How odd,' Azalea said again, and I nodded, my legs feeling weaker than the chase across the city warranted.

'I just hope we weren't seen,' I told Azalea as I pulled her down the street away from the windows. 'That man – he was the one I photographed when we arrived at the hotel.' 'The man that choked you? Oh Babs.' We stared at each other in mounting excitement and wonder. 'Blackmail,' Azalea said, reading my thought. 'Poor Reverend Burnett puts the money in the newspaper and never knows who gets it.'

'How could they have anything on him? In so short a time, I mean.'

'I don't know – but if they pull it often enough – on lots of people – they'll have a tidy sum. Quite an operation. Holiday makers must have fairly unlimited money. Mike must set them up and this guy takes their money. A possibility, Lea'.

'How will the Burnetts manage for the rest of the holiday?'

'Mrs Burnett may have her own money. And credit cards. But if she has to pay for everything, she is bound to suspect something is wrong.'

'He could ring the card companies and say he just lost the money and wait for replacement money from insurance. How does that work?'

'Not sure. He might have been threatened, you know – warned that something would happen to his wife and maybe he's no good at lying to her. Or anyone. He's a Vicar after all!'

We were now safely back in the Mirabellplatz and Azalea said her feet were killing her, so we took a taxi back to the hotel in the old town. As we lay on top of our giant quilts resting before dinner, we roamed over the subject which had temporarily taken our attention off Angelique. I was glad of the diversion from my attack.

'If it was that photograph,' I began, 'the one Reverend Burnett received – how could it be compromising? He's only done the same things the others have done.'

'He went out on the tour last night.'

'With his wife.'

'Yes. How am I going to scrape food from my plate for Angelique? Shall I explain I suffer from night starvation?' 'Take some tissues down. I'll cover up your moves.' I looked up at the ceiling, thinking hard.

'You're an angel, you really are, Babs. Some other females would have been raving mad about getting involved with Angelique, but you're taking it all in your stride. Uncle Charles knew what he was doing when he detailed you for this job. And heavens knows, I didn't realise there was so much to it.'

'Mm? Remember Colin Barnes being put in that room – to share a bed with a man he had never even met. Suppose he had been photographed. He could have been another 'touch'. You can imagine how horrified he'd have been.'

Azalea looked thoughtful. 'And we scotched it by offering to change rooms. We must be getting in their hair. They had three perks going at once, if you think there was anything about our room having no proper lock.'

'Yes. I suppose so.'

'Let's go to the police, Babs. You can produce your shot of the man that attacked you.'

'It's his word against ours. What proof have we? No, let's think this out. We can use the shot later. Besides, we've no time. We're always moving on.'

She nodded. 'What can they possibly have on Reverend Burnett? If ever a man was in love with his wife ...'

'Exactly.' I wished my heart would stop racing so uncomfortably. 'He won't want her to be hurt. And if any scandal reached his parishioners! Help!'

Angelique, who was resting on one corner of the quilt, looked up in surprise at our raised voices.

'So he pays. He has no choice. We've got to do what we can.'

'He'll be upset if he knows we've been watching him.' Getting up from the bed, Azalea scooped out enough tissues to wrap up a brontosaurus bone, popping them in her all-purpose bag.

Previously, when we had paid off the taxi, we had gone into the meat shop and bought some sausage meat for the pup. It turned out to be garlic sausage but Angelique didn't appear to mind. Azalea put what was left of it under the bed where it was followed by the pup who had quickly got the hang of the routine.

No one could say Angelique wasn't intelligent.

There was no chance to dine with the Burnetts for their table was filled, and immediately after the meal they disappeared. The Reverend Burnett appeared rather easier in mind, which was something at least. Determined to do any tour that Mike had arranged that evening, it was an anticlimax to learn that nothing had been arranged.

Soon after eight o'clock, Mimi bounced in again, looking delicious in her own clothes. Drawing us into a corner she said, 'I've been dying to know how you got on. Is everything all right?' This was accompanied by such an elevation of eyebrows that we knew she referred to Angelique. We gave her all current data about the pup, but by tacit agreement made no reference to the Reverend 's blackmail or anything else. With all the goodwill in the world, Mimi might let slip something in the wrong quarter. 'Make the most of tonight,' Mimi advised. 'We're off tomorrow at nine o'clock.' She pinned a notice up on the notice board. 'I know it's all printed in the itinerary, but you'd be surprised how few people read it.'

'We've scarcely seen Salzburg,' moaned Lea. 'We'll have to come back. Do you notice we keep on saying that?' 'Yes, we'll end up like the Frasers, who've seen everything but keep returning for another look.'

Just then Colin Barnes came out of the dining room into the lounge, and gravitated towards Azalea as if he had been a needle and she a magnet. 'If there is anything you want to do tonight, I'll help you do it,' he said earnestly.

We were drawing up a schedule of sightseeing by night when Mr Findlatter joined us – rather warily, as if unsure of his welcome.

'Could we make it a foursome?' he suggested diffidently. Immediately assuming he was reacting to my exhaustion and nervousness from that afternoon, I felt miserable. I found him attractive and had started to warm to him. Then, after this afternoon's attack, I felt I had had enough of the company of men for the time being. I was tired, short- tempered. And owlish. In a phrase, I was throwing out mixed messages.

'Can you spare the time?' Yes, positively owlish. Azalea shot me a quizzical look, to which I answered with rolled eyes.

Oblivious to the sudden drop in the social temperature, Colin plunged in happily: 'We could hire one of those horse-drawn cabs.'

'What a marvellous idea,' Azalea said. 'Let's tell him to take us absolutely everywhere. It'll be so romantic, seeing old Salzburg in the moonlight.'

I could have pinched her. 'Yes, romantic,' I replied flatly, feeling nothing of the kind. Fortunately, Mr Findlatter had not been put off.

We stopped a driver and his trotting horse in the Residenzplatz and made a later date with him. First, he said, he had to go home to feed and water Milli (his horse) and have a meal himself. While we waited, we wandered about the square in front of the cathedral and had a look at the tombs, and in no time at all, Milli and her master were back and we were bowling along the quiet streets of the old town. Upper windows were open to catch the warm night breeze and the smells of cooking mingling pleasantly with horse and harness. The streets were dark for a few short hours before the bakers started yet another day in the middle of the night.

The castle was now floodlit; a breathtaking, fairy place, where fountains glistened in the dawning starlight as we passed. The old buildings had a magic air about them that was a cross between Disney and faded elegance. Milli's owner sensed we were not in a mood to talk and he kept the horse at a slow, steady pace and with a deep sigh, I resigned myself to just forgetting it all for an hour in the hope that inspiration would strike, the mysteries would be solved, and I would be safe. Azalea and Colin seemed to have dropped into a mutual, relaxed state, leaning toward one another with the gentle sway of the carriage. I turned to study Gareth Findlatter's profile, not quite as fine-chiselled and handsome as it had seemed that morning. His nose seemed a little large for his face – like Pinocchio's. I wondered what he was keeping so close to his chest. Funny thing about secrets – they're either alluring or alarming. At least I wasn't being pressured into making conversation.

'You're very quiet,' Gareth Findlatter said tentatively. 'Did you know someone was following you? I've seen him twice today.'

My heart leapt, and I could have kicked myself for it. 'A man in lederhosen and a feather in his hat?'

'No. An ordinary sort of chap. It was a while before I noticed him. Just medium height, light hair, a dark suit and an old mac. Could have been anybody. I mean, there are certain types you recognise straight off: the business man, the tourist, tradesmen ...'

'Azalea attracts men, haven't you noticed?' I said, trying to keep the conversation light. She giggled. 'Perhaps he was a spy.'

'Who would want to follow you,' enquired Colin. 'Someone hoping to snatch your bag?' At once he had reduced the matter to its absurd minimum. But of course, if Hyena Face knew the mobile had been in Azalea's bag …

'He'd have a shock if he'd snatched Azalea's bag,' I said. 'All bread crusts and beef shanks,' I said a bit too loudly. I looked at Gareth, embarrassed and grateful, knowing he had warned us to put us on guard, and dipped my head slightly in thanks. My esteem for him rose a few points. Maybe he was a man to be trusted. I should talk to him.

Though the city was as beautiful as ever, some of the glitter seemed to have gone and we were glad to call in at a weinkeller recommended by our driver, whose name, Azalea discovered, was Willi. After taking out a quart of beer for Milli, he downed another quart at our suggestion himself.

'It's ages since we ate,' Azalea sighed hollowly.

'No problem,' said Mr Findlatter and ordered onion soup which came in great heartening bowls floating with cheese and served with thick slices of grey bread. I never saw Azalea down anything faster. Adventure evidently did not take away her appetite. My thoughts continued to whirl. Someone must have been in the Mirabell gardens and seen us. Someone detailed to see that the money in the newspaper did not fall into wrong hands – and of course Azalea was aware of this. Scatty though she seemed at times, there was little of value that escaped her. Was she scared now?

'How is the pup?' enquired Mr Findlatter, hoping to endear himself to someone.

Azalea reflected. 'Probably hungry.' She put a slice of bread in her evening bag, horrified to find she had not evacuated the scraps filched earlier from the dinner table. Mr Findlatter appeared to find amusement in this, but made his face blank when I winked at him. Mildly, he suggested, 'She doesn't have to be fed at all hours.'

'She can't stop eating, poor darling. I suppose in time she'll readjust,' Azalea said fondly, having recovered her sunny temper.

Thought of the pup, hungry and perhaps mourning, rather took the edge off the party spirit for Azalea who was fidgeting to get back to the hotel like any mother to her child. Some of the streets we returned by were very dark – others still bright with the floodlights that shone on the historic buildings and fountains.

Mr Findlatter moved closer to me as we passed through a dark patch of road. His arm slipped comfortably behind my head. His face was close, and suddenly his nose didn't look too big at all. His grey eyes smiled into mine, as he said softly, 'Enjoying your holiday?' Suddenly I wanted nothing more than for this moment to never end. I was afraid to breathe for fear it might change the mood enveloping us.

'I'm not sure,' I said quietly, and fell silent, watching Colin Barnes who could scarcely keep his hands off Azalea and had to grip them together between his knees. There was a dreamy expression in her eyes as she turned to him and said simply, 'Do remind me to buy a hat for my godfather before we set off in the morning.'

Mr Findlatter exploded with laughter, causing both Milli and Willi to glance back, and soon we were all laughing. When we arrived back at the hotel we paid off Willi, and gave Milli a pat and some of the bread. The sound of Milli clip-clopping home down quiet, deserted, cobbled streets was very sad indeed.

'Can I show you the pigeon loft?' Mr Findlatter murmured in my ear. He seemed reluctant to let it end as I was. That was a different way of putting it, I thought.

'What's so special about it?' I said, turning to Azalea and telling her I'd be up in a minute.

'They've got staircases and flap doors – most fascinating,' he said persuasively.

'I'm sure. I'll have a look at it in the morning. Goodnight, Mr Findlatter.'

'Can't you call me Gareth?'

He didn't actually put his hand on my arm but somehow I had been detained. I almost melted: 'Well, Gareth, then!' And to cover my confusion I asked, 'Are you continuing the tour. You gave the impression you might be leaving it.' He was most attractive in the light from the lamp at the corner of the building. And even though I was pretty certain he was a man I could trust, I reminded myself he was still an unknown quantity. We needed a talk, but now really didn't seem like the time.

I was just about to say so when a door opened down the side of the building, streaming light out into the night, casting in silhouette the man that had taken the newspaper from the little boy of the Mirabell Gardens. My jaw must have hit the floor.

Gareth saw my face change. 'You look as if you've seen a ghost.'

'Perhaps he lives here,' I stammered.

'What are you talking about?'

I looked up at those gorgeous grey eyes, where worry and strength and romance all mingled together. And I wanted to tell him, explain everything. Ask his advice. He was a policeman of some kind. But that fear, not knowing for sure if he could be trusted prevented me. Like this afternoon, I felt pinned to the floor unable to move forward. 'Nothing,' I said at last. 'At least, nothing I can explain just now. Good night.'

I brushed past him, eager to reach Azalea and the possible safety of our room.

All was well with Angelique, Azalea busy with a mopping-up operation. At first she did not notice my tension and then asked lightly, 'Your Mr Findlatter proving awkward?'

I stood still in the centre of the room, trying to fit the pieces together, unable even to get ready for bed. 'No. Yes. Both I guess.' I told her I had spotted the man who had taken the newspaper from the little boy. I felt weak and jittery again.

We lay awake for a long time, listening to Angelique's twitchings and groanings and muffled barks. She seemed to have a disturbed subconscious. Or it might have been the garlic sausage.

CHAPTER FIVE
THE ALPS

A Dreadful Accident!

Almost before the shops were open we were out, glad of the sanity of daylight, exercising the pup for whom we had bought a leather collar, and looking for a menswear shop. This was soon found and Azalea's hunt began. Knowing her of old, I took no part, and when she had run through most of the stock, guessed that her final choice was imminent. Angelique shifted her position and gave me a look of understanding, recognising my silence for one of despair. I'm not sure whether it was the feather in a certain green hat that did the trick, or the fact that I thrust my wristwatch before her eyes, but we were presently outside on the pavement, congratulating ourselves that we had at least five minutes in which to hare back to the hotel before Mike left – presumably with or without us. Mimi, who was getting used to us by now, had our bags on the coach. Her look of anxiety cleared; she admired the hat volubly as did almost everyone else on board. They said it suited Azalea. Mike glared ahead, not committing himself.

Grossglockner Pass is a 3,700 metre-high section of the High Alpine Road that meanders through the Alps, much of it following paths first made by the ancient Celts and Romans. It was hard to imagine them making it on foot, pack animals plodding behind. We picked up the road heading south out of Salzburg toward Villach. It glides easily through national park, the land protected and preserved for future generations. Retaining walls of local granite shore up the highway where needed, making the road comfortable for the coach. As we looked out of the windows, however, the scenery looked distinctly precipitous. We have small mountains in England. But they would barely play footstool to this range of magnificent giants, with the Tyrolean blue skies over snow-covered peaks poking out of a dark blanket of Alpine forest – all on such a vast scale!

'It's only been opened a couple of days,' Mimi sang out. 'If it had been closed we should have had to detour over the Brenner Pass.' She made us feel it had been opened specially for us, but we had an idea the melting snow had something to do with it. Some of the tops were still mantled, there being deep snow on the summit, where, despite brilliant sunshine, we were glad of the heating in the coach. Once through the Hochtor Tunnel, Mike was recovered sufficiently to ask, 'Would you like to see the glacier?'

Naturally we chorused Yes, so he followed the spur road that led to the Franz Joseph Hohe (Hohe being height). We were now about eight thousand feet up, in rarefied air, and were able to look in stupefied wonder at the twelve-thousand-foot summits of the Grossglockner to the stupendously great glacier below. Numbed by the spectacle and the breathtaking cold, we felt that nothing thereafter could compete. In this, of course, we were wrong. If the scenery were less dramatic lower down, it was no less beautiful. It was warmer too.

Hour by hour we wove through the valleys, trusting to Mike's skilful driving. Everyone was enjoying the sudden burst of warmth after our chilly tour of the various viewpoints (Mimi kept insisting we stretch our legs) and the quiet descent into the valleys which promised a less nerve-wracking run to the more nervous amongst us. Personally, I have felt safer – and probably been safer – in a plane, and at one spot, I was sure that Lea was clutching Angelique so tightly that she gave a grunt in protest.

I think we were all feeling more relaxed when suddenly the windscreen exploded in a myriad pieces and bespattered everyone in the front half of the coach. Toughened glass or not. Mike swerved and tried to straighten up as he applied the brakes. He was already in low gear. There was a moment of suspense – a thrill of horror went through the party as the coach skidded across the road and went quite gently over the edge, to rest against a boulder. The vehicle shuddered but did not turn over or slip further down. There were screams along the coach, but such was the air of relief that we were not to go hurtling down into the valley which was steep enough, even at this lower level, that no one made a fuss about the glass.

'Anyone hurt?' asked Mimi as she helped us out onto the grass where the wind was keen, then attended to a cut on Mike's forehead. With the blood trickling into his eye he made a heroic figure and lost some of his bad temper when we made a fuss of him and even praised his driving. Mimi soon had him patched up.

Miraculously no one was hurt, although the pebbled squares of glass were in everyone's hair and clothes. We picked each other over carefully while Mike assessed the damage done to his coach. After a while he said in disgust, 'The wheel is finished. I must ring for a replacement coach.' It was interesting to note that he had no air of relief about the safety of his passengers. It was rather as if he were annoyed that his schedule had been rudely interrupted. His nerves were obviously made of steel. With a final kick at the offending wheel, he muttered something to Mimi and not waiting for her reply, set off at a rapid pace on foot, down the slope, to reach the road at a lower level. The rest of us remained above, still shaken.

Wemys voiced the question in all our minds. 'What's going to happen now?'

Mimi answered calmly, all her training and experience evident. 'We'll have to wait until another coach comes, and then we can continue our journey, although I doubt if we'll reach Bled tonight.'

Uncle Charles – insurance! flashed through my mind.

Wemys looked even more agitated. 'Another coach?'

'Yes, there's a village down the road. Mike has gone to phone headquarters from a landline. There's no mobile reception here. Probably a coach will be sent from Villach or Klagenfurt. There may be one nearer.'

'What'll happen to this coach?' Wemys enquired. He seemed as upset as the most shocked among us. Strange! He'd not been on the inner side of the vehicle, so he hadn't got splattered with glass or faced the drop as we slid over the edge. It had been quite a moment – one I wouldn't care to live through again.

The impact of the bursting windscreen and the near-accident had at first made us all voluble, but now we fell silent.

Mimi patiently considered her answer. 'The coach will have to be lifted back on to the road and the wheel replaced.' 'I mean – where will it go?' Wemys was angry. I saw Gareth Findlatter looking at him, and became thoughtful myself. Was Wemys reluctant to lose sight of the coach because it contained something of value to himself? If so, how would he solve his dilemma? As he realised we were all looking at him and listening, he caught hold of himself. 'Sorry – nervous reaction, I suppose.'

'Of course, it's been a shock.' The Reverend was white-faced. 'We can only give thanks to God we're all safe. When we read of such accidents, we never think it will happen to ourselves.' He was holding his wife's arm tightly under his and they began to pace nervously, obviously unable to keep still.

'What about me making some coffee?' Mimi said. Some of the men assured her there was no danger of the vehicle sliding further down the slope, and we gave a cheer as she clambered in. Her assured manner, plus the delicious coffee, did much to restore our spirits, and soon everyone was chattering volubly.

Selecting a sheltered spot, Azalea began sketching the view ahead – some pines stark against the sky, with gray rocks in the foreground which had rolled down almost to the stream. Near her, Angelique lay with crossed paws, watching the party which was now beginning to split up – some going for walks up and down the road to offset their stiffness – others climbing to various viewpoints. If anyone noticed the dog, no one mentioned her. Only Wemys stayed within sight of the coach; he couldn't seem to settle to painting. When a police car came up the hill and drew in to the side of the road, he was the first on the spot, listening to all that was said, though I doubt if it did him much good – it seemed to be in some kind of unintelligible Austrian dialect.

The police made their survey, shared a few jokes with Mimi, and then departed smartly, going up the road to a turning point. As they re-passed us we waved, and they grinned and waved back.

We settled down to waiting. With a plaintive air, the pup patted Azalea's shoe. 'I know, love. You're hungry. So are we all.'

I wondered how long it would take Angelique to learn English.

A fair amount of traffic passed us but though people glanced curiously at the coach, no one stopped. We were all feeling rather limp when we heard a cheer from down below us and saw the Ted Frasers pointing out a bus coming up the road. It must have been built about the time of the Ark. Possibly it had had the same architect, but it was evidently roadworthy, for it came screaming up to us and shuddered to a halt. Mimi's face was a study as she looked at Mike seated beside the driver, a thin old man who appeared to be having the time of his life. As he jumped down on spidery legs he looked as if he was going to embrace our little courier.

'This is for us?' Mimi gasped, trying to control her sense of outrage and keep face before us as we crowded round.

'Just as far as Villach,' Mike replied impatiently. 'I've arranged for the coach to be towed in. We can't wait for it to be repaired. Another one is being sent tonight.'

'You mean we're staying at Villach for the night?' Mimi asked.

As Mike nodded, she turned to us. 'We were going to have a meal there. It's a comfortable hotel. You'll be all right. We'll go on to Bled tomorrow.'

We waited as the old man went up the road to turn his bus. We entered it in some curiosity, for the vehicle was a museum piece, with embroidered curtains at the windows and paintings on the walls and ceilings. If our British censor had seen some of the more erotic paintings he might have winced. Lea had her sketch pad out like lightning.

Feeling like members of a circus troupe, we trundled into this little border town. Our hotel was on the outskirts – as comfortable as Mimi had promised, and the staff unperturbed at our descent on them with such little notice. No one wasted time in the bedrooms but hastened to the dining room where waitresses came in beaming. An extra special meal had been laid on.

We revelled in genuine Carinthian dishes – leberknodelsuppe, kalbskottelet, followed by melt-in-the- mouth milchrahmstrudel. And gallons of heavenly coffee served every way we liked it. It has been suggested that the root word for Carinth is based on one of the Celtic words for friends. The food made it easy to agree.

'I don't care what they call it, it's delicious by any name,' Azalea concluded. Angelique's groans of pleasure confirmed it when she got her share later. She sounded as if she had difficulty in breathing because of the tightness of her skin stretched over her full tummy.

Modestly I translated for her. 'Liver dumplings in beef broth, veal cutlets in egg and breadcrumbs etc, and cream pastry with vanilla sauce.'

'Divine,' she sighed. 'I'm not surprised Mimi married an Austrian. Have you noticed that Wemys is missing it all?'

'Also Mr Findlatter,' I said. 'What it is to have a troubled conscience.'

'I can guess where they are, poor devils.'

We cornered Mimi after the meal. 'Has the coach been rescued.'

'Yes. Why?'

'What garage has it been taken to?'

She looked at us doubtfully. 'You're the third party to ask me that. You've no need to worry about your heavier luggage. It will be transferred to the new coach which has already arrived.'

'Quick work,' I said admiringly. 'Where did you say the garage was?'

I think it was then that a doubt intensified in our courier's mind. She looked hard at us. 'It's on the Tirolerstrasse. Why does everyone seem to want to know? Is there something going on that I don't know about. Or is it a matter of insurance? '

'No, of course not,' Azalea assured her. 'Oh, Mimi, we're not like that.'

'Well, I work for a good firm here. I don't know how the insurance will be settled. Perhaps our firm will be covered for the coach expenses and the English firm – Magic Carpet Tours – will cover the extra hotel expense.'

Thankful that she was no longer considering us capable of some underhand work, we pursued this angle and when she excused herself, went up to our room.

'Obviously Wemys won't be able to do anything until it's dark,' Azalea pointed out.

'What sort of thing had you in mind?'

'If he has to transfer something from the first coach to the new coach. In a way he's lucky...'

Mentally agile as I had to be where Azalea was concerned, I could not quite catch up with her here. 'Lucky?'

'Yes, they're bound to put the new coach alongside the old one. You can't think Mike would carry that lot of luggage any distance. Suppose we walk Angelique along there tonight?'

'But what about ...' She knew who I meant – the anonymous face, Mr X, if you like, who followed us about. Would he still be with us in Villach? It wasn't pleasant to think we might be observed as we walked along deserted streets at a late hour. A look of disappointment drifted across her irregular features.

'I was just getting interested.' She took the cobbler's faded rosebud and carefully pressed it between the leaves of her drawing block.

'Goodbye, Mr Chips,' I said.

'He was sweet.' Her smile was nostalgic; already she was storing up memories. I just hoped she lived to enjoy them. I was worried. Perhaps we should do as advised (or had it been threatened), and mind our own business? A word with Uncle Charles might not come amiss. He would surely not expect us to stick our necks out too far?

'Oh, I forgot to call Uncle Charles. He'll need to know about all this anyway.' Azalea stood watch while I dialled his mobile. Getting no answer, I left a message and tried the apartment. The housekeeper, Mrs Joincey, answered. Enunciating clearly, I asked, 'Mrs Joincey, will you ask my uncle to phone me in Split? At the hotel. We shall reach there two days from now.'

'Split?' The elderly housekeeper sounded vague.

'You'll give him my message? Split, Croatia?'

'I'll do that. Is everything all right? Are you enjoying yourselves?'

'Yes, it's lovely,' I assured her, gave her my love, and rang off.

I shrugged my limited progress at Azalea and we stepped into a shop for some chocolate. When I turned with my spoils to Azalea, I spotted her through the front window, talking to Gareth Findlatter. I hadn't even seen her leave. His back was towards me, and to tell the truth I was a little relieved that he had followed us – or I hoped he had. It was nice to think someone was looking out for us, but I wasn't about to tell him that, I thought as I crossed the pavement. I was glad of the chocolate in my hand though I didn't offer him a piece.

'Did Wemys get his little job done? You missed a superb meal.'

'So I've just been told. It's evidently the sort of thing a person enters in their diary.' There was a shade of amusement in his voice and something in his eyes which told me he had seen me making my entries in my little book for Uncle Charles's benefit. And conjectured.

'Are you going to tell me what you're up to.'

'Are you?' I admit I had to smile.

He added, 'Mr Wemys looked pleased with himself, so I imagine he's put his affairs in order.' It was a half confidence at least.

'You saw him?' Azalea asked.

'Not exactly, but I think I've found where he concealed what he was carrying. Most ingenious.' His voice was bland, almost admiring. 'In the heavy luggage compartment outside the coach. The metal lining panels hadn't been screwed back tight and there were small scratches on the heads. He must have secured it between the coachwork and the panel.'

'So you'll continue the tour?' I asked, not looking at him.

'If Wemys does, I must.'

By mutual consent we began to walk along the pavement. The evening air was cool, particularly on the corners where the cross currents met. Azalea glanced at him in exasperation. 'What can he possibly be smuggling out?'

'I wonder.' His expression was maddening. 'Why don't you ask him?'

'Because we'd get the same result we get from you,' she snorted. 'Not much.'

He smiled, his face transforming himself, as if by magic, back into the form of a charming, guileless young man. 'If you two girls aren't too tired, perhaps you'd come and watch me eat? I missed out on a meal, remember?'

'Very well,' I said grudgingly. If Wemys had made the switchover there was no point in our making ourselves wretched watching at a deserted mouse hole. Or did I mean rat hole? 'We can order drinks.'

'Make mine beer,' Azalea said. 'We can guess it's a picture – we've grasped that from the scene in the post office at Heidelberg. But I mean – is it some famous painting? A masterpiece?' She fell back a step to keep her eye on Angelique who was investigating a fascinating smell on a lamp standard.

He swung round. 'Strange as it may sound, I literally don't know. I do not know.'

'You mean you're wearing your shoes out following Wemys and you don't know what you're after?'

He grinned and fell into step again as Azalea and the pup caught up with us. 'Not exactly. That's what makes it so difficult. I'm pretty sure too that Wemys won't hide the painting or whatever, in a similar place in the new coach.'

'Why? Any special reason,' I asked, looking hard at him, and resisting a desire to slap his ears down.

'I fear Mike is on to him.'

'Oh. He'll have problems then.' I thought of our driver's propensity for scams.

'Let's forget it for a while,' he urged, and we were in agreement.

We spent an enjoyable time in a weinkeller, watching Gareth make short work of a savoury dish of pork, and listening to some music coming from a rattly old piano. At a nearby table, an elderly gentleman was plainly fascinated by Angelique and the uneasy feeling that he might have recognised her began to grow. We had stopped trying to explain so it was a relief when he leaned across and said with a compassionate air, 'Why do you not give the little one what she wants?'

'We try,' I said, smiling at him and thinking how clever he was to have a wart exactly in the right place to keep his glasses from sliding down.

'She keeps asking, and so nicely.'

It was true I had noticed that the pup was trying to attract Lea's attention, teetering on her hind legs as she scrabbled with her forepaws.

'What does she want?' I asked him.

'Bier.' He smiled shyly back.

'Beer? Won't she grow up into a canine delinquent?' I gazed blankly at Lea, who had managed to follow the conversation, mainly because of the gestures. And the word beer.

'We can control it,' she said, as she poured a small quantity of beer onto a used plate, half expecting the pup to decline it. Angelique's rasping tongue was specially made for beer drinking, we decided, when she finally looked up, plainly asking for more. We gave her some and watched her set about it.

'You see?' The old man was triumphant. We were considering inviting him to join our party when the pup created yet another diversion. The pianist had retired, and a man with an accordion took over, starting a happy tune which set our feet tapping. It must also have set Angelique's nerves on edge for soon her howls drowned the music, convulsing the people at the tables and bar. We were soon ringed around with spectators. As we hurried out – much later – tankards were raised to our health.

Angelique continued to cry even when we were outside, her memory dying hard, but I think she really kept it up because she loved the comfort Azalea offered. As we neared the hotel Gareth enquired: 'Room all right? You don't want to change it with mine, or anything?' There was a smile in his voice.

'No ... we do not,' I said, playing along.

Azalea added for me, 'Thank you, though,' and smiled back at him before putting the pup back into her all-purpose bag. I wished I could feel as easy with Gareth as she appeared to be.

After a platonic goodnight I skittered up the stairs ahead of them. The night was uneventful, peaceful and quiet. I was awake for some time.

For some reason I felt mad as hell.

CHAPTER SIX

SLOVENIA

A Romance in the making

We stayed on the route of the Alpine Road known as the E55, crossing the border quickly into Slovenia. The topography through the Alps continued to be breathtaking every second, with every mountain peak distinct from its neighbour and fabulous in its own way. The coach had begun the descent into the Slovenian region, giving us a slice of changing topography every few minutes as we dropped gently down into the urbanized areas. The air inside the coach became warmer and drier as well. The richness of colour and texture made me wish I could just reach out of the window and touch it all as the evergreens blended quickly into beech and mixed hardwoods. Even little bluebells nodded their welcome from warmed patches of melted snow.

A stunning vista of mountain rivers dropping in and behind peaks and valleys burst open through our windows, harbingers of the more open spaces we were to see in our further descent, level summits given over to grassy meadows, wavy and silken in the sun. This corner of the world had been inhabited since Neanderthal days, and situated as it was, a highly-contested piece of earth for nearly as long. But, as with any nation, it is the people who make a place, not boundary lines. A lesson one learns very quickly growing up in the travel business.

Mimi had been giving us a little lecture to that effect by microphone about the history of Slovenia, Croatia, and Bosnia-Herzegovina, which was interesting but difficult to follow without a score card. I had had courses at uni about it all, and even then it was hard to keep it straight. Therefore I doubted if much of it was sticking in the minds of the other passengers. Azalea seemed as far away as usual, which meant she may have been listening or contemplating the obstacles to world peace. Or a recipe for liver dumplings.

In the end, the Romans, Hapsburgs, Ottomans, Nazis, Illyrians, Croatians, and Communist Russia all had their turn at conquering this majestic and enchanting land until – as if history finally stuck a finger in the record book – it reached the millenium in its present form.

Mimi wound up her presentation by informing us: 'They are a pleasant people, an honest people. I'll be surprised if you don't like them. Don't be put off by their reserve – that will melt if they take to you.'

She stressed the you and we recognised it for a warning. We must behave as if we were ambassadors of our own country. 'And please try not to leave any litter. You won't find any.'

She left us to brood. Were we English a dirty, untidy lot? It rather looked as if we were; she would not have had her piece ready if it were unnecessary. I considered giving her a little perspective by taking her to New York City on holiday.

The new coach sped smoothly on under Mike's expert handling, once he had mastered its idiosyncrasies. He seemed extraordinarily happy and good-tempered whereas before he had seemed furious at having his schedule upset. He made jokes with the ladies whom he had previously avoided. I caught Mimi watching him, though her manner was as usual. From her we learned that we were to stop only one night at Bled, instead of two as arranged, thus catching up on the itinerary. Could this alone count for his changed temper?

'Mike is a louse,' pronounced George Lonsties sometime later. 'And you can quote me. Right from the beginning I distrusted that fellow. Anyone with eyelashes like his … ' He gave a sound I've never really believed in when I've seen it written down. 'Pshaw!'

Azalea made a sympathetic gesture – even patted his arm. 'He's not a ladies' man,' she comforted. 'Any woman could see through him. Any woman who isn't congenitally defective.'

George Lonsties blinked. 'What on earth are you talking about? The ladies are falling for him as fast as autumn leaves.' He looked rather pleased at his simile.

'Not really. They all know Mike loves only one person – himself. They are merely whiling away some of the tedium of the trip. They aren't after what Mike is after.'

'And what is he after?' A wide grin had started to spread on Lonsties' broad face.

'Money.'

Not expecting this answer, Lonsties looked deflated and then thoughtful. 'I'd better warn Daisy,' he said, and I thought this sounded rather odd, for I had gained the impression that money was what George Lonsties was after – lots and lots of it.

'I doubt if you'll need to. The Misses Watford look as if they have been able to take care of themselves for quite some time now.' Her limpid gaze denied any attempt at double-entendre.

'You're a nice kid,' he said impulsively and looked almost wistful. I thought he might be thinking up ways of getting even with Mike.

We were seated on the stone terrace of our red-pantiled hotel in Bled, having arrived an hour before. Our hotel had been the summer palace of a king. That palace brought the locals hopes of visiting potentates, and a whole tourism industry catering to the rich and famous was born. The stateliness and opulence of the rooms was well beyond my imagining: high ceilings hovering over gold brocade, papered walls and polished granite floors adorned with enormous oriental rugs – vibrant, sophisticated – fit for a king. Gilt-framed Venetian mirrors adorned all the rooms, which were large and charming, and both the hot and cold taps in the bedrooms elegantly ran cold water into antique basins! But what's a palace without a few quirks? I didn't bother making a note in the mobile.

All the balconies were wide and sprawling, the view only hindered by the graceful curve of turn-of-the-century style balustrades and posts. Placid, turquoise Lake Bled filled our view; Bled Castle lay nearly directly across from us, slightly to the northwest, perched far out on the edge of the white granite cliff, 130 meters up. Thick woods grabbed hold around and beneath it where they had been holding on for hundreds of years, like the mane of a majestic and impossibly beautiful lion, curtained by the Julian Alps whose tightly grouped peaks protectively encircled this lake valley region and imparting to Lake Bled a definitely Mediterranean climate, away from the fierce, cold winters and icy Alpine winds. The lake was only 4 miles across and all the pamphlets said it could be easily walked around in an hour. Our coach party went silent as we all gaped openly, mesmerized by the sudden change from the mountains we had just left. It was a little like waking up in Brigadoon. The feel of the lake area was of a well-manicured park, picture-postcard ready at all times.

And there in the middle of the lagoon-sized lake stood St. Martin's church, little more than a tall steeple poking out of thick broad leaf trees on a little island. It was romantic in the extreme, and a favourite spot for honeymooners. We were all visibly impressed except, of course, for the Ted Frasers who had seen it before. Once we were checked into the hotel they moved quickly to the far end of the terrace, miserably wondering what was for dinner.

From the travel brochure supplied by Magic Carpet Tours I read out, 'Bled, with its glacial lake cradled in the Julian Alps, and dominated by Triglav, Slovenia's highest peak, is a place of incredible beauty where one can get away from the madding crowd.'

We only partly agreed with this. 'The trouble is,' pointed out Azalea, 'we take the madding crowd with us! Not that we're a noisy lot. We're just all there, doing all the things everyone else wants to do.'

'I wonder what the foreigners think of us?' asked Lonsties, and laughed as I corrected him with 'Don't you mean, What do the locals think of us foreigners?'

When Azalea and I had first entered our room we had been charmed by the freshly-picked rosebuds which lay on our pillows, and the accompanying note which said in English:

Welcome to Slovenia and our hotel.

We hope you will have a happy holiday in our country.

'Marvellous,' Azalea breathed. 'Can you imagine such a greeting to tourists in England?'

I could not. Visitors to Britain would probably be met with the news that they couldn't have a drink because the bar was closed, or food because the kitchen staff was off- duty or on strike.

Mimi arrived, her red hair flaming in the sunshine. The heat, which was making us feel languid, did not apparently affect her this way. She was not in uniform but was wearing a green cotton dress, and white sandals. She looked marvellous – crisp and cool.

'The water is 20°C. Just right for a swim,' she encouraged. Some of us brightened.

Some of us did not. I doubted such a degree of warmth in a lake fed by streams from icy glacial summits.

'Warm springs,' Mimi explained with a grin which showed she had sympathy with our reluctance to bestir ourselves. As she dropped her voice in passing Azalea and myself, we felt flattered. 'I'm going for a dip in half an hour. If you like, meet me by the side entrance – near the fish pond.'

We nodded and Azalea added, 'We'll see if Angelique can swim.'

'Will the fish be safe?' I asked, recalling her prowess with cats.

'I don't suppose Mimi meant we'd swim in the fish p...' She broke off as she saw my fixed stare and realised I wasn't serious. 'Isn't it a relief that the scenery isn't passing us. It's staying put and we can look at it.'

'Until tomorrow.' It was a relief to be out of the coach.

George Lonsties suddenly stood up. 'Well, I must be off. I told the girls I'd take them up to the castle. I just hope I haven't forgot the route.' As he passed behind us he asked, 'By the way, who is Angelique?'

Azalea opened her eyes wide and glanced at me. 'Angelique? Do you know who she is?'

'Search me.' We looked at George Lonsties as if we suspected his ears must be playing him tricks. A little baffled he went off to meet 'the girls' and we departed to get ready for our bathe.

As we ran down to the side entrance of the hotel with Angelique in the shoulder bag, we met Colin and Gareth coming in together. They eyed our swimsuits and towels, and after a second of unbridled enthusiasm looked us in the eye with a hint of a smile.

'Oh, I say,' Colin lit up.

'May we join you,' asked Gareth.

I have never been much of a flirt. Azalea however took to the situation like a bikini-clad girl to the water. 'Yes, do come along. Mimi is taking us to a private beach. Aren't we lucky?' She and Colin walked arm and arm toward the lifts. What choice had Gareth and I but to follow.

When we were all ready, we joined Mimi who was waiting by the fishpond, complete with beach bag loaded down with bottles of beer. Hearing the clink of bottles, Gareth offered to carry it for her and I gave him a good mark. It wasn't really far to the bathing beach: we just skirted a path of forest where there were gigantic trees, passed a twin waterfall, climbed over some fallen tree trunks, balanced along a sliver of rock with a sheer drop of thirty feet, and there we were. The beach might have been undiscovered since the dawn of time – that is to everything except the biting flies. They loved me. They loved Colin too but they seemed to avoid the others who could not understand our restless state. Needless to say, I was the first in the water, despite its freezing cold.

What had Mimi said? Warm springs? They hadn't made any difference to the bit I was in. But the others were ecstatic and no one appeared to notice that the pebbles were agony to their feet. Mimi looked as complacent as if she had personally supervised the pouring in of the water herself. More than ever in his swimming trunks Colin looked lean and hungry, to Azalea's concern.

'You ought to eat more ... take vitamins ...' she said and began a long, earnest harangue about food, until he interrupted her with, 'I've an appetite like a horse. I couldn't possibly eat more.'

This rather took the wind out of her sails. Also she had overlooked the fact that she had about as much figure herself as a broom handle. In a swimsuit that was surely at least fifteen years old, she looked hardly more than a schoolgirl. Despite this, there was a grace in her limbs and Colin could scarcely take his eyes off her. He loved it when she offered to oil his back, and in return helped her put her long hair on top of her head.

Angelique sat with her back to the water until we were actually in it, perhaps hoping it would go away if she ignored it. When we were immersed she ran in and out with little cries of distress. How could we have abandoned her? In time, her anxiety got the better of her feelings of self- preservation – she paddled towards Azalea and climbed onto her head. It was from this vantage point that she faced the shore and saw something that set her barking.

'Someone along the trees,' Gareth said. 'Your private beach isn't so private after all!'

Mimi grimaced her distaste. 'We can't expect to have the whole lake to ourselves. There are tourists at the other hotels too.'

Remembering the camera, mobile, and watch I had left among the rocks I began to move towards shore, glad even of the excuse to get out of the cold water. It was a relief to find my effects undisturbed beneath my dress. All except for my phone. My mobile – my lifeline and log – was gone. Stolen!

First I was angry, then I was scared. And the longer I had to think about it, the more I realised what I had to be scared about. My mind raced. Should I mention it? Now, later, at all? To Gareth, to the police? What to do? Keep fighting my own battles and win through, or accept help and win? Or lose the battle? Or even my life or, worse still, someone else's? My mind was in turmoil.

Gareth followed me. 'You seem jumpy!

'Just watching my interests – and Azalea's,' I said, picking up my towel and rubbing myself dry. 'She exists on another planet? Hadn't you noticed?'

He stood before me, hands on hips and shedding water in cascades down his strong legs and arms, an undeniably attractive figure. 'Of the two of you I would say Azalea would make her way more easily through life.'

'Really? Then why do I always feel as I have to look out for her?' I had a moment of jealousy. Maybe he'd prefer a dizzy blonde to charm her way out of the situation!

Gareth invaded my thoughts: 'I can see she disarms people – just about everyone she meets. She doesn't need a weapon handy.'

'She's just been lucky so far. She usually has others to rescue her. Men mostly, and me. So tell me. What do I have that you so disapprove of.'

He let his gaze fall gently up and down my body, stopping to rest comfortably on my eyes. He stepped forward and I could smell the faint tang of sweat on his muscled skin, see fine particles of sand dried to his skin. 'Visibly, nothing. You must know you are beautiful. Men must have told you.'

I was leaning in for the first kiss even though my mind was whirling, when he added: 'You pack a hidden wallop. I've felt it once or twice.'

I was ready to wallop him now, frustrated with myself as much as anything, so I surprised myself when I answered softly, trying to keep the mood romantic, 'Perhaps I saw something nasty in the woodshed.'

The heat from his body warmed my skin as I drew closer. His pulse quickened beneath at his throat. Up close, I could see tiny, dark hairs that traced the curves of his pecs, and I suddenly wanted to touch them. I was feeling an arousal unlike any childish passion I had known before. It was deep and real, linked to my knowing and liking him. Trusting him, and in a weird way, being mad at him.

I was a million miles away making this discovery when he asked me a second time, 'Did you?'

'Did I what?' The trace of a knowing grin quickly brought under control twitched at the corner of his full, curved mouth. The need to feel embarrassed registered somewhere on a level with my common sense, and I pulled myself back out of the biochemical vortex I was being drawn into. He seemed a lot closer than he had a minute ago.

'Um, no,' I laughed nervously, forcing myself to be still so I could focus entirely on his grey eyes: funny how I hadn't noticed the slight almond shape at the corners, or how they took on a deep blue when shaded by the thick forelock of unruly hair he was forever pushing out of his way. I felt the return of his gaze, pausing first to glance casually down my chin and throat and back up into my eyes, as if he were studying me, committing every detail to memory.

Feeling self-conscious about my injured neck, I stepped back a pace. So did he, and turned to go. He'd obviously intended to go further. Would he think I wasn't interested? I was thinking of calling him back and telling him about Uncle Charles, which would have made me feel a whole lot safer. But that would have ruined the mood even more.

I was going to have to watch myself. I was falling fast and it scared me – but so did all holiday romances. Besides, I guessed that Gareth was not on this tour for his health or pleasure. He was on a mission of some sort, and had hinted at being a cop. Who knew? He did look tightly wound, as if he could spring in any direction at the required moment.

This passionate encounter had run out of steam!

Even later, when we were all relaxing in a breeze that blessedly kept the flies at bay, he was not wholly at ease, but kept sweeping a watchful glance around. Which served to validate my fear of attackers lurking around every corner.

It was when I decided to take a shot of them all on the beach that I realised the card had been taken from my camera, too. I automatically blurted out: 'The card has been taken out of my camera.' Of course I shouldn't have been surprised.

They crowded round, full of questions. Azalea snapped out, 'That man in Salzburg – the one we saw taking the newspaper money. I bet he's followed us to get back the photo we took of him!'

Mimi looked bewildered. 'What are you talking about? What man? What money?'

I tried to smile. 'You're better not knowing. You'll be safer.'

'Safer!' Her pert little face whitened. 'What's going on? This tour is my responsibility. I must know what I'm dealing with.'

'No,' I insisted. 'it's probably over now.' Like hell. I was really being stupid.

'Well, he didn't really get anything.' Azalea shook out the all-purpose bag and a clump of dried veal dropped onto the pebbled beach. Angelique snatched it up and began chewing in earnest. 'Where's your phone, Babs? I don't see it.'

'Yeah, I know.'

'I'm going mad. Will someone explain? I can't leave it here.' Mimi was justifiably worried, and getting angry at our reticence.

'No really – you're better off this way,' I said. 'For now. If we spilled the beans everyone would have a wretched holiday. No, we must finish the tour. Can you trust me for just a few more days? I promise, we'll explain everything.' I felt everyone might just have a go at me soon, so kept saying 'we' as though we all did know what was going on and I had kept them informed.

Lea and I exchanged glances. Mimi clearly didn't like this on a professional or personal basis. I tried to console her by saying, 'Please. Just do me a favour? Don't tell Mike about this!'

As Mimi didn't like Mike, I thought she might have been pleased to keep something from him, but my inspiration immediately backfired. She was seemed alarmed about having own misgivings borne out. I'd obviously only whetted her curiosity further: 'Mike? What's he to do with this?'

'We really aren't sure at this point, Mimi. But there is some tie-in.'

Gareth spoke up for the first time, his voice soothing and controlled, like one who had seen – and handled – this sort of situation before. 'Just give it a few more days, Mimi. Really, it shouldn't take much longer than that. Then everything will be explained. But for now, it's just safer for you if you don't know. Trust that I know what I am about.' That carefully repressed Scottish accent and determination was leaking out around the edges.

'Well, all right then. For now. I don't feel too happy about not informing my employers. When will this business be settled?'

'By the time we leave Italy, I should think.' Gareth answered very concisely, as if giving a professional evaluation. If he wanted to ask me questions, he restrained himself remarkably well. Azalea looked as comforted by his manner as I was, even if Mimi still required some convincing. She went back to her room, pleading a need to shower and change. I feared it was to spy on Mike.

We walked back to the hotel to relax, and I have to admit I shared Azalea's hopes when she whispered, 'With that phone gone now maybe Hyena Face will leave you alone. Your Uncle Charles got the photo the moment you sent it. So there's nothing that bastard can do about it.'

'Except trace the number to my Uncle Charles.'

'Oh no. I hadn't thought of that.'

I had. I needed to find a phone. 'Colin, do you have your mobile on you?' He handed it to me from a plastic shaving bag. I would just have to take the chance of warning Uncle Charles by text, then wipe the message and record of the call off Colin's phone.

'Txtd pics discovered. Be on guard Hyena Face. Mobile stolen. Usual suspects.'

No, that didn't sound quite right. Gareth was walking over, and left me with no alternative but to hit SEND and hope Uncle would understand. Well, he was going to call me in Split in any event.

I was just clearing the call and walking back over to return Colin's mobile where he and Azalea had settled together on a flowerbed retaining wall, when Gareth caught up with me.

'Just let me know if you need help,' Colin was saying. 'Right away!' She nodded gratefully, resting her sweet, blonde head on his shoulder.

'Just a second, Barbara.' Gareth's voice, saying my name, made me melt.

'Certainly, Gareth.'

He gestured toward a corner where there were some more stone seats backed by flower beds with no one in earshot. 'Let's get something straight. I didn't question you in front of Mimi but I think a few explanations are in order now. About that man – and some money.'

I looked him straight in the eye before remembering that he had accused me of packing a hidden wallop, so softened my voice so I wouldn't sound officious. 'Azalea and I think that the case we are working on, and what you are working on, may have got tangled up together.' I paused to revel in his aroused interest. Clearly he was impressed. Score one to me.

'We might as well tell him, Babs. It's about Mr Burnett.' Lea and Colin had joined us. 'Colin thinks it would be better if we combined forces.'

'Safer too,' Colin added. I noticed his arm draped protectively about my little Azalea's shoulders. Yes, there was more to this Colin Barnes than an innocent kid.

'Oh, I see.' A whole new set of conjectures appeared to be shuffling round in Gareth's mind. 'Go on.' I saw he'd had a shock. 'Is it some racket? Is that why you didn't want Mimi to know?'

I nodded.

'A racket,' asked Colin, fascinated, as he only knew a little of what was going on. He seated himself beside Azalea so closely that she had to shuffle along the stone seat, now warm from the sunshine. Somewhere near a bird sang madly, trying to compete with the waterfall which splashed into a pool.

'You nearly got pulled into it too,' Azalea and I said in unison.

'I did? How?'

'The hotel rooms scam in Heidelberg the first night.' Azalea leaned in closer. 'I believe you were to be photographed with Wemys.'

'And blackmailed? But I haven't any money. Besides who really cares back home.'

'You would have paid,' Gareth said quietly.

'I really don't think so,' answered Colin equally quietly. We were all impressed.

'Well, dear Mr Burnett did. I really think you'd have been sickened at the very least, and who knows – they could have got violent. Besides, they don't usually ask for all your money. Just a nice round sum – something people can afford to buy their way out of a private nightmare. They only need a couple of hits on each tour – from other countries too – and remember, they move on every day or so – it must add up in a season. That's what we think, anyway,' Azalea concluded.

'Was Wemys in it?' asked Colin, disgusted.

'I doubt it. No, he was just being used.'

I studied their faces. Colin was shocked, but Gareth's fleeting expression had been one of relief. He asked abruptly, 'What about? You said he paid.'

For a moment I felt embarrassed. 'I happened to be in the bank when Mr Burnett was there and saw he was getting lots of money out. I couldn't see whether they were large notes or what denomination – but he got as much as he could on several cards.' I avoided his eyes when I saw the smile growing there.

'Poor devil! I wonder what they've got on him?' was all he said.

We were all conjecturing when Colin interposed. 'That night club? Nothing much happened – rather tame, I thought.'

'Did the Reverend leave the party – even for a moment?' Gareth pursued.

'I didn't see him leave – he always seemed to be with us when we got out to look at some building. Of course I wasn't paying particular attention, especially in the night club.' Colin sounded defensive.

Azalea squeezed his arm. 'You couldn't know.'

He brightened, glancing at her gratefully. 'Did you see what happened to the money after Reverend Burnett cashed it?'

'Yes. We followed him to the Mirabell Gardens, and do you know, we nearly lost Angelique to an over-conscientious woman there.' Her voice began to rise with her indignation.

I took up the story as Lea was momentarily diverted. 'We saw Mr Burnett buy a newspaper and then later leave it, unread, on a bench in the gardens. We were pretty sure the money was in it, because we approached him after he had left the seat and pointed it out to him. He picked up the paper, and later returned it to exactly the same position when he thought we had gone. A little boy collected the newspaper and ran off with it. We followed and saw the man he gave it to.'

Gareth looked astonished. 'Did this man see you peering at him?'

'No, of course not,' I said impatiently. 'I'd snapped him previously when we arrived. I didn't know who he was. I still don't. I just thought how picturesque he looked in his lederhosen. And I saw him again last night, when – when you wanted to show me the pigeon loft.' Here, I felt Azalea's gaze on me in deepening interest.

'Is he the one who gave you the marks on your neck? I have noticed. Don't look so surprised – you looked like there had been some sort of incident when you got back to the coach. Besides Wemys was telling everyone about it.'

'The idiot!'

'Not really. People talk about upsets when they are pushed together like this on a coach tour. So, it sounds as if you two really managed to stir up a hornets' nest. Right in the middle of my investigation.'

'?' Finally he'd made an open admission. 'Speaking of which,' I added, 'I thought we were to share information!'

'Haven't heard anything to convince me of the kind. Your reticence has been phenomenal, and given the possible danger, extremely unwise – whatever your reasons, screwed up or otherwise. Pardon me for saying so! But I'll keep a closer eye on you from now on. And Colin will too, won't you?'

'Of course!' said Colin enthusiastically.

'Whatever.' I gave in gracefully, relieved that Gareth was going to look out for our safety and, even better, that his intentions were not criminal. It's all I wanted to know. I turned the conversation toward our concerns for the Burnetts. 'I don't know how they'll manage without money. It's very expensive getting it from credit cards'

'Should I offer to lend him some?' Colin enquired. 'I don't need much really.'

'You're a lamb,' Azalea told him, and he went pink with pleasure, adding to the interesting shades of sunburn and peel already on his baby-soft face. 'But perhaps I'd better do it, and then he won't be embarrassed thinking we all know about it. We could all chip in enough for him to get by.'

We were agreed on this, considering that Lea would be most likely to perform the act of kindness with the least possible pain. She would watch for her opportunity. If only Mrs Burnett would leave him alone for a minute! But she was so anxious about her husband that she scarcely let him out of her sight. Maybe it was too late to cover for Mr Burnett, with his wife, but we had to try, not knowing what he may have told her.

We were pretty sure he hadn't told her anything. Problems solved for the moment, the meeting began to break up. The sun was waning toward mid-afternoon and the breeze was freshening. It was paradise.

When Colin said he would like to see inside the castle, we made arrangements to meet him later and went up to our room which was beautifully cool, the shutters having been closed against the afternoon sun. We collapsed on our beds. Angelique backed out of her confined quarters and panted her way to coolness, assisted by a huge, improvised water bowl – the waste bin, which had her on her hind legs lapping from the top.

'Holidays are so exhausting,' Azalea muttered. 'I shall need a rest when I get home.' She turned her face towards me. 'That was a new smartcard you put in your camera yesterday.'

'I was hoping you wouldn't remember.' I closed my eyes, thinking how heavenly it was not to have to move. What a pity I couldn't stop my mind revolving.

'Where is the other one?'

'Here, somewhere.'

Under the bed, Angelique sneezed before starting on a lower note of panting. The air was warm and still.

'Azalea, I've been thinking. Do you want to go home? Uncle Charles would understand. We could hand over our findings to date and let him carry on.'

She reared up and stared at me. 'Go home? Besides, do you want to leave Gareth?'

'What's he got to do with it? Anyway, he'll leave the tour the minute Wemys does.'

'I couldn't bear to go home with everything unsolved. I'd go mad thinking about it. Look, if you think I might hold you responsible for anything that might happen – I shan't! I absolve you absolutely.'

I stared back. 'Just so long as you do realise something very unpleasant could happen. I'm proof of that.'

'Naturally, not being a complete idiot. We've rumbled more than one more kind of scam. They might try to stop us going home to split on them.'

'This doesn't scare you? You appreciate that Mike is pretty sure to know. And he's our driver – with us all the time.'

'We can't be sure Mike knows – about Mr Burnett, I mean, or indeed us. He'll have his own ways of making extra money. He might not be in on the bigger scams.'

'Hm. He was awfully pleased about something when we left Villach!'

'Yes, but he might be squeezing Wemys now. Don't you remember Gareth said Mike was around when Wemys was at the garage? He might be on to him.'

I thought about this for some time and was nearly drifting off to sleep when Lea sighed. 'If we are going up to the castle with the boys, we'd better get ready.'

'Must we?'

'I can't disappoint Colin. He's a sweet boy.'

'And getting sweeter every minute. You'll have to disappoint him one day.'

'Not today,' she said weakly, and swinging her legs to the floor, trod on Angelique's tail which she had carelessly left available. The next five minutes was spent in loving Angelique who played up sickeningly but gradually accepted good health again.

All smiles, we went down to meet Gareth and Colin. To be sure, Gareth had not said if he were to accompany us to the castle but I had an idea he'd be around. I was right. He detached his long, muscular length from behind a table, and Colin appeared like magic from the reception desk where he had been looking at postcards. He said earnestly, 'Have you noticed the spring flowers are about over? They're full of seed pods.'

Lea looked at him kindly and allowed him to carry her sketching materials. 'Are you a botanist?'

He coloured. 'I'm interested in flowers. I don't want to mislead you. My job ... I'm a chef.' He looked relieved when the worst was out.

He need not have been worried. From Lea's radiant smile one would have surmised that she had been waiting all her life to meet a real live chef. She simply couldn't help liking people and making them like her. It was as natural to her as breathing. It was also what caused a lot of misunderstandings.

All the way up to the castle – and it took about forty-five minutes of hard slogging – they discussed exotic foods, some of which I'm sure Azalea had only read about. It took her all her time to poach an egg and balance it on toast. I've often suffered from her cooking, which is generous but uncontrolled! Her cooking speed is either full on or off. But it made interesting listening, and presently Gareth commented on my withdrawn state. His grey eyes were so warm and friendly, his mouth curled so good-naturedly, that I forgot how he looked when he was angry: bleak, calculating, cold.

Without thinking, I smiled back and wished this was an ordinary holiday without sinister undertones.

'That's better,' he said, moving closer. 'And don't spoil it by a crack about my having a vacation from watching Wemys.'

'I won't. I wonder where the Burnetts have gone?'

'Across to the island to have a look at the church. Did you know, it was said at one time that if you made a wish when the church bells were ringing, it would be granted.'

'You must tell Azalea. She believes in that sort of nonsense – horoscopes and all. Apparently we're in for trouble.'

'Really? Nothing about meeting a tall, fairly dark stranger with the initials G.F. and having a romantic attachment?'

Declining to reveal Lea's prediction that I was to meet someone special, I answered lightly, 'Can I get back to you?'

'Strange. I had a feeling the hand of fate was moulding my life this week.'

I tried not to be beguiled by his teasing voice – a most charming, rusty, velvet voice. Common sense told me the deep timbre was probably caused by his having too many colds during his childhood. I had the imperative urge in this exquisitely beautiful spot to eschew all caution – the insinuating holiday virus, like yeast, working in me.

Some distance ahead, Azalea said dramatically, 'He looked at it and said, 'stick it in a bucket'.' Knowing Lea, the mind boggled.

Gareth and I glanced at each other and shared a grin. I called out, 'What are you talking about?'

Azalea whirled round, upsetting Angelique, who only just got out of the way in time. 'What? Oh, the art master told me to stick my first attempt at a landscape in a bucket of water.'

'Did you?' asked Gareth, fascinated.

'I burst into tears and horrified the poor man. I thought he was being sarcastic but he told me a water colour landscape was often improved by dowsing it in water and then drying it off. All the hard edges are mellowed. Of course, it's a professional technique. I don't suppose I ought to mention it really.' She scooped up Angelique who was visibly flagging. Gareth looked after her, puzzled, then laughed softly to himself.

Near to, the architecture of the castle was impressive, almost fantastic. Their need to build such thick bastions in the eleventh century revealed that they'd had their problems even in those days. Inevitably the place was now a museum. Several buildings housed an actual museum, a chapel, restaurant, a herbal gallery, a mobile wine bar and a printing outfit. We wandered about until we were tired, and when I elected to have another look at the magnificent panorama of lake, forests and mountains, Azalea decided she wanted to make a quick sketch of the carved, wooden devil we had encountered earlier. The portrayed malevolence was disturbing; she felt that others might like to be disturbed by it too. Colin went with her as of divine right and we sat on, absorbing the view and feeling the twitching muscles of our legs relax. I had my finger hooked in Angelique's collar, suffering her reproachful glance and whine. It was made plain that she considered me a poor substitute for Azalea. Gareth took in the situation with a sympathetic grin at my reproach.

'She probably thinks of me as a poor relation,' I said easily, and smiled.

'Shall we go dancing tonight? You can't live your lives round a dog, no matter how cute.'

'I suppose not. I'd like to dance – if I've any energy left in this heat.'

'A band is coming to play at the hotel. Young Colin spotted it. He's a dab-hand at languages.' His voice was admiring but I had an idea Gareth too might be a natural linguist. When I laid traps for him he sidestepped them neatly with an air of understanding that was infuriating. But I leaned over backwards trying to be fair to him – a situation of which he took every advantage.

It was something of a relief to see Azalea returning with Colin in attendance. She was always so transparent that I could tell at once that she was disturbed. Not so Colin, who appeared to be amused.

'Tell all,' I ordered kindly.

She was purposely obtuse. 'I finished my drawing. I'm rather pleased with it. I've made a list of the colours and shall paint it later – or perhaps do another.' She showed us her sketch, which was horrifyingly effective, before putting it away.

'She hasn't really finished it,' Colin guffawed. 'She just wanted to fade out of the scene.'

'Colin!' Her gaze was reproachful but he continued to look happy. 'I don't like gossiping. That poor woman! She must have wished the floor would open up.'

'For heaven's sake,' Gareth said, laughing lightly at Colin's confusion over Azalea's sensibilities.

Colin couldn't wait tell all, and exploded again. 'Excuse me. It was the Lyons. At least, we know them as Mr and Mrs Lyon. And this older woman rushed across to her and shrieked, 'Darling, fancy meeting you here. Is Ron with you?' and Mrs ... er ... Lyon went scarlet and said, 'No, I'm here on my own' just as Mr Lyon went up to her and said, 'I'm baked in this heat. Let's go back to the hotel and have a drink before dinner.' They tried to carry it off – saying that they'd met on the tour, but I don't think their reputations back home will survive.'

'At least they're beyond blackmail now.' Lea shrugged, looking heavenward as if for answers. Gareth and I exchanged a meaningful and interested look.

'Lea suspected they weren't married. How awful for them! Did they see you?' I asked.

'I hope not. It would be too embarrassing for them. They seem such a nice couple too.' She could find no amusement in the situation so Colin quickly composed his expression. I released Angelique who was trying to choke herself in an attempt at reuniting with her goddess. The meeting was affecting – they might have been separated for years.

Happiness restored, we left the fortress, luckily not meeting the Lyons. On the way down, we saw Wemys contentedly painting a view of the lake and the island; he didn't appear to have a care in the world. We were too far away to speak, but we waved and he made a gesture with his brush in return. Out of the corner of my eye I saw Gareth's face harden, but a moment later he was laughing at Angelique's antics. Investigating an itch at her rear, she had overbalanced and done a double somersault on the steep path. Deeply offended by our lack of sympathy she retired behind Azalea for a while to brood.

'Wemys is a lonely soul,' Azalea observed. 'He doesn't seem to make friends.'

With an engaging grin, Gareth said, 'You need to know who your friends are in that game.'

'Do you think he's an art forger?'

I never did get an answer.

CHAPTER SEVEN
STILL IN SLOVENIA

Cliffhanger!

The scenery was breathtaking, but all of it sharply straight down. Angelique had tottered too close to the edge of the cliff. Dipping her nose to scent the air over the edge, her little puppy paws started to slide in loose stone and thin dirt, so she scrabbled along the limestone where it snubbed off in a steep slope.

Azalea gasped in alarm, not even daring to call her for fear the pup would be startled and drop into the lake hundreds of meters below. Aghast, we watched as Angelique suddenly appreciated the dangers of her position and started scrabbling back to safety. I found myself willing her to back away quickly onto the sparse grass where we stood. She was almost back up, tail down, when she took that one last curious sniff, and her paws slid. Azalea stooped to grab her, and the pup looked back at her with scared and trusting eyes. Then she was gone with a pitiful whimper. The world seemed to stop.

'Oh no!' Azalea had her hands to her mouth. 'Oh no, oh no!' The men went to the edge and looked down but there was no sign of Angelique – only a cloud of dust which slowly drifted across the face of the bluff. We looked at each other in horror. It wasn't possible for tragedy to have struck so swiftly, so cruelly. Azalea was beside herself.

'The poor darling! And we had been laughing at her. I should have had her on a lead. I didn't think she would run off like that.' Tears flowed.

The men were considering ways of going down but she stopped them. 'You can't possibly risk your lives – it's too dangerous. It's a sheer drop. I can't let you.'

They looked at her in perplexity, trying to ignore the tears filling her blue eyes. Colin suggested in desperation, 'We could ask if there is a safe, short way down.'

'What's the use,' she asked anxiously. 'The poor darling couldn't survive a fall like that. She was probably killed straight off. If she were alive, she'd be crying. We'd hear her.'

Filled with an utter dismay we listened to the profound silence of the sun-steeped countryside.

'We'll get a rock climber to go down,' Gareth said, reacting practically.

On this we were agreed; we could not leave Bled without knowing exactly what had happened to Angelique. As we turned to go sadly down the path, Azalea murmured, 'Another place I shall never forget.'

She was too choked up to continue and we were silent too, not knowing how to comfort her. It could have been a funeral procession in which we were burying all that was brightest and dearest to us. It might have continued for some time, if only Azalea hadn't kept glancing back. At her sudden shriek we all whirled about, thinking she'd lost control of herself.

Down the path came Angelique, racing after us, panting with her exertions but apparently no worse for her adventure. How she had found her way up to safety would always remain her secret. In sublime faith she hurled herself into Azalea's arms and there was another rapturous reunion.

For a moment only. Reacting with shock, Azalea picked her off and held her at arm's length, shaking her, then quickly hugged her tightly. 'You naughty, naughty dog. You gave me the fright of my life!' Tears flowed, alternating with more hugs …

I welled up a little myself, surprised how fond of Angelique I had become in only a few days. In many ways she was a headache, but having become precious, she was worth a little discomfort. In no time at all she had recovered her nonchalance and was the cause of some concern as she disappeared amidst a bed of purple iris at the lake's edge.

In desperation, Lea said, 'We must buy a lead.'

I pointed out that she could not then pretend the pup wasn't hers when people warned her that a small creature had taken a fancy to her.

Almost immediately, someone did. As we entered the hotel grounds George Lonsties straightened up from looking at the view and said, 'There's a cute little pup following you.' He put out his hand to Angelique who gave the whirring noise in her throat. After which, Lonsties looked pained and did not make any further advances.

'It's always following me!' Azalea looked helpless – as if she could not prevent any animals pursuing her if they wished to. He gave her a long stare and then wagged a finger. 'So this is Angelique. Suppose I tell Mimi?' He didn't mean it. He was smiling.

'She knows,' said Azalea.

'So does everyone else by now, I should think,' I muttered. 'We found the pup – or rather, she found us – in Heidelberg.'

'And you got her through Salzburg to here?' He roared with laughter. 'That beats all. It surely does. Let me know if you get into difficulties. I'll help all I can.'

'Mike doesn't know,' Azalea said softly.

'He won't from me.' Lonsties looked delighted to have the opportunity of doing Mike one in the eye. 'Did you know there was a dance here tonight? Will you girls dance with me? I want to make Daisy jealous.'

So it was serious – his growing attachment and involvement with the younger of the two sisters. We agreed to dance with him as part of his campaign so long as it did nothing to make 'the girls' too antagonistic to us – we would hate to start open warfare on such a confined trip. Lonsties grinned.

'I don't propose to go as far as that. I just want Daisy to know she isn't the only pebble on the beach.'

'Money attracts money,' Azalea turned her head and mumbled so low that only I could hear it.

Though he was grinning, there was a desperate look in Lonsties eyes – almost one of appeal, and enough to make one uncomfortable. As I recalled the elder Miss Watford's cold, probing look, I thought she might take good care of her sister and that it might be easier if he charmed her first before trying to charm Miss Daisy. Also, what was George Lonsties really after? There were times when he lost his benevolent Father Christmas look. Perhaps Azalea was right. If it were a pose, it must be second nature to him now. But Angelique hadn't been fooled, and was wary of him. It was rather interesting!

The cliché that life is full of surprises is as true as most clichés. As we crossed the terrace of the hotel we saw the couple we knew as Mr and Mrs Lyon enjoying a cooling drink. They looked radiantly happy.

Azalea's eyes sought mine to see if I had noticed. We could hardly wait to reach our room after making a date with the men about dining and dancing later. The door had scarcely closed behind us when Azalea said, 'Did you see? The worst is over for them. The truth is out and no one can do anything about it.'

'They've grasped the nettle,' I agreed thoughtfully. 'They can enjoy themselves from now on.'

'I wonder. I wonder how many people it will affect?'

'Well, they don't seem to be bothering about that now.'

She kicked off her shoes and was amused to see Angelique retrieve them for her. 'She's forgiven me. We've forgiven each other.' She looked up from loving the pup, an air of puzzlement clouding her face. 'I always used to think when making a decision: What will I wish I had done when tomorrow comes? That way I got a longer view at things. But it can be inhibiting. Perhaps tomorrow I might wish I had done differently today. Because I might be in another mood.'

'Were you thinking of anything specific?' I ventured, not really wishing to probe the devious workings of her mind.

'We are fully adult?'

'Well, I am. I can't speak for you."

She ignored my pleasantry. I waited, dismayed at the thought she might be trying to tell me gently that she was about to embark on a relationship with Colin. It would be like having an affair with a calf, I thought. A calf had once washed my face in an excess of emotion after I had given it a piece of apple.

With a most serious expression, she began, 'The most sensible, the most adult thing to do, would be to inform the police.'

I took a deep breath. 'About what?'

'Oh for Heaven's sake, Babs – who's the adult here? What's wrong with you? About all the scams – about poor Reverend Burnett

– about the attack on you in the park at Hellbrunn gardens – about our suspicions!'

'All right, all right but that's exactly it! They're just suspicions. What proof have we? I've been over and over this. We could be sued for libel, or slander, or whatever, if we couldn't prove anything! Uncle Charles might be dragged into it. There could be a huge law suit. He might be furious if I brought it out into the open now. There must be other ways of dealing with it. It's no good going off at half-cock. The only definite thing is the attack on me – but who's to say why it happened? It's not certain I'd be believed about what the attacker said to me.'

'You might be right.' She considered my point.

'Besides, the police would be bound to detain us – and everyone concerned – until they'd made a thorough investigation. We're in a different country too. They might send us back into Germany. Imagine the headlines in the newspapers!. Oh my God – Uncle Charles would be hairless! And if we couldn't pin a thing on anyone – and I doubt if we could – where would we be?'

She sighed. 'I see what you mean. In prison most likely for wasting police time. I just hope we don't regret not telling someone in authority.'

'Several of us know,' I pointed out. 'And remember, you were the one who wanted to stay when I suggested making for home.'

As though a curtain had been lifted, she said, 'Oh, I'm not worrying about my personal safety. It's Angelique I'm concerned for.' When she saw I was speechless, she added, 'She might be safer at home. She could easily have been killed today. We don't know what we might get her into.'

'She must take her chances, the same as the rest of us,' I decreed, sounding a lot more confident than I felt. 'She looks happy enough

– very different from when we found her. You need have nothing on your conscience.'

She gazed fondly down at the pup, who was sleeping with her head on a shoe. 'Yes, she's accepted the situation. I suppose we might as well do the same.'

Soon after, I went along the corridor for my bath. Another olde-worlde hotel experience! We had quickly got the hang of the hot-water system. If you waited for a bath just before dinner, you hadn't a hope. As we had plenty of time, and I had also spotted another bathroom nearby, I didn't hurry, but luxuriated blissfully, feeling outraged when someone rattled the door handle. Shouting a rude reply, I arose like Niobe and did some effective towelling, accelerating my movements as I became aware of the glass panels of the door. Glass, clouded, but thin.

Hurling on my dressing gown, I tidied the room and hurried past the man outside the door without looking at him. Had I been silhouetted against the light? We did a sidestep, avoiding each other.

'I thought you had gone to sleep,' Gareth said. 'I saw you go in ...'

'Oh, it's you. There is another bathroom.'

'Yes, but someone beat me to it. Besides, there were compensations in waiting.' He smiled pleasantly. 'It was good of you to switch the light on.'

'Yes, well, um… ' I stammered, cleverly caught between moral outrage and a real turn-on. To which he answered with a superior laugh. I fled down the corridor, all sense of wellbeing gone – slammed our door and shouted to Azalea, 'The nerve of that guy! He's too cocky by half!'

I suddenly realised I was fuming to myself. There was no sign of Azalea or the pup.

A tenuous mound on the floor in front of the wardrobe mirror sent a tremor through me. My heart began to thump as I went slowly across and picked up a handful of Azalea's hair. Chunks of her silky blonde hair were scattered all over the place as if she had been attacked mid-haircut, and there had been a violent struggle. I felt myself grow sick with shock. Had she been kidnapped by Hyena Face, and the blackmailer? What would they do to her? Was this to serve as a warning to me too?

My heart sank as I plunged my hand into the mass, gazing at it in despair, one part of my numbed brain still thinking that I should keep a lock to remember her by, the other, half-aghast at the thought.

As the door opened behind me I whirled round, ready to defend myself. Azalea, with the pup grunting under her arm, skidded in and pulled up short at sight of me.

'You look like Delilah with the head of Samson. What's the matter?'

I swallowed. 'Nothing. Everything's fine. I just thought you'd been kidnapped and your fair locks left as a warning.' My legs turned to jelly yet again, on this trip, but this time it was more with relief after the initial shock. Lea had cut her hair!

'This business is getting you down,' she said, trying to be serious but fighting a losing battle as the funny side of the situation became uppermost. 'I'm terribly sorry,' she gasped as she collapsed on the bed with laughter. 'Angelique played with the hair as I cut it. I hadn't time to tidy it up. I heard the bathroom door click and I flew to catch it before someone else did.'

Relieved, I began to smile, then begrudgingly laughed. I realised Azalea had simply no idea how she looked with her shorn head! I sank onto the other bed and we simply giggled and then howled with laughter at each other, though for different reasons. Every time I caught sight of her hairstyle I went off into another paroxysm. It was possible we were both a little hysterical after the various recent shocks, but whatever the cause, we enjoyed ourselves. Wiping my eyes at last I became practical. Tactfully I suggested, 'There are a few wisps of hair that need attention.'

'You're so clever at it, Babs,' she said admiringly and came like a lamb to be shorn. For several minutes I snipped and shaped and when she had washed her hair, it fell into a short layered style with plenty of fullness after we blow dried it. From the right angle she looked about seven years old. From another, absolutely glamorous – in other words, perfect.

'It feels marvellous to be without it,' she said, stroking the nape of her neck. 'I decided on the spur of the moment. I knew we'd be swimming every day– at least as soon as we're on the coast.' Happily, she swept up the hair from the floor and put it in the litter bin.

'You're not saving a lock for Colin?' I suggested. 'He could wear it next his heart.'

She brooded on this, seeing beyond my words. 'I don't want to hurt him. I know, I'll tell him I'm a flirt. That should put him off a bit.'

'You aren't anywhere near a flirt.' I looked at her helplessly. 'Do you always have to be so damn kind to people?'

'They're so lovely to me.' There was weak apology in her voice.

I couldn't help laugh at her but my ribcage ached and I stopped abruptly. 'I give up,' I said and looked out another dress for her. She took it with an air of triumph.

'You see? You're lovely to me too.' She tried the dress on – a simple shift, which disguised the fact that I was more – shall we say – voluptuous than her. I was forced to concede that the colour probably suited her blondeness more than it did my brunette. Combined with her new elfin haircut, she looked hot. Hot. Hot. Hot. Colin was going to be in deep, no matter what Azalea told him.

Angelique looked her over and slowly waved her tail, evidently approving. We gave her a piece of cheese to occupy her time until we could return from dinner with her second course.

Puzzled by my request that she leave her evening bag in the bedroom, Azalea followed me down the stairs into the hall where the men were waiting. Colin's indrawn breath was audible to everyone within ten yards.

'You've cut your hair.'

'Yes, do you like it?'

'It's beautiful,' he said fervently. I doubt if he noticed I was there too. Gareth did. As he fell into step beside me he murmured, 'You look so different in your clothes. Beautiful, though.'

I had to bite my lip to keep from laughing.

At the dinner table, in a room elegant with lace draped across the massive windows framing the views of the lake, we settled down with keen anticipation for our food. At least, we provided the keenness; the food was slow in arriving. The wine waiter was the first to appear and occupied some time in which he tried to teach us about Dalmatian wines. Lea ordered a glass but didn't dare drink it on an empty stomach. When the soup plates arrived (large enough to keep goldfish in), we became excited but had to contain ourselves for another ten minutes until the soup was poured into them. It was only just worth waiting for, and we had long forgotten it when the second course showed signs of arrival.

We waved to fellow passengers, discussed every topic we could dream up, and gave the thin, dark waiter a cheer when he bounded up to us with a trolley of food and began serving us at lightning speed. Again, we were not given a choice, but served with some minced beef wrapped in cabbage leaves, unexpectedly delicious, and served with potatoes and a side plate of lettuce in oil and vinegar. For dessert we were given a choice between compote, which we declined after seeing it, and cheese with fruit. We chose cheese and fruit, swapped it between ourselves. Coffee was an extra. So was the dancing.

Towards the end of the meal, which occupied eighty minutes, a group of young men assembled on a dais in a corner of the room where there was a grand piano. Lively Slavic music began to drown conversation. It was some time before we recognised Yellow Submarine which no doubt was being played in our honour.

'How- charming of them,' Azalea breathed, and forgetting the pangs of hunger which still assailed her, dashed immediately to thank them, in consequence of which we were given another rendition. We clapped, and they stood up and bowed, handsome guys all of them, probably a mixture of national origin, including Turkish, which might have accounted for some of the weirder music. But we loved it, and them.

When I was dancing with Gareth – rather strenuously to keep in time with the insistent beat of the music – he said, 'In a moment, when I turn you to face the doorway, take a look at the man there. I'm pretty sure he was the one who followed you in Salzburg.'

Almost missing a step, I looked casually towards the doorway but there was no one there except a cleaning woman who had come out of the washroom to watch the dancing. Gareth danced me out to the terrace, through one of the windows that was open, but we could see no one except strolling couples and a group playing cards. The women were in heavy shawls against the cool of the evening and I rather wished I had mine when Gareth led me among the bushes beyond the tables. The night was dark, the shadows deep enough for an army to hide in. I drew back, thinking of the man who might be watching.

Gareth looked down into my face, his expression sombre. 'I hope you know what you're doing.'

I tried to shrug it off. 'I've had my orders. I know what I'm doing, but I'm not sure about the others.'

He indicated a stone bench. 'Shall we sit down?'

'Is it safe?'

His dark eyebrows were almost meeting. 'I won't make a pass at you if that's what you're afraid of. Unless you want me to.'

'I meant – shall we be eaten up by mosquitoes,' I lied in exasperation. 'Besides, and more to the point, what about that man out there?'

'Exactly, let's disarm him – whoever he is. I'd like to have a closer look at him. So if you could appear to be absorbed in me...'

'Actually, I'm feeling rather cold.' I allowed him to lead me to the seat and didn't object when he put his arm round me.

I sensed that he was listening intently to all the sounds round him as though he were trained to a super awareness. If it hadn't been so serious it would have almost been comical. After killing a couple of sneaky, winged enemies, I said dryly, ' If I stay out here I shall have to fight for my life.'

He didn't hear me. I could feel his muscles coil for a spring and a second later he shot off into the darkness and I heard a scuffle across the path behind some trees. There was a crash and a yelp of pain before Gareth returned with his prize: a man of about thirty -five, who objected to having his arm locked behind his back. His struggles obviously caused him even more pain, for he finally gave in, and stood there with his head down, not looking at me. From what I could see, our prisoner was of average build and looks, with brown hair and wearing a dark suit of smooth cloth without any particular pattern. He did not give the impression of having expensive tastes; there was nothing about him to draw the eye.

'Take a good look at him so you'll recognise him again and can identify him.' Gareth shook the man by the back of his jacket. 'What's your name? What are you playing at?'

The man shrugged and said in careful German, 'I do not understand. I do not speak English.'

Gareth laughed, but there was no humour in it. 'Don't give me that.'

Looking almost embarrassed, the man remained silent, only protesting – again in German – when Gareth pulled his head back so that I could see his eyes. They were brown, and at the moment had a malicious look in them. I was glad when he looked at the ground again.

'Right, then, we'll see if the Militicja can make you talk.' Gareth hauled him along the path away from the hotel, towards the village. I was undecided about following as I had the distinct feeling that Gareth was not really going to the village but had every intention of making the man talk himself. The following moment proved there was no need for a decision on my part. The intruder appeared to stumble and in going down tripped Gareth, giving him a clip with the back of his hand. The darkness swallowed him, his progress marked by the swish of bushes as they were bent at his passing. I hadn't the slightest desire to follow him and turned to Gareth who was slow to rise off the ground.

'Are you hurt? We've lost him. Frankly, I'm not sorry. I wouldn't want to have the Militicja breathing down my neck for the rest of the stay in Slovenia.'

He rubbed the side of his neck. 'I'm all right. To think I fell for that old trick!' He sounded disgusted with himself. 'At least he knows we are on to him,' I said. 'What's worrying me – he's not the same man we saw taking the Reverend 's money.' Nor was he Hyena

Face, I thought. 'He's not?' Gareth was dusting himself down. 'He's certainly the chap I saw twice in Germany.'

'Let's go back to the hotel. I've had enough for one night. I'm going to bed.'

'I'll come with you. I mean, it's a good idea.'

I could just see the curl to his lips. 'I hope your head won't ache,' I said with a fine lack of warmth, and swatted an insect gloating on my arm with positive ferocity. As soon as we stepped inside the dining room Azalea rushed towards us.

'There, you are! I'm going along to see if Angelique is all right.'

'I'll check for you. I was going up anyway. We have to start early in the morning. Mimi says Mike wants to show us the Postojna caves.' I was gabbling, and it was obvious that something had happened.

'What's up,' she said, her look going beyond me to Gareth. 'The man following you finally caught up?' We didn't answer. She grew very still. 'Quite a thought.'

'At least I've had a good look at him,' I pointed out. 'Perhaps he's not connected with the shady business on the tour, or the blackmail racket? Perhaps he's connected with Wemys?'

'For what reason?' asked Gareth, his eyes bright as they watched me.

I shrugged. ' He must know we are interested in him. He may want to get rid of us …. scare us off.'

'He hasn't scared me off yet,' Gareth answered.

'Nor me,' echoed Azalea, coming to life. 'I'm having far too good a time to go home. Which reminds me, I don't think I want to see inside the caves. I'll make do with the pictures. I don't fancy nearly an hour underground.'

This was a new Azalea to me. Unless... 'You think Angelique would be nervous?' I guessed, and enjoyed seeing her blush.

'I can't run round on a little railway with her. Suppose she ran off – I might never find her again. No, I'll stay above ground and you can tell me about it.'

As it turned out, it was Azalea who saw and marvelled at the largest known caves in Europe, and it was I who looked after the pup. Ever since the regrettable incident of the blackmail of the Reverend Burnett (we were convinced it was blackmail) Lea had haunted him, hoping for a private conversation until even Mrs Burnett began to look at her in a perplexed sort of way. At the entrance to the caves, which were about two hours or so distance from Bled, the Reverend Burnett hung back and gave Azalea her opportunity.

'My treat,' Lea sang out. 'You are my guests.'

'My wife doesn't care to go down,' the Reverend explained. 'She's a little nervous of caves.'

'But mustn't miss them, must he, Mimi,' she appealed to our diminutive courier as she ventured to shepherd us through the entrance.

Mimi's radiant expression encompassed us, checked us, and if she found some of us wanting, she made no comment. 'Yes, indeed, they're wonderful. They have everything! Stalagmites, stalactites – even underground lakes and waterfalls.'

'Yes, do go, dear,' urged Mrs Burnett . 'I shall feel so guilty if you miss it.'

'And I'll look after the pup,' I said, pushing Lea forward so that the impetus, and her own enthusiasm, swept the Reverend Burnett after Mimi. The caves swallowed them and I walked back into the sunshine with Mrs Burnett, who looked rather bereft. Long after her beloved was out of sight, Angelique kept up a pitiful whimpering, changing the note to one of outraged howling when I gave her a light poke to her side. Obviously there had to be an explanation to Mrs Burnett who thought the whole subject quite delicious. At least it took her mind off her husband for an hour. It was pleasant to see her worried countenance lighten and I hoped Azalea was making progress with the Reverend.

After a pleasant walk we arrived back at the entrance to the caves and it wasn't long before the coach party emerged blinking into the sunshine. They were generous in their praise and sense of wonder – all except for Abby and Ted, of course, who had seen it before and found something to criticise. They objected to the lights going out even though the object had been to reveal the multi-faceted colours.

'I wouldn't be a mole for anything,' Abby remarked gloomily making one wonder why she had gone into the caves in the first place.

It was obvious Azalea was seething with emotions other than her sense of wonderment at Nature's prodigality, and as soon as we were spinning on our way towards Rijeka, where some of us were to board the coastal steamer to Split, I said urgently, 'Well, tell all.'

She took a deep breath so I knew it was to be a long story. 'It's as we guessed: they took a photograph in the nightclub. He was playing the Good Samaritan in the men's room and, well, was caught in the act.'

'You don't mean he was doing anything he, um, shouldn't?' I ventured.

'No, no. He was trying to help this other gent whose shirt tail got caught in his trouser zipper. The Reverend bent over to hold his pocket penlight to shed some light on the situation and someone took his photo with the other guy.'

'Did he recognise him? Was he from the tour?' I asked

'No. Not at all!' She was adamant.

'Imagine what his parishioners would have made of it! We know the rest. Putting the money in a newspaper and leaving it in the Mirabell Gardens! Did you tell him we had followed the boy?' I asked.

'No. I didn't want to worry him. Let's hope the whole thing is finished for him.

'He told you all this freely?'

'I had to coax him, tell him we were worried about him. And that we'd seen the paper which had been picked up by the little boy. I think it was a relief for him to talk about it all. And he nearly cried when I told him we were all chipping in – Gareth and Colin, and us – so there would be no need for him to tell his wife. He said it was like a miracle. I felt sorry for him. He's such a nice man.'

I said, 'I must admit he looked a whole lot happier when he came out of the caves!'

'I even thought of slipping the cash to him in envelopes!'

'And have Mrs Burnett sick with worry that he's having an affair with you?' I was exasperated. 'Little notes being passed!'

Lea's mouth formed a startled 'O' under equally arched brows. 'I hadn't thought of that. Then Colin must do it. He's so kind he wouldn't hurt a fly.'

A description I would remember later.

As we were well in hand for time, Mike graciously agreed to detour a little to take in the fashionable resort of Opatija. Here we found roses rioting up the palm trees and all the inhabitants with simply unbelievable tans.

'One hour,' said Mimi. 'And one hour only. We have to be in the port of Rijeka in time to catch the afternoon steamer to Split. The party splits up there – sorry, no pun intended! So you must all chose. Either sail down the coast, or if you wish to stay with the coach Mike intends to visit the sixteen lakes of Plitvice in Croatia.'

'Which would you do?' asked Azalea, adding, 'No don't tell me. I want to sail down the coast. It'll be heavenly to be in the fresh air and sunshine.'

Mimi smiled and gave us a wink. 'Other things too.' When we looked intrigued she explained, 'You'll have a chance to meet the natives.'

'First thing, I vote we eat,' Azalea said.

At lunch on the terrace of a hotel overlooking the tideless sea at Opatija, I asked Gareth what his plans were. 'I have no option but to follow Wemys, and I heard him telling Mimi he was going with the coach. So, I'll see you tomorrow at the hotel in Split.' He looked me over critically. 'Be careful of shipboard acquaintances.'

I returned his look calmly. 'Yes, big brother.'

A smile warmed his eyes. 'My feelings are not exactly brotherly. Surely you've guessed.'

Well, nor mine either, I added mentally. I smiled warmly by way of a reply. I was happy to hear Gareth say it, but I have to admit to a pang of regret that this holiday was not an ordinary one for either of us; we were suspicious of each other by very nature of our assignments. But all the same, it was kind of fun.

Despite the drawbacks I was determined to obtain some enjoyment from the situation at hand. I gave full marks for the meal of sardines and salad, with pork on skewers, which was served without undue delay after my explanation about our lack of time. The waiter was attentive and could speak good English. At once Azalea was into a conversation that continued with zest every time he hovered near the table. I heard drifts of '... Your brother planning to go to an Art school. Yes, I'll write the address down. If you just mention my name at the house in Hill Street, my old landlady will look after him ...' And later, '... No, I don't suppose you could. The rubber would be too tight.'

Obviously the conversation had changed its course. We all declined the inevitable compote and accepted the ice cream with murmurs of appreciation. We drank up our wine and smiled at the waiter, who was bowing us out without any appearance of servility, and well within the hour. He accepted the ballpoint pen which Azalea gave him with a pleasure that seemed genuine.

'You mark my words,' Azalea said a minute later when we were powdering our noses. 'The next time we call in here, he'll be manager.'

'I don't doubt. But what had rubber to do with it?'

'What?' She was uncomprehending for a second only. 'Oh, he likes to scuba dive. He would have given me lessons if we'd been staying. Free.'

'What was the parcel he gave you?'

'Meat scraps for Angelique. It was very sweet of him considering she tried to bite him when he put my cardigan over the chair.' She sighed with the contentment that a filled stomach brings. 'Thank you again, Babs, for letting me come on this trip with you.'

'Don't mention it. You're better than any soap opera.'

She was a little doubtful of the compliment but let it pass. A few minutes later we were bowling away from the promenade and up the hill towards Rijeka. The undulating coastline was really beautiful and we watched it dreamily – the forest-clad slopes gradually giving way to a mere domestic countryside.

At the busy port of Rijeka, Mimi said fondly, 'I'll meet you in Split. You'll love it, I promise. It's all built round Emperor Diocletian's palace – about two thousand years old. He was born near there, and built the palace for his retirement.'

Overhearing, Mike muttered, 'Two thousand year, nien. Seventeen hundred years it is.' He had brought us expertly to the quay where the steamer waited and those of us who were to sail south went aboard. Though the sea port was busy, everyone seemed to make time to watch the boat leave the pier. The gangplank went up behind us, reminding us that we were only just on time and there was reason behind Mike's impatience. As we began to slide out from the quayside, we waved to those left in the coach, feeling superior, but also a little sad at the parting. Almost at once the interest of being aboard ship claimed us.

Angelique was almost the cause of our being put ashore, for the cabin steward surprised us by coming in with fresh towels and the pup flew at him in fury.

The steward, a mere boy, stared first at Angelique and then at us as if he couldn't credit what his eyes told him. He would have backed out – no doubt to inform one of the officers – had Azalea not put her hand on his and looked so appealing that he stayed to look intently at her. I wondered how long they would manage without words, for he obviously hadn't much English, and she certainly hadn't any Croatian. I tried what little I knew and he brightened, turning to me eagerly. With the innate dignity of the Slav, he said he would keep our little secret – particularly as we were leaving the boat in the morning at Split. Here his gravity crumbled and he giggled helplessly as Azalea tried to separate the pup from his trouser leg. Angelique had got a good grip and was enjoying herself immensely. When at last he was free, he gave us a salute and stepped out of the cabin, closing the door almost in the face of the purser.

At the exchange of words we held our breaths, expecting a knock on the door, but none came and we dared to breathe again. Azalea looked at me, perspiration dewing her temples. 'Phew. How much longer will our luck hold? I couldn't bear to lose her now.'

When she had fed the pup and placed her on her oldest cardigan, we left the cabin, taking the key in the innocent hope that no one would disturb her.

On deck we found the air delightfully cool and after walking round and watching the pirate island of Krk, we found ourselves mixed up with a party of four students who were dying to try out their English and discover what impression they might make on two English maidens. On the excuse of finding us deckchairs they hovered near, smiling and gazing into our faces, letting nothing escape their eager, intent eyes. A slim, wiry youth with thick hair slicked back off a narrow forehead presented a vivid face to us, and told us he was called Kobasica. I laughed and exclaimed, 'That means sausage.'

Aside, Azalea murmured, 'He's certainly a dish.'

Kobasica smiled sheepishly. 'I make mistake. I not guess you clever English lady. My name is Juraj.' He introduced his three companions to whom we gave our names in exchange, and when they learned we were just down from the uni too, they plied us with questions which we did our best to answer.

Attracted by the gabble, Colin Barnes drew near, not surprised to find who was at the heart of it. They included him generously in what I can only call their entertainment. They sang sea shanties and folk songs, told us stories of the people who lived along the coast and even danced the kola, weaving in and out and gradually pulling us into the circular dance. All the time their dark, beautiful faces showed that they were filled with intense pride in their nationality, that they were eager for the future and that they did not dislike the English.

We were forever passing islands: as one faded from sight another came into view. Some were tree-covered, others starkly bare – limestone karst which had been thrust up from the sea in some gigantic upheaval. The further south, the barer the islands grew.

'Many earthquakes,' Juraj explained. 'Many towns and villages under water. Make for ghosts, yes?'

We believed everything we were told, caught up in the magic that is inherent to the Dalmatian coast. As the light began to fail, we drew to the sheltered side of the ship and watched man-made lights springing up on the islands. When the gong for dinner went, we made a move towards the dining saloon but the students drew back in sudden shyness. They had no money for dining splendidly on board; they showed us their provisions – long loaves which they would eat without butter, mysterious sausage-meat shapes, pickled baby marrows, and wine which they drank from the bottle. Even as we slipped below deck, they were toasting us and our swift return. It was an unforgettable experience.

In the dining saloon the engine throb seemed nearer and we had to keep running up on deck the better to see some landmark or lighthouse.

Colin watched Azalea's face in some natural jealousy. 'They say there are a thousand islands.'

'A thousand islands,' she repeated dreamily. 'Shall we buy one?'

The idea charmed him. 'You could paint while I did the cooking.'

This jolted her out of her fantasy. 'And what would Babs do?' she asked demurely, seeing the dangers of an island existence a deux.

When I could stop grinning, I said, 'I could protect you from all the Kobasicas of this world – as I do now.'

'Bless you. Oh, isn't it heavenly? You are clever, Babs, to have an Uncle Charles.' She broke off as I kicked her. 'I think I'll go to the cabin to see if Angelique is all right. ' As she moved away she added darkly, 'Also to get a bandage for my ankle.' Colin followed her like a faithful dog but she said clearly, 'Good night ,Colin. See you in the morning.'

I watched him mooch off down the deck, not envying him his thoughts. Gusts of hot air came up from the engine room; I moved upwind and leaned over the rail for a last look at the coastline. The lights were reflected in the clear water; we were proceeding so smoothly we might have been on a placid lake. The mountains were becoming higher and more bleak; the rising moon edged little shelves of cultivated earth among the bare rocks – and always there were the dark shadows of caves. Snatches of song came from the students who had moved to the prow of the ship; they were singing about a man who swore he would come back to the islands and claim his love. It was the same song sung the world over by men who were homesick. Many of the words were snatched away by the breeze but I knew the theme. Were the students going to sleep on deck? Or would they, during the colder hours, move into the warmer saloons?

'All alone?' The genial voice could only come from George Lonsties.

'And enjoying it,' I said softly.

'Ouch.' He pretended to turn up his jacket collar.

I laughed and said, 'Goodnight, George. It's been a wonderful day.'

'Sweet dreams,' he chuckled and padded further along the deck, his large figure melting into the darkness. Something had pleased him. Was he making progress with Daisy despite Miss Watford's protection? A moment later he was back at my side. 'A word to the wise,' he said, still looking benevolent, and yet, in the half-light, rather wolfish.

'Yes?'

'Your friend, Mr Findlatter ... I thought you ought to know ... he carries a gun.'

'What?' The whole peaceful mood of the evening was shattered.

'Yes. Thought it would shake you. Didn't see it properly. I was just passing his door when the maid surprised him and I saw he was examining a small revolver. Couldn't tell what sort it was.'

'Could you have been mistaken?' I had to force the words out – I felt winded.

'Oh yes, but I don't think I was.' A trick of the moonlight hid his eyes under his bushy brows but I could sense his enjoyment of my consternation.

'Perhaps he has his reasons,' I said weakly.

'Perhaps he has.' He laughed and went off, whistling under his breath. No doubt this little piece confided to me – and everyone? – had made his evening. So Gareth carried a gun. What of it, if he was cop of some sort, as I assumed. Lonsties was just being mean. Wasn't he?

Out at sea, a great fish leapt into the silver light. Though I watched for a time I did not see it again – only the expanse of dark water, and the foam fanning out behind us. Something was making me sad. Perhaps it was the singing of the students who were coming along the deck. I slipped down the companion way and along the corridor. As I entered the cabin, Azalea who was already in bed on the bottom bunk with Angelique said, 'All is well.'

'It was decent of you to let me have the top bunk,' I said.

There came a sleepy chuckle. 'Not really. I was afraid Angelique might fall out of the porthole. I had to open it, it was so hot in here.'

When I had finished my toilet, I climbed up – watched by an astonished pup – and gazed out through the porthole. I was on the starboard side. I could see nothing but smooth water as far as the horizon. The throb of the engines was soothing but I guessed I would not sleep for some time. Then I realised what was really getting to me. Gareth with a gun. Whatever it was – he was in deep.

And so was I.

CHAPTER EIGHT
SPLIT, CROATIA

Sparkling Seas and Dreadful Danger

Mimi said contentedly, 'To me, the main fascination of the Dalmatian Coast is that the ships come right up into the town. You disembark, you cross the road – and there you are in the middle of things.'

Though it was only about six o'clock in the morning, she was there to meet us at the pier as the steamer came in. Split Harbour must surely be one of the most beautiful in the world: the ship tied up in front of the Emperor Diocletian's palace with its palm-fringed promenade and flower beds, all seen against a backcloth of grey mountains. In the background were bright, white box buildings capped by terracotta-coloured pantiles, nestling between the mountains; with the gorgeous, light-blue water of the Adriatic in the foreground, this had to be the most beautiful spot on the entire tour!

It looked as if it could easily be across the sea in Italy, but Croatia was famous for clearer, cleaner, bluer water. And from what I could see only having just landed, everything – buildings, pavement, grounds, and people – was crisp and fresh as if minted that morning just for us. In the early morning with the mist still on the water, the place had an almost unearthly beauty. Even at such an early hour, the shops and many squares were humming with activity, for new Slavs, like the old are sold on the idea of early rising, with a sleepy siesta during the heat of the day.

'The shops and offices close for a few hours during the afternoon,' Mimi instructed us as we waited for Mike who was having a shoeshine and catching up on the local gossip. 'But they open for the korzo, the promenading of locals to see and be seen.'

The humming note we heard proved to be the chattering of the people on the massive stone walk as they went to their places of work. Voices and footsteps bounced back from the walls of the palace, an insistent thrum as roaring and constant as hundreds of pigeons being fed.

We could see the end of the market place, already busy with people, and there was such a brilliant array of colourful objects for sale that we determined to buy at least a rug to take home. On Mike's return, we suggested he might wait a few minutes, but he made no reply; he only gave Mimi a look that almost took the curl out of her hair, and started the engine roaring. Azalea and I exchanged arched eye-browed glances. Eager to be on his way to set up his next victim, perhaps? We roared off to our hotel.

The hotel faced south, round the headland, with fine views of the bay and coast. We approved our bedroom, which was charming, and boasted a balcony overlooking the sea, and a bathroom in which everything worked for a change. After becoming orientated, we walked across from the dormitory block to the dining room, a large building which had one wall almost entirely composed of sliding glass panels. Diners could rhapsodise over the breathtaking view of the islands.

To our joy we were given an egg with our expected continental breakfast of two rolls and tepid coffee. Before we had finished our meal, both Colin and Gareth were in attendance. We basked in their flattery; it was surprising how attached you can become in so short a time. But perhaps all holidays are like that – a little life within a lifetime.

When we had exchanged notes about our respective journeys, Azalea said with satisfaction, 'Cruising down the Dalmatian coast must be one of the best holidays in the world ...'

All eyes rested on her with affection; we should have been prepared by now for her next remark but we were not: 'Something quite awful is going to happen here. I can feel it in my bones. Did you know I was a bit psychic? The horoscope points to trouble too.'

Gareth said lightly, 'I never knew someone's psyche was in their bones. I thought that was rheumatism.'

We asked him about his journey by road. 'Interesting,' he answered. 'Of course the highlight was the Plitvice lakes and the way they cascaded into each other. It was also fascinating to watch Mike.'

'Why? More scams?' asked Colin.

'No. George Lonsties played a trick on him – offered him some chocolate. Mike took several pieces.'

'Well? What was so fascinating about that?'

A ghost of a grin played about Gareth's well-cut lips. 'It was Ex Lax.'

'Will he have it in for Mr Lonsties?' I asked.

'No. He doesn't associate the two. He just thinks he caught a bug. Mimi gave him some pills. We had an awful lot of stops – some in the most unusual places.'

It was impossible not to laugh but we tried to control it when we spied Mimi doing a round of the tables. She had various helpful suggestions for our day but we voted first to explore the beach, with a spot of sunbathing in mind followed by a swim. We also planned to visit the town and palace during the afternoon. I remembered that I wanted to buy a rug to take back home.

'Don't miss the oldest suggestions or complaints box in the world,' Mimi pointed out. 'It's in the wall, under one of the archways near the sea front. Please, if you need help for anything – there's a tourist bureau in the square near the cathedral. This is a splendid cultural centre – there are museums and art galleries and castles, even a pirate's fortress a few miles up-coast.'

She lingered to tell us a little about Diocletian who had become Emperor at 40 and abdicated at 61, to live in splendour for his remaining eight years. It was a sobering thought; it also showed that Mimi did her homework. After collecting our swimming gear from our room and Angelique from the balcony, we wandered down the many and varied stairs to the pebbly beach. Down there it was undeniably hot, and after a while we were glad to seek the shade of a tree.

On one of the terraces Wemys was painting; he too must have found it too hot to be comfortable, for he called to the attendant to fix an umbrella between him and the sun.

When he saw this, Gareth stretched himself and proposed a swim. Had he been watching Wemys all this time? I wondered, as I tested the water, marvelling at its clearness and colour. The travel posters had not lied. Every pebble, every rock, every living creature was clearly visible, the translucency of the soft blue water confusing as to its real depth. It was a shock to put your foot down to the floor of the ocean and find it not there but much deeper down than you thought.

I was floating on my back when I heard Gareth say loudly, 'Damn the man!' His arms flashed in the sunlight as he sped towards shore. Over his shoulder he called, 'Be seeing you,' before he found his bathrobe and ran up with it towards the hotel, taking a short cut through the pinewood. It was then I noticed Wemys was not seated beneath the umbrella, placidly painting. From the beach he had been hidden from us, but out at sea Gareth had been able to observe he was no longer a part of the scene.

As I came out of the water, Azalea looked at me enquiringly but I could only shrug. With Colin we waded further along the shore, finding sandy coves quite deserted except for the lizards which darted for cover at sight of us, but soon came back. It didn't take long for Angelique to scatter them. Meanwhile our solemn, sunbathing ritual continued. Conversation died away. Complete silence reigned on the beach. After a time I became bored and decided I would go up to our room for a shower before lunch. Besides, I was thirsty and hoped to track down a drink.

'I'll come up too, when I can find the strength,' Azalea whispered. 'At the moment I feel too drunk. Isn't the sunshine glorious? It's almost met in the middle of me. I'm grilled on both sides.'

As I waded back, preferring this to a scramble over the sand hills and rocks some of which were quite steep – I found the dazzle of the sun on the water was blinding.

Only my feet were cool for the heat was unbearable. At a small, pinging sound I looked round, to see a pebble sink to the sea floor. It had come from the bluff immediately above me. As I glanced up, shading my eyes, I heard a whine and something flew past me, and would probably have hit me, only that my foot slipped and I went down onto hands and knees. The water was only a foot deep but sufficient to drown in as I lay along the water line face down, pretending I was unconscious, my mouth only just out of the water, trying to gather up strength if my assailant should try to finish me off. I was an easy target for his gun – unless he thought he had hit me and came down to make sure. Everything in my beach bag was sodden, but there was a handy fruit knife in there.

I waited, my heart beating heavily, and then I knew why he hadn't come. Children came round the rock, chattering, but their noise, which sounded like a heavenly choir to me, died away as they spied me. I managed to smile at them before picking myself up and continuing on my way to the hotel beach and the steps, trembling but determined to make it back to relative safety.

I walked mechanically, the white stones blinding me, and not able to see into the shadows cast by every bush and shrub. A dull ache had started in my head though I knew I had not been hit. After a shower, I took a couple of headache pills and lay on the bed, appreciating the light breezes which blew in across the veranda. I could feel my rapid pulse begin to slow and finally resume its normal rhythm. When Azalea finally came up I was almost in command of myself. Was I getting hardened to all this? Had I imagined the incident? Neither.

'I feel like a bit of chewed string,' she said cheerfully as she put Angelique down and went into the bathroom to get her a drink of water. As she came out she glanced across at the bed on which I lay and looked at me uncertainly. 'Babs? I get the impression … Has something else happened to you?'

'Unless I'm going out of my mind, something has,' I said prosaically. 'I have the distinct feeling that someone shot at me. It could have been someone throwing stones but I don't think so. Or a kid with an air rifle. Oh, I don't know. I really don't.'

'Shot at you?' Her whole body went tense. 'Oh Babs! Did you see him?'

'No. I just heard a whine. I happened to be falling at the time, so it probably saved a nasty injury – or my life.'

'What are we going to do? I assume you don't want to tell anyone!' She studied the floor as if she might find inspiration there. 'I told you there would be trouble. This is the beginning!'

'Only the beginning? Oh lord! What am I going to tell Uncle Charles when he phones? He'll have us back on the first plane if I tell him about this. After all, it might have been something I dreamed up. Once something happens for real, everything else that's probably innocent, gets out of proportion. Besides, I'm feeling better every minute.'

Her face lightened momentarily before she began brooding again. She didn't believe me either. 'Who could it be? Would the man from Salzburg follow us so far? Or could it be The Shadow?'

'Who?' I asked, startled.

'You know. You said he was wearing a pullover with an M and S label.' She was referring to the German stalker on the patio in Bled where Gareth had taken me to dance.

'Oh yes. It could also be Wemys.'

'What do we know of any of them? We might be close to something they don't want us to know about. They don't realise we haven't a clue.'

Our brains went round and round the subject but still coming up with mere conjuncture. After a while Azalea said, 'We'll go mad if we stay cooped up here.'

When we were ready, we walked back to town by a short cut along the foreshore, finding it very rewarding. My spirits were rising; I only looked over my shoulder every two seconds for a lone gunman! Two little boys combed the shallow water for shellfish which they trailed after them in plastic bags. They were so sunburned as to be almost black – and this in spring. We kept within the sight of people all the time.

As we stepped onto the promenade proper, a London bus trundled past and Azalea gave me a hard pinch. 'I'm dreaming. I must be.'

'A wartime gift?' I suggested. All this was blessedly taking my mind off the earlier incident. 'And still going strong, bless it.'

We dived happily into the open market looking for souvenirs and soon had to buy a string bag to put them in, for Angelique objected to sharing her shoulder bag. Before coming out I had changed some money, and after putting a little aside for the Reverend, found to my delight I had enough to purchase one of the smaller fringed rugs. I determined to buy as brilliant a one as I could find and pored over them while Azalea chose a lace tablecloth at a nearby stall, adding it to her wooden stork and a box covered in shells. When I had looked doubtfully at the latter she had explained that it was for her landlady's little daughter. Normal life went on and felt glorious. I even began to believe I had only been the victim of an unruly kid.

It was impossible not to realise the rug makers favoured oranges and reds, but I was determined to track down a blue one. With this in mind, we moved further along and explored more stalls inside the palace precincts, going in by a side entrance, down some steps.

Two nuns passed us as we approached the cathedral – originally built as a mausoleum for the Emperor and now guarded by a black granite lion which had once languished in Egypt some three and a half thousand years before. It was as we were going up the steps that Azalea said in anguished tones, 'Angelique's gone!'

She ran down again, but I stayed at the top, the better to view the square, paved smoothly in ivory-coloured stone. Almost at once I saw the pup – a confused Angelique who had been caught up in the backwash of the nuns' passing and been swept beneath the voluminous robes of one of them. Only her frantically waving tail was visible as the nun strode on, following her companion.

Azalea looked back at me in agonised entreaty, but I was literally holding my breath for fear the pup would be trodden on and could not speak – I just pointed. Following the indicated direction, Azalea saw the plume of a little tail now and again, and the skittering legs which were trying to keep up with the long strides whooshing the nun's heavy black habits around her. We were convulsed with a multitude of feelings as we followed at what we considered a safe distance for we had no wish to offend. Before the stupendous statue by Mestrovic the nuns came to a halt and confronted us.

'You wish ...?' Gentle eyes reproached us. Azalea almost gave a curtsey as she pointed to the hem of the nun's heavy robe. Perplexed, she lifted it a fraction and Angelique came from under, panting, into the air.

In a moment the nuns were laughing delightedly and we were able to join them with nothing on our conscience. 'So sweet,' they murmured, their very presence a benediction. We parted good friends and almost immediately were surrounded by the students we had encountered the previous evening.

'What is this?' One of them pointed to Angelique. 'A long-haired mouse?'

Angelique half-closed her blackcurrant eyes and the familiar whirring note began in her throat.

'She doesn't like criticism,' I explained.

'She understands only love,' Azalea supplied conclusively.

'Ah, love ... that is what we all understand,' he said sentimentally. 'May I write to you? To improve my English, you understand, and because you are a so nice girl.'

We exchanged names and addresses though I guessed we would not hear from them again. Then, impelled by some self-imposed time limit, the students ran off and we continued our tour. As we came abreast the harbour again, we saw two destroyers anchored, and Canadian sailors as thick as fleas. My heart sank for I knew Azalea would be involved before long. It was not possible for her radiantly friendly look to pass unnoticed. For a while I made us tag along behind the Burnetts whom I had spotted – hoping the sailors would think we were their daughters. Under their auspices I bought a blue rug and rolled it up under my arm. It was quite light.

Remembering we had missed lunch, we went into a cafe and treated the Burnetts to lemonade and ourselves to something more substantial. The lemonade was made from home grown fruit, which puzzled us for we had seen both blossom and full grown fruit on the same tree. Rather clever, we thought.

After a while Reverend Burnett said with a twinkle, 'We had planned to go along the coast to the Marine Museum, so if you will excuse us? I don't think you will be lonely long. I have noticed the same faces looking in at you several times. Thank you for your hospitality.'

His forecast proved correct for the Burnetts had scarcely left before a couple of brawny boys approached us and asked if they could buy us a drink. The tall one said, 'We heard you speaking English, and it's such a treat to hear English when you're in a foreign country. You don't mind, Miss?'

'Surely the other thousand or so sailors speak English?'

He looked hurt. 'They aren't young and pretty. No ma'am. They sure ain't girls.'

Azalea took pity on them and they were soon showing us snapshots of the families they had left behind them, and promising to look us up in England – if ever they got there. Recognising Angelique as a top favourite, they made a great fuss of her. They also dissolved like snow in summertime as Colin Barnes came up to us and said,

'So that's what you're up to.' He looked pleased to have routed them. 'Oh, you've bought a carpet. Can I look?'

I unrolled it, attracting the attention of an elderly gypsy woman who came up and fingered the rug, staring darkly into my face, her eyes wild as a hawk's. She said something unintelligible and I shook my head, resenting her hand on my arm. After giving me a strange glance she left, and I thought no more about it until we were walking towards the cathedral again – hoping this time to see inside – when I was again approached by the same gypsy creature. She stared hard at the rug, muttered something which I could not catch and seemed puzzled when I did not answer. She gestured as though she wanted to lead me somewhere.

Colin grinned, 'Perhaps she wants to sell you another one?'

I shrugged and continued walking, ignoring the woman, who continued to follow. I was certain she was no beggar, for the Slavs are independent and resent charity. Suddenly I spotted Gareth emerge from the cathedral across the square, and my heart began to race as I watched him move as if on the run. Or the chase. After a swift look round from the top of the steps he ran down and through the archway that led to the market. My hand went up to attract his attention but he did not see me.

'Shall I go after him?' urged Colin.

I shook my head, still clutching the rug, for the woman looked as if she was laying claim to it. I had lost sight of Gareth, adding to my irritation. Perhaps once we were in the cathedral she might drop back. As she continued up the steps with us, she said impatiently, 'I show you the house. You waste time. Come!'

I shook her off impatiently. 'You're making a mistake. I don't want to see your house.'

Colin stepped between us and ushered us into the cathedral, patting the granite lion on the way. It was some sort of sphinx, we all decided, and maybe Colin hoped it would bring us luck. I moved toward the circular interior of the building, and didn't notice Azalea hanging back in the entrance as though reluctant to enter. She made a great pretence of being fascinated by the stone shaft of the belfry tower, before minutely examining the magnificently carved door. At last she stepped inside and slowly went around to pause at the picture of a Madonna over a side altar.

It was beautifully cool beneath the domed roof, which was upheld by massive granite pillars supplemented by slim columns of porphyry. I was gazing in some awe and quite distracted by the Romanesque choir piece, when I heard Azalea give a little yelp.

'Angelique has found something!' Her voice quavered, her face white as chalk. 'Somebody, I'm afraid. I knew there was trouble waiting for us in here. I nearly trod on ... ' Colin and I rushed towards where she gazed down at the figure sprawling in the shadow of the altar, terrified it was Gareth. Angelique whined but grew silent as Azalea picked her up. Doubtfully Colin began, 'Perhaps we shouldn't touch him until ...' It wasn't Gareth, that much I could tell.

'But suppose he isn't? Perhaps we could do something for him ...?'

There was something familiar about the figure. Slowly, gingerly, Colin lifted the head and we bent to see the face.

Mike Radnin, our driver.

CHAPTER NINE
MORE CROATIA

A murder is discovered and Gareth faces arrest

Mike Radnin looked hopelessly dead from the wound between his eyes. A little round hole with some discolouration round the rim. A bullet wound?

'Oh God!' Colin licked his lips, his hands dusting against each other as if he would wipe away all contact with Mike's dead flesh. We stared at each other in the gloom, not knowing what to do. At first the shock felt overwhelming – but, thankfully, Angelique brought us back to reality. She struggled to be put down and when Azalea obliged her, ran to Mike and began to nip his trouser leg, pulling at it with her sharp teeth. It was the trick she had learned on the steamer – how long ago that seemed now!

'Come away,' Azalea said and ran outside into the sunshine. The peaceful scene below the steps was much the same as before our grizzly find. People wandered about the tables set out for their refreshment; some were busy with their cameras, others went in and out of the information bureau.

The information bureau! The people in there would know what to do. Thankfully, we went in and told our story. Immediately, officials went to close the cathedral doors before anyone else stumbled over the body, keeping in those already there in case the police wanted to talk to them as witnesses. Azalea was shaking so hard that the pup looked up into her face. Colin seemed in a trance – I had to speak three times before he realised I was addressing him. He was in shock. I suppose we all were but over the past few days I had had more practice, and my continuing resolve to tough it all out was standing me in good stead now.

'We must find Azalea a seat,' I said. 'Could you get us some coffee or something to drink?'

He was glad of something to do, found a table and chairs for us and got us a coffee. By the time it was served, two men from the Militicja walked into the information bureau, coming out a moment later, one going to the cathedral, the other approaching us. He was a slim man, sunburned and very smart in his uniform. He bowed, smiling pleasantly as he put his hand on the back of the fourth chair.

'May I?'

When he had seated himself he looked at us each in turn out of keen, dark eyes. 'It must have been most unpleasant for you,' he said in good English.

He listened to our story almost without comment, though a look of puzzlement crossed his attractive face at Azalea's earnest theory: 'He was a Taurus, and it is a bad month for them. He probably couldn't have escaped his fate even if he had gone to Samara.' From Azalea's 'antiquities' period. He wisely decided not to follow this up.

'I see.' He studied her face and his became gentle with compassion. 'Now, if you will give me your names and the hotel at which you are staying? Also your room numbers, please.'

He scribbled busily. 'Your driver Mihajlo Radnin was often through here. He was a stranger to you?'

'We met him first time on Sunday morning,' Colin said.

'Perhaps my colleague will be able to tell us something when he has finished his investigation. But this will delay your journey, I'm afraid. How long do you plan to stay in Split?'

'Three days,' I answered. 'I think.' Uncle was supposed to call our hotel today. What was I going to tell him? News of Mike's murder was sure to reach him before long, bringing him down here to rescue me. I was almost that close to throwing in the towel and saying, enough is enough. But it wasn't. Someone had tried to kill me, then succeeded in killing the blackmailer. Was Mike indeed the blackmailer? And if so, had he succeeded only in blackmailing Wemys? Was Uncle Charles in danger? Highly unlikely!

Smiling tremulously, Azalea began, 'It's such a relief that you speak English. It really is good.' As her face became illuminated, the policeman's smile answered hers with quickening interest. Already Azalea was recovering and, equally, I felt that I was going into a decline. I had a murderer to catch now. Things were getting more and more serious and dangerous.

'Thank you,' he said. 'It is too bad that this happened to spoil your holiday. You were enjoying my country?' he enquired.

'We love it,' she answered. 'Everything except the fruit compote. And cheese without biscuits. Oh – that wasn't here, was it? Sorry.' My, her mind worked in strange ways. Food was the furthest thing from mine.

A strange spasm crossed his face; he looked hard at his little notebook, snapping it shut and returning it to his pocket. 'Further enquiries will have to be made. I will call on you this evening at your hotel.'

He rose to his feet. 'At nine o'clock. Please be available.' With a polite bow he left us and went to join his colleague and another man who was about to enter the cathedral. They seemed to know each other for their arms went up to each other's shoulders in a fond gesture. A doctor?

'How long shall we be detained?' I conjectured aloud. 'Also, we shall need another driver. Poor Mike. But he was a man who must have collected enemies.'

'It'll be a terrible shock for Mimi,' Azalea said gloomily. 'I feel terrible – and I scarcely knew the man. It's just that we're involved. Your Uncle Charles ...' She broke off, remembering that we were not alone.

I started practising how I would broach the topic of the dead driver / petty criminal (even blackmailer) to my uncle. I suppose could just wait until he learned about it through the usual official channels. Also, if we were to be delayed, the Dalmatian coast was a splendid place for it.

Alittle crowd was beginning to gather; curious stares were directed at us. It was time to move. The thought of Gareth having a gun descended on me with all the bludgeoning power of a pole axe. On wobbly legs I followed the others from the table. George Lonsties would be sure to mention to everyone this detail if he hadn't already – just not the kind of thing normal passengers keep to themselves. This aside, Lonsties seemed to have had a reason not to like Mike and would not mourn his passing. So, was he just an ordinary passenger?

As we walked slowly back to the hotel our brains seethed with conjectures. We couldn't find Mimi so left a message for her to contact us, hoping the authorities would get to her first and tell her. For the rest of the afternoon we stayed in our room, trying to read, or write letters, but giving it up, and pottering about doing small chores. I went down to the internet café off the lobby and sent off an email to Uncle Charles explaining I had 'lost my phone,' and therefore would wait to hear from him here, at the hotel. Funny – he still hadn't phoned!

Angelique sensed our unease and stared into our faces, several times giving a gruff bark, unlike her usual shrill crescendo – as if pleading with us to snap out of it.

Looking hard at a shoe she was polishing, Azalea said quietly, 'You knew Gareth had a gun?'

'I suppose George Lonsties told you. Damn him.'

'I suppose he's told everyone by now. I didn't want to mention it in case it worried you.' She glanced at me and then away. 'We don't know if it was Gareth's gun that killed Mike.'

I looked from the balcony at the garden below; it would have to be watered soon or everything would shrivel up in the heat. 'We saw him coming from the cathedral just before we found ...' Here she hesitated. 'Facts add up, but I still don't believe he could ...'

'Not always.' I wondered why she defended him. 'Anyway, it could have been worse.'

'It could?' She stared uncertainly.

'If it had been one of us that was killed.'

As the knock came on the door Azalea held the pup's nose. A chambermaid said, 'Telephone for Wills. Please to come.'

'I wonder why Uncle Charles didn't just ring our room. Or is it Mimi? Weird,' I said in relief at the prospect of speaking to either, and bounded along the corridor and down the steps to the reception office, which was by the dining block. I took up the receiver and gulped, 'Uncle Charles?'

'How's my favourite niece? Are you enjoying yourself? Be careful how you answer. They may be listening in the office.'

'I can't – enjoy myself – not any more. It's too awful. Our driver has been murdered.'

'What?'

'This afternoon. In the cathedral. Lea nearly fell over him. He'd been shot, I think.

'Lea found him? Is she all right? You poor child!' Uncle Charles was obviously finding it hard to conceal his anxiety. 'Don't say any more. I'll try and get there by tomorrow. After all, I've got plenty of contacts and I'm owed a lot of favours.' He paused only fractionally. 'Are you all right?'

'Fine!' Except I may be next, I thought. 'As well as can be expected.'

'Well, look after yourself.' No truer words.

As I put down the receiver I faced the curious stare of the clerk. 'Madam says that the driver of your coach is dead? Mihajlo Radin?'

'Yes. The police will be here soon.'

He looked excited and no doubt wished to inform his colleagues. 'Excuse, please,' he said and disappeared. I walked slowly back across the garden feeling the heat beat against me, glad to reach the coolness of our room. Tiredness washed over me as I explained to Azalea that my uncle was expected next day.

With some regret she murmured, 'I suppose we'll have to go home now.'

'And everything will come out and he'll be angry I didn't call him. He may never trust me again, Azalea. I may never be a partner. I'll always just be Little Babs. Damn.'

Azalea tried to give the proper, soothing response but it was no good: I needed to find out who had been victimising me and see him punished. Worse, the finger pointing would start with Gareth, and if Uncle Charles had even an inkling I was extremely attracted to Gareth, well, then the overprotective uncle role would really go into overdrive. There was just no way Gareth killed Mike. I could feel it.

This sense of loyalty filled me with a certain embarrassment; I couldn't understand myself. If he were a murderer, he deserved to be caught. Did I believe what I wanted to believe because I cared for him? I had to admit I enjoyed his company very much. He was amusing and charming. But – let's face it – there was a cold, calculating streak in him when provoked. But murder? I suppose it all added up to why I had never fully confided in him.

But it was time to bathe and dress for dinner, for as Azalea was constantly lamenting, there was never any time on these tours to do what you wanted. Like solve a murder for instance. Or fall in love properly – or even good old- fashioned lust.

At dinner, to which we took Angelique, the dining room buzzed with the news of Mike's murder. 'Isn't this something, eh,' George Lonsties said with every sign of enjoyment as he made his way to his table. Mimi was rushing around talking to everyone but seemed to avoid us. She hadn't responded to our message. We called her over in the end and told her what had happened in general, without revealing all. We had begged her patience previously and now, far from solving anything, we had got in deeper, but she seemed to appreciate our confidence and we were soon companionable again. We assured her of our support, and sympathised with her task of calming passengers. She had a lot to do – company bosses to talk to, I supposed – and I resolved to get Uncle Charles to offer help and thanks.

It seemed incredible that such a powerfully-built man should now be a limp corpse on some doctor's slab, a subject for autopsy. As we looked round the room we could not see either Wemys, or Gareth, and though we lingered over an already long drawn-out meal, they did not put in an appearance. This was very worrying for all manner of reasons. Was Gareth all right? Was he hiding for a reason? We went on to the terrace for coffee and to watch the dancing which had started. The light was fading rapidly, and tonight of all nights we were all acutely conscious of being foreigners in a strange country. The music came to a sliding halt to allow an announcement to be made: it was a request for all the travellers on the Magic Carpet Tours coach tour to gather in the lounge of the central dormitory block.

We had finished our coffee, so we put Angelique in our room, discovered we were already in the central block and made our way to the lounge. This was striking in its décor, the vivid murals made up of seascapes teeming with marine life. Azalea sank into a chair and leaned her head against a baby seahorse. Almost immediately we were asked to the end of the room where the man from the Militicja whom we had met previously began questioning us. He was perfectly polite and even more thorough in his probing than previously. At his side was a young man taking notes. Not all the coach party was assembled – who was missing and did we know why? We could not know the latter. Had we known ichel Radnin before this tour? Yes, he knew he had asked the question before but sometimes when people were shocked, they forgot details and later remembered them. Did we like him? Azalea was careful in her reply and I was grateful for this, for I did not wish them to pursue the angle that we might have some grudge against him.

Was he a popular man?

Then Azalea again hesitated.

I supplied, 'Not very.'

'Why do you say this?'

'You asked me for my opinion.'

'Ah, but I meant why did you consider him unpopular. Was he rude?'

'Sometimes. I think it is because he had little patience with clients. He's a good driver – I mean, he was a good driver. But his personality is – was – perhaps not right for this particular job.'

'He did not mix well, no?'

I asked, 'Was he killed by a bullet?'

He looked at me intently and said, 'Why do you ask?'

'The hole in his head rather indicated...'

'You should not have touched him.'

'I didn't. Our friend Colin Barnes turned him over to see if there was anything we could do for him. It's usual when you see someone on the ground. They might have fainted, or had a heart attack.'

He put his hand to his mouth and looked sideways at his clerk who was smiling openly. 'Er ... yes, I see. Do you know of anyone on this tour having a gun – legally or illegally?'

Avoiding looking at Azalea, I said, 'I don't know of anyone.'

She repeated my words for we did not know for sure that Gareth had a gun. It was only hearsay and could have been put about by George Lonsties to make mischief.

The time of our finding the body was again checked; we said we could not be more exact. A little wildly, Azalea added, 'The next time this sort of thing happens to me I'll be sure to check the time by my watch. You too, Babs?'

'Rather. The next time I shall run off in the opposite direction; I shan't be around to be helpful. Let other people find the corpses.'

Here our interrogator relaxed enough to offer us his packet of cigarettes; when we declined he lit up with every sign of enjoyment. 'Your passports, please.'

These were scrutinised and returned to us with a smile. I gathered the photographs did not flatter us. He wouldn't have been blamed if he had arrested us on the photographs alone – we both looked as though we had criminal tendencies! 'You would not object to your room being searched?'

'Not at all,' I began and then caught Azalea's worried frown. Angelique! If we had been weaving a tangled web, it became unwoven that very minute.

From along the corridor came a shrill scream followed by barking, a slammed door and hysterical crying. Right on cue.

Our questioner gestured and his clerk ran out and brought in a sobbing girl – one of the chambermaids who had obviously just become acquainted with Angelique. As they questioned her she grew calmer. I translated for Azalea's benefit.

'I went in the room to turn down the bed. I was picking up what I thought was a nightdress case when it turned on me. It was some sort of fierce animal.' It had attempted to 'savage' her, she declared. She had only saved herself by slamming the door before the thing could leap on her. Here there was a fresh burst of sobbing. Taking advantage of the lull, Azalea stood up.

'It's a cute little puppy dog we found in Germany. We couldn't find the owner, and we couldn't leave it behind, so it is going the rest of the way with us. I'm sorry if it startled the young lady, but it was only defending our possessions. It is a very good watchdog.'

In turn, the man translated to the frightened girl, who stopped shuddering and even essayed a weak giggle. She had been alarmed by a little dog. She could not move from the room fast enough to tell of her the adventure to her workmates.

Azalea was sad, picturing the consequences. Her little darling being driven out into the wilderness!

I asked our interrogator, 'Would you please send someone to search through our effects? We'd like to get it over.'

He bowed. 'There is no need, madam. All your rooms were searched while you were at dinner. You are free to go. The gun which killed Mihajlo Radnin has been found.' His words caused a sensation in the crowd which had gathered in the room. In the confusion that followed, the Reverend Burnett made his way to us. 'Are you girls all right? You've gone so pale.'

'It's all been rather a shock.' I appealed to the man in uniform. 'Have you finished with us? We'd like to go to our room and see if our dog is behaving.'

He relaxed visibly. 'Allow me to escort you. I am curious about this creature!' With a nod to his clerk to continue, he went with us down the corridor along which a refreshing breeze now blew.

'Allow me,' he said again as I fumbled with the key in the lock, which was a sort special to the country, and could be turned round and round without releasing the spring. We imagined we would learn its secrets in time. There was a fresh burst of staccato barking, changing to a note of hysterical relief at sight of us. Angelique was so effusively welcoming that we realised she had something on her conscience. Not only the attack on the maid, but a pool in the bathroom. Hastily I shut the door and we all went out on to the balcony, where Angelique cemented a friendship with the Croatian.

'This so fierce creature,' he laughed when we were all seated and he had accepted the boiled sweet Azalea offered. In an intense sort of way he was very good-looking. 'I am Marko Dubci. I am so sorry you have been disturbed. If there is anything I can do to make you stay more pleasant, please tell me. I am at your service.' He did not unwrap the boiled sweet but put it in his pocket. I felt rather cheated.

'Shall we be able to leave on schedule?' Azalea asked, wide-eyed and looking so wistful that a monkey would have parted with its last flea for her.

'Surely? Although I cannot really say this yet. You understand? It is unfortunate that it has brought a shadow over your holiday. We would like you to be happy in Split.' 'Oh, we are, really. We love it!' she said fervently. 'It is so beautiful – and the people are so pleasant.'

He looked gratified, as if the whole place were his responsibility and pride. With some reluctance he put Angelique off his knee and stood up.

'Where did you find the gun?' I dared to ask.

He looked at me thoughtfully. 'I cannot say. At the moment it is best to reveal nothing.' When he had replaced his hat on his handsome head he saluted, and left us to our thoughts.

In a moment, Colin Barnes, looked in, concerned for Azalea. 'I dashed to the photographer's before it closed. I only just heard about the meeting in the lounge. They didn't keep me. Gosh, I'm hot. How about a swim in the moonlight.'

We thought this was a marvellous idea and said we'd meet him outside in three minutes. His room was only a few doors from ours and we could speak across the balconies. Such balconies would prove child's play for romantic Romeos. Or burglars. Or people who wanted to steal a gun. Or wanted to kill me.

Grimly I donned my swimsuit, reflecting that if the gun had been found there would be little chance that I would be shot at again tonight. And where was Gareth. Sweating it out somewhere, keeping a low profile? Waves of horror made me go weak.

We were a subdued trio as we cautiously felt our way down the many steps to the beach. I had forgotten my torch and couldn't be bothered going back for it. Cool air fanned us, making the water seem cooler by contrast, and we were soon under, swimming languorously back and forth amid the chosen rocks. An idyllic experience if only we hadn't all been worried.

On the gentle breeze were borne other scents – wallflower and lilac – mingling with the spicy sea wrack on the ledges of the rocks.

In the silence broken only by the lapping of the water, and a deeper gurgle as it sucked round a hidden cave, a nightingale began to sing. Treading water, we listened, entranced.

'Ahoy there!'

Recognising the voice, my heart began to thump. 'Gareth? Is it you?'

We swam in, surrounding him, astounded that he appeared so calm. 'Have you been to the police? They called us all together to question us. Do the police know who murdered Mike? Where were you at dinner?'

'Here, steady on. One question at a time.'

I asked quietly, 'You do know that Mike was murdered in the cathedral this afternoon?'

Although it was dark I knew he was looking at me. 'Yes, I know. I saw him. I also saw I couldn't do anything for him. I was after Wemys.'

'We saw you. Did Wemys kill him?'

He hesitated. 'No, I don't know. I can only guess. But that's no good in this game.'

'The other day Mr Lonsties said he saw you with a small gun.'

He started. 'Then Lonsties is lying. I don't possess a gun.'

'He said the door was opened by a maid just as he was passing and he saw you handling it.'

'He couldn't have. Besides, if the maid had seen it she'd have reported it.'

My spirits began to rise. I wanted to believe him. As the night air blew cold on us we decided to leave the water and get dressed.

'Have you talked to the police yet?' I asked as we felt our way up the steps.

'Not yet. I had a meal in town. I walked back along the shore path and heard you splashing about in the water. I recognised Angelique's bark. Then you all went quiet.'

'We were listening to a nightingale.'

'Romantic.'

'Very. Well, so long as you are prepared – about the police, I mean. They're very polite. Marko Dubci is charming.'

'Is he, indeed?' Gareth's voice was grim as we emerged into the lights below the kitchen quarters and went up the last slope to the gardens towards our dormitory block.

There was nothing charming about Marko Dubci as he stepped out of the shadows and addressed himself to Gareth. He was not alone. 'Mr Findlatter? We have been waiting to talk to you. We would like you to explain about the gun which killed Radnin.'

Gareth was tensed as though for swift movement. 'What gun?'

'The gun we found in your room, in your bag, Mr Findlatter.' I think I stopped breathing at this point.

'If there was a gun in my bag then someone put it there.' His voice was as hard as his unyielding expression.

'We will discuss it,' said Mark Dubci. 'Come. Our car is waiting. We will talk more comfortably down at headquarters.'

He did not actually touch Gareth, but stepped closer, and his colleague moved in behind as they escorted Gareth to the car which stood in the forecourt. A slight inclination of the head from Dubci showed that he acknowledged us, as we watched transfixed, sea water still trickling down our legs and making pools on the garden path.

'Gosh!' Colin said, staring after the car as it whirled away in a cloud of dust. His mouth had fallen open; he only closed it as the dust reached us.

I tried to stay calm. 'I don't believe Gareth had anything to do with Mike's death. Someone is framing him – the real murderer who wants to distract attention from himself. It would be easy enough to get into Gareth's room either from the balcony or by the door. I'm sure all the keys are the same. In this heat, all the windows onto the balconies are left open.'

Azalea gave me a look full of sympathy. 'The gun could just as easily have been found in our room. Think how awful we'd have felt if it had been found among our clothes.'

Disconsolately we wandered back to our room, Colin urging us not to worry too much on the grounds that if Gareth were innocent he had nothing to worry about. This advice was regarded dubiously. We were in a foreign country; we did not know their procedure. Colin said he would let us know if Gareth returned. We thanked him and for a long time sat out on the balcony, pretending to watch the bobbing lights at sea on the tuna fishing boats, but really straining to see the darkness beyond the dining terrace.

At last the mosquitoes drove us indoors, where Azalea began her masterly campaign to defeat the flying menace. All doors and windows were closed while she sprayed with insecticide and we retired to the bathroom with Angelique, to repeat the process in the vacated bathroom when we were ready for bed. I will say this for it – it was effective, if a bit stifling to have to sleep in a sealed room with the bodies of your victims. For warmer nights we would pursue Azalea's second plan – that of pulling the lace curtains across the open shutters and smothering ourselves in anti-mosquito cream, another layer of cream to be added to it when we awakened. This was not wholly effective, as the bedcovers kept sliding off and exposing the soles of our feet, which we'd neglected to anoint!

Just now we felt safer with the windows closed, all things considered.

CHAPTER TEN
FAREWELL TO CROATIA

In which Uncle Charles joins the team

We talked into the small hours so it was only natural we should be late in waking and even then, we felt as if we had weathered some awful storm.

Dragging herself onto the balcony, yawning fit to dislocate her jaw, Azalea was petrified to find she was looking straight into the eyes and grinning face of the gardener who was sinking his bucket into a well – one of several in the area. Falling back into the room she asked, 'What time is it?'

'Help. It's nearly afternoon. Charles could be here any minute.' My simultaneous thought was for Gareth. I felt I couldn't function properly until I knew if he was OK.

Trying to rush, yet chained by a lethargy which made us stumble and get in each other's way, we gradually completed our chores while longing for a strong cup of tea to help us pull ourselves together. When I muttered this, Azalea said pertly, 'You once accused me of being insular. Don't be so insular.'

It was as near as we got to quarrelling the whole trip. Besides it takes two and I knew she was dying for a cup of tea as much as

I was. The only thing that's wrong with a foreign tour is not being able to get a good old British cuppa; I must be sure to tell Uncle Charles!

Finally, we were ready, and walked along the cool corridor to be met by the full blast of heat which was making the flowers wilt. Only the lizards seemed to approve, though we found even one of those dead, and as dried up as a piece of string.

We were on the terrace and counting the minutes to an extremely late breakfast, when who should come walking up to us but Uncle Charles. My emotions were conflicting; I had never been so glad to see anyone. Thrusting away a weak desire to burst into tears all over his handsome, lightweight suit, I became at once cool, calm, capable. His handsome face was rather grim until he saw us, when it softened into a smile.

'Uncle Charles!' I said, hugging him. It was like a piece of home. 'You haven't met Azalea.'

As I looked from his tall, compact frame to Azalea who was not looking her best this morning, I wondered what he would make of her, but I need not have worried for she had him in the palm of her hand in ten seconds.

'I've heard so much about you, I've been dying to meet you, to thank you for letting me accompany Babs!' Her interest was so genuine, so flattering that he was charmed. 'Do you girls want to come home?' he asked, weakening his position.

We immediately chorused, 'No!'

He nodded as if he had expected that. 'I've already been on to the police who are following the usual line of enquiries. I couldn't help them. Apparently your coach driver was not popular because he was always on the make, so they imagined several people who might have a grudge against him.'

In a small voice I asked, 'Did you hear that our driver was shot with a gun which was later found in the room of one of the passengers in the coach?' I looked round; there were several people within earshot. 'Shall we go to the end of the terrace? There's a bit of shade there.'

Uncle Charles directed that coffee be brought for us, asking (to my surprise, in Croatian) that it be 'as hot as hell'. The waiter grinned and presently served us with a most delicious brew accompanied by iced water.

'Oh, Mr Madden!' Azalea sighed blissfully. 'If you could only continue the tour with us it would be so much more enjoyable.'

His amused glance locked with mine. 'Didn't Babs tell you it was a working trip?'

'Of course, but we're combining business with pleasure.'

I interposed hastily, 'I'll give you my findings to date. I'll write out a list later – it's quite a lengthy one.'

'It's not necessary. Just read them off to me from your mobile.'

'Well, I …'

'That many!' He pulled a face. 'Really? It just goes to show.'

'No, Uncle. It's not that. You see, my mobile was stolen. And the memory card from my camera. We think it's because of the picture I sent you. Of the … '

'Hyena Face?'

'Yes, partly. And by the way, where have you been?' I added. 'I've been trying to get you for days.'

'Well, by coincidence, my mobile disappeared as well. It did turn up again just before you called. I was worried – that's why I phoned the hotel.'

And my mobile still hadn't showed up either. Was there a connection? Did people know I had been keeping Uncle Charles informed, and knew how to find him, or had he just been careless?

'However,' he continued, 'I got a flight in and out of Germany. I sorted out those hotels you were talking about. Amazing what you can achieve in twenty-four hours! I asked about Mike Radnin at all the usual stops, and only one person told me about his blackmail scheme. Fairly easily as well.'

'Let me guess. The fat hotel manager in Heidelberg.'

'No. His wife, on the sly. Said Mike had been blackmailing her for months. Her father had stolen several paintings from a hiding place in the basement of the town hall when the Nazis were run out. Sold all but one on the black market.'

'And forced her to con guests at the hotel ...' I put in.

'So he can rush in and threaten them with the evidence!' This was Azalea. 'What a rat!'

'He's a dead rat now,' I added, wondering how many souls he had made miserable. The list of suspects in his death was limitless. 'At least he won't be bothering the Reverend anymore.' Azalea and I explained the story in great detail now that we had time.

'I shall have to make it up to them. A free trip somewhere, perhaps.'

I should have been happy things were winding up. The blackmailer had had his just desserts and victims were free. Including my uncle and his clients. 'So I guess our mystery is solved, Uncle.'

'Then why do you look so miserable. Is it a man?'

Azalea answered for me. 'No. If she runs away now, not knowing who tried to kill her or why, it will haunt her for the rest of her life.' She knew just what it would take to convince him.

He didn't answer right away. 'Azalea, I wonder if you would give us few minutes.'

'Sure. I'll see if I can get that picture of Hyena Face printed downstairs in the I-café.' And she was gone.

Uncle Charles said, 'First of all, I've always been proud of you. Even when you were very young you were a tough, smart little girl. Smarter and tougher than either of your parents, that's for sure.' I had to smile at that; he was right. 'You're not weak, Babs. You're your own person. That's why you hate being afraid.'

I cried softly for some time, making a mess of several linen napkins and all the while my Uncle Charles comforted me. And told me how proud he was of me. That I had to stop beating myself up about it. 'What's done is done, sweetheart. We all have to move on.'

'That's why this is so important to me. I want to do well for your firm. And for myself.'

He doused another napkin in a pitcher of iced water. 'Here. Now why don't you pull yourself together and I'll order us something tall and cool to give us a nice boost.'

The drinks came, Azalea dawdled, Colin didn't coming looking for her, and my Uncle Charles and I were able to have the conversation we should have had a long time before. I felt so much better about everything. Well – almost everything. I was still afraid of being shot and, not surprisingly, would be until Hyena Face was behind bars.

Once we'd sorted my head out, Uncle Charles sat back. 'Now you can tell me about this Gareth!'

'I think he's some sort of retired military or police type. Private agency now – on a case. I don't believe he shot Mike. Nor shot at me. He's a fine person, someone you can depend on.' Uncle Charles smiled at me, eyes twinkling. 'No, I mean it. There's this vein of cold, hard steel that runs through him. Straight-edged and true. Sounds a bit corny, I suppose.'

'Not at all. You like him very much.' I nodded, never breaking eye contact. 'Then that's good enough for me.'

He hugged me tightly, and whispered a little advice in my ear. 'If you feel strongly about him, then give him your best, and expect the same from him. Relationships are give and take. And it takes honesty to keep the balance. So be honest, Babs. Don't keep anything back. And he'll most likely do the same.'

I knew what he meant. 'Just be myself.'

'That'll do.'

'Well, what's this then? I get sent up the river and come home to find you in the arms of another.'

'Gareth!' I flew to him, holding nothing back. And that is how my Uncle Charles witnessed our first but brief kiss. We turned to face my uncle as I presented Gareth to him. Gareth took it rather well, I thought. Flushed cheeks and a small bead of sweat on his upper lip. He was very flustered as Uncle Charles offered to shake his hand. 'Uncle Charles, how do you do, sir.' Uncle Charles asked for more details of the trip down to the police station, and the gun.

'Well, I managed to clear everything up and convince them we are on the same side.' He was just about to explain when Azalea joined us, oddly enough without Colin trailing after. 'I finally proved to them I had nothing to do with the shooting because of some work I am doing. I think what clinched it was that the gun had been wiped clean of finger prints. If I had been careless enough to leave it lying around, I certainly wouldn't have gone to the trouble of wiping it clean. I'll explain more fully later, I promise.'

'OK, Gareth. So what's your line. Private, is it?'

'Yes, but can't say exactly what right now.'

'Were you in the military?' He guessed shrewdly.

'Yes sir.' How did he do it? I'd been trying to get something like that out of Gareth for days.

Uncle Charles nodded an okay. One man of the world to another. 'So I gather from the police that your driver was not popular.'

It was Gareth's turn to stare. 'You've been in touch with the police, sir? May I ask on what grounds?'

'You may. My name obviously didn't convey anything to you when Babs introduced us. I own the company of Madden's tours.'

'I forgot to tell you. My uncle is Charles Madden.'

'But your name is Wills.'

'That's right.'

I was grateful he'd not been given the whole annoying mouthful (Madden's Magic Carpet Tours), which always made me writhe! I was not prepared for the effect produced on Gareth. After the first digestion of the fact, a curious spasm crossed his face and resolved in a stifled laugh.

'Excuse me, sir,' he chuckled. 'It's just now it all occurs to me what Barbara and Azalea have been up to. You put them up to snooping on this tour.'

'Yes, I did, in a word. To see what was going on with my clients. It's not all that funny,' began Uncle Charles mildly, seeing Gareth still smiling.

'Sorry, sir. I'm not laughing at you. It's just that at first I thought Azalea here was an art smuggler along with Wemys. And that Barbara was her sidekick.'

'I like that,' I said punching him in the arm. Azalea laughed and thought it very funny. Explained a lot about Gareth's general reticence.

'When all the time she was doing a little job for me – vetting the tour arrangements. Good heavens, when I think what might be going on all my other tours!'

'Things like this go on everywhere,' Gareth said in a matter-of-fact way.

'You really think Wemys is an art thief? He's been a client for a few years. Can you at least give me an indication of what you think he's done.'

'The man who is employing me has a right to privacy. I could tell you If I thought it wouldn't go any further...'

He looked at Uncle Charles who spoke for us. 'I think you can depend on our discretion.'

Gareth still looked dubious. 'If what I tell you is repeated Wemys could bring a good case for defamation of character.'

'We understand,' I said.

My uncle looked at us.

Azalea said, 'You have my word.'

'And mine,' I added. 'I have a lot more to lose.'

Gareth pulled out a chair and seated himself. 'Briefly, I have a hunch, and it is little more than that – that it's Wemys who has smuggled a valuable painting out of England and has already placed it somewhere abroad. Perhaps sold it, though I think not – it would be easier for him to dispose of in Italy. But at the moment it's hot property.'

Azalea said eagerly, 'Wemys was upset when the coach had to be changed so we naturally thought -whatever it was – had to be transferred.'

'It's my opinion that Mike Radnin got into the act,' said Gareth. 'He may have seen Wemys transferring the painting and tried to cut himself in on the profits in one of his blackmail schemes. Instead, he got himself killed. I followed Wemys to the cathedral after he had bought the blue rug in the market place.'

'A blue rug,' I repeated in rising excitement. 'I was stopped twice about the blue rug I'd bought.' That's what the gypsy lady was on about.

'I think Wemys rolled the picture in the rug, ready to hand over to friends who would hide it for him until he left. Mike thought he was going to get paid, and instead ... I found him in the cathedral. He was already dead and I didn't want to be mixed up in that little lot. When I came out, I'd lost Wemys. I've thought since he may have run up into the belfry tower and would be able to watch everything that went on down below. Anyway, I lost him. He could have waited up there until the coast was clear, unless he was found by the police. He would have had to talk his way out.'

'Interesting,' commented Uncle Charles, bright-eyed. 'Could you go back a bit and tell us why you think Wemys is a crook – possibly a murderer?'

'You do understand why this should be kept to ourselves? I've told the Militicja all I'm telling you. That's is why they released me once they'd checked it out. Besides, Wemys or anyone could have planted the gun among my things.'

'Did you say it's only a hunch you're following?'

Gareth nodded. 'I'm a private detective retained by Sir Leopold Reynolds. You've heard of him? He buys up works of art – not only as an investment but because he genuinely loves beautiful things. Anyway, he sent a painting for cleaning to Jacques Astel who always handles this for Sir Leopold – just a routine job as he thought.'

'A painting he'd just bought,' enquired Azalea.

'No. He'd had it many years. He got a telephone call from Astel who was terribly excited about what he had found under the painting. He'd had it x-rayed and wanted permission to uncover the original painting.'

With bated breath Azalea asked the question for all of us: 'Who was the original artist?'

'Rembrandt.' He smiled round at our awed faces. 'Worth about a million pounds at least. Of course there was a risk involved – that of losing a painting worth five thousand pounds to gain one of …. ' He waved his hands. 'There was also the chance that some flaw had caused the original to be edited over.'

'Did Sir Leopold agree to take the risk?' asked Azalea. I noticed she had just returned to her childhood habit of biting her nails when on edge.

'Yes, he told Astel to go ahead. He came round immediately to talk it over with him. When he got there Astel was suffering from the after-effects of a heart attack, though there were signs that he'd been involved in a struggle. The picture had gone, of course. Sir Leopold called in the police, and in a private capacity asked me to scout around. I put several men on the job – tracing the movements of anyone connected with Astel over the last six months – and I soon got a list of three people who interested me very much. I worked on these myself. Wemys fascinated me. He was an artist himself; he'd been in the office the day Astel died. The police could find nothing on him. But they were interested in the painting he was sending abroad – to be picked up Poste Restante. Interpol dealt with what proved to be a red herring.'

'You believe then,' concluded Uncle Charles, 'that Wemys has stashed the painting somewhere in Split – finding it too hot to hold after Mike Radnin's murder?'

'Yes. My guess is that he'll try to get it into Italy – either by bus at Trieste – or by boat. It will be easy to dispose of in Italy.'

'The cradle of Art,' Azalea said dreamily.

'Yes. I fancy the idea of a boat. What's to stop him slipping across during the night? That's why I went to see an old acquaintance. He owns several boats – lets them out to holiday makers – uses them for tuna fishing – anything that comes to hand. He lives down the coast at Omis.'

'Can we help,' Azalea breathed, her eyes gleaming. 'You have helped,' Gareth assured her. 'Wemys has been so busy watching you he hasn't always noticed me. I'm sure he's been as puzzled as I have. By the way, where is Angelique?'

My embarrassment showed as I explained to Uncle about the pup, but I was loyally supported by Azalea who took all the blame to herself. 'We left her in the bedroom for a while. This heat is a bit too much for her with her thick coat. I thought we'd have had a deputation from the manager by now – asking us to remove the poor creature.' Amused, Uncle Charles suggested, 'He has other more pressing worries on his mind. If you like, I'll have a word with him – make it worth his while to overlook a small trifle such as cute dog.'

'A pedigree – well, something, I'm sure,'Azalea insisted. 'You can't help noticing her style.' She sighed in pure pleasure. 'It'll be splendid not having to worry about her while we're here. You make it seem so easy. Isn't it still a man's world. Sometimes!'

Gareth and Uncle Charles looked at each other but would not be drawn into an argument. As we walked arm in arm, I whispered to Uncle Charles that I really was very happy for him. 'And I am very happy for you, my dear. I like Gareth, very much. As you say. One who can be depended upon. Good Scottish morals, after all.'

After the long tall drinks which we all enjoyed together now, almost celebrating, we took Uncle across to our room to make Angelique's acquaintance, and it was another case of love at first sight. Presently we went out on to the beach, enjoying the cooler part of the day, Charles having donned a rakish-looking sports shirt. The stripes of this garment against his sunburned skin made him look a pirate.

As he stared out to sea he observed, 'There are caves all along this coast – have you noticed? When the Germans invaded during the war, the Slavs hid some of their valuables in caves. Down at Orebic, in the south, there is a place called the Riviera of the Sea Captains – old salts who have come to retire and built fine villas. I was shown over one villa by the widow of the last sea captain in that family. It was a priceless museum piece, though still lived in most comfortably.

'For hundreds of years the captains had brought home their treasures from all over the world. There was a Chinese room, a South American room, a Russian room – and so on. The Nazis stole a lot but the family managed to hide some. I understand the villa is under state protection now and the delightful widow a curator.' Uncle Charles broke off to say, 'There's a young man trying to attract your attention.'

Azalea looked round and beckoned. 'It's Colin Barnes. He's on the tour too. He's so nice. Come on over, Colin, and meet someone.'

As if he were a politician seeking votes, Uncle Charles shook hands with Colin too, but I craftily lost him a vote by introducing him simply as my relative and nothing else. If Colin thought it unusual for an uncle to drop in and see me in such a place as Split, he made no reference to it, but listened to him respectfully, perhaps a little out of his depth. Without any trouble at all, Uncle Charles dominated the scene, until quite suddenly, overcome by his recent snack and few drinks, the heat and the inviting beach proved too much for him. He succumbed to silence, and finally, slumber.

Our swimming and splashing did not waken him but as we flopped down near him he roused himself and said sheepishly, 'Must have dozed off.''

We refreshed him with real lemonade provided – at a charge – by an attendant in his kiosk near the steps. As we were all drinking, my eyes kept resting on Gareth who always looked most impressive in his trunks. I decided happily, that if he wanted to show me pigeon lofts, or tuna-fishing boats, or anything like that, I would let him. I also had the feeling that he knew it too, for the smile that had never quite reached his eyes, warming them, was there now in full force, making them shine wickedly.

Out of the blue Azalea asked, 'I wonder why George Lonsties said he saw Gareth handling a gun?'

'I've been thinking about that,' Gareth responded. 'Perhaps he has a guilty conscience and thinks I'm trailing him for some reason. The only thing he's achieved is to draw attention to himself. I've no idea what his game is, so he's not really significant, for the moment at least.'

Azalea and I smiled at each other. She said, 'We've decided he wishes to entangle with money. Of course he's a Leo.'

'Well, I am going to speak with the detectives handling this case and find out what I can about this Wemys from our company data base. Find out when he surfaced. Be careful, all of you.'

'You too, Uncle Charles,' I answered, hugging him. 'And I'll remember your advice,' I whispered.

'Let's all get together soon. I'll be around in general, though not in your hair. Oh, and I'll have a word with your courier. Sounds as though she has been doing an excellent job all round.'

And off went Uncle Charles, scampering down the tricky steps, pausing under a thick-leaved orange tree to look at the bay. Then up again and out of sight behind the ilex and olive groves. He was moving quickly, like a man with a bee in his bonnet.

Silence weighed down on us again, but the conversation with Uncle Charles was still going round and round in my head. So much to think about! The heat was less oppressive, and Lea and Colin began languidly discussing sight-seeing plans. From under the towel with which she was protecting her head, Azalea mumbled,

'I'd like to see the Mestrovic Gallery. Mimi tells me the sculptures are powerful, passionate, brooding. I can't wait to see them.' Seeing Colin's face, her voice trailed off as if she had died. Politely but not too enthusisatically, Colin murmured, 'I'll take you. Later ...'

With a meaningful glance at me, Gareth said, 'I'm going to the harbour to check over the boat I've borrowed from my friend at Omis. If I need it in a hurry, I want to be sure everything is trim, and I can handle her. Care to come?'

'I'd like that.' It was exciting to be working with him on a case.

'Let's go, you two.'

As Azalea and I dressed in our room she said, 'Remember the gipsy's warning?'

'What's that?'

'Beware the dark stranger.'

'I was told to beware holding back.'

Azalea flashed me one of her patented smiles.

I changed the topic. 'Are you taking Angelique?'

'Yes. She'll be unhappy if I leave her alone until dinner time. She's really very good, isn't she?'

It was an appeal and I answered darkly, 'She knows her place.'

At the foot of the terrace I went one way towards Gareth, and she went in the opposite direction to meet Colin. Their look of mutual pleasure must surely have been mirrored in my own as I saw Gareth's eyes light up at the sight of me. As we wandered along the promenade we saw George Lonsties in the distance but he turned away, pretending he hadn't seen us. Neither of us cared very much. Gareth said, 'I talked to Mimi just before you came, and she said arrangements had been made about a new driver. I think she's more shaken up than she lets on.'

'Yes, and we haven't been frank with her about Mike's scams.'

'I think she's guessed – or learned from the police.'

It was still very hot but a breeze along the shoreline made walking pleasant. 'Where's Wemys?' I asked. 'Don't you have to keep an eye on him today?'

'Not at the moment. He's fast asleep in his room, like Sleeping Beauty. I looked in on him before I came out.'

'He could be pretending.'

'I doubt it. I put a couple of sleeping pills in his after- lunch tea. I noticed he always orders tea and I saw the tray set ready as we went in. He should sleep until dinner time. Besides, I doubt if he'll make a move before dark. He has all night to work in.' Gareth smiled at me. 'Are you not working at your job either?'

I hung my head. 'Don't laugh. Yes, I've made several notes. Not that they'll do any good – my mobile still hasn't turned up.'

'It will. If you had it, what would you report?'

'The coffee is never hot – and that's because it's put into those tiny, individual pots. By the time it gets into the cups, it's tepid. One large pot for the table would ensure hotter coffee. Also, the length of time between courses is too long.' 'As you say, a national characteristic. Why rush? You're on holiday? It's like the Spanish manana. The Slavs will probably have a word for it too.'

'They have. It's probably prekosutra – the day after tomorrow!'

We were feeling very happy as we found the Labud and went aboard her by climbing across two other boats which were riding the slight swell. Though described as a tideless sea, the Adriatic rises several feet – more during high tides or bad weather.

'What is your friend called?' I asked as I seated myself. I had no wish to help him in his survey. 'He's named his boat Swan'.

'Petar Vratmic. I've known him about seven years. We've fished together. He's a fellow I'd value having around if ever I was in a tight corner.'

'I'd like to meet him. He sounds interesting.'

'You can if you like. I was just going to propose a run out to Omis – you'd enjoy seeing the place. It's not far. It really is fantastic – just a fishing village with a few streets at the mouth of the river and under the cliffs. They're really sheer – about a thousand feet, I'd guess.'

'Let's go.' I settled back in the stern to enjoy myself, having every confidence in his handling of the craft. He certainly had no difficulty in starting the motor. When we were a little way out, I looked back at the harbour and the whole dramatic coastline.

Gareth said, smiling at me, 'This is the first time I've had you to myself. You do rather cling to your friend.'

'Do I? It's just that we're on holiday together. Besides ...' I looked away from him.

'You've had no reason to trust me? I could say the same about you.'

'I suppose so. It feels a relief to be able to act naturally.' On impulse I asked him what he thought of the shots that had been fired at me in the water – or rather, the one shot, following the thrown pebble that had attracted my attention. 'Why should anyone want me out of the way?'

His expression went grim. 'Wemys may be nervous, but it could have been someone else.'

I read his thought. 'George Lonsties. Why?'

'Search me. You've made a few of us nervous. People with guilty consciences often see danger where there isn't any.'

I nodded. 'Let's forget it for a while. Isn't it heavenly on the water? So smooth and clear.' I trailed my hard over the side until I saw a dark shape rise some distance away. 'Sharks?'

He laughed and shook his head. 'Probably a dolphin or a tuna. Petar likes to fish at night with flares. They send a boy to the lookout and when the fish are sighted, they go out.'

All too soon we were running into the little harbour of Omis, charming with its long beach of clean sand and backing pinewood, until we looked upwards and saw the sheer savagery of the cliffs. Into one of them had been carved a building which only enhanced the wildness of its surround. Gareth tied up alongside a jetty and we went ashore to an open-air cafe where he directed me to sit at one of the tables. I chose one under an oleander, for since we had come off the water, the land felt the hotter by comparison.

Gareth strode into the dark interior of the house up which vines grew, returning several minutes later with a slim, dark man, tanned as are all the men on this coast. His smile was singularly radiant because of a gold tooth.

'Barbara, meet Petar.'

We shook hands and there were some pleasantries, before Petar asked the question nearest his interests. 'How you like my Swan? A fine boat, eh?'

'Very smooth,' Gareth said.

They talked engines for a while until Petar said with a serious intent expression, 'The man you describe to me – Veems – he has been here.'

'Wemys? Here?'

'Yes, he come last night. He come see my friend Ivo Brovac – a little matter of a boat.'

'So I was right.' The keen expression on Gareth's face sharpened. 'When he comes again, could you phone me?'

Petar repeated his number. 'I will phone, and I will arrange with Ivo for the small delay while you come.' He laughed and slapped his leg. 'Until then – you enjoy yourself, yes?'

There was no doubt about it – Petar liked girls, for he made expressive eyes and all but nudged me in the ribs.

'Shall I leave here?' asked Gareth.

Petar shrugged – a remarkable performance for it involved the whole of his rangy frame, his trim waist, his wide shoulders, finally fanning out to his lean finger tips. 'No, you take. Put it down to expenses, eh?'

'Hvala.'

Still a business man, despite sentiment, Petar asked, 'What you drink? Slivovitz?'

'No thanks.' Gareth turned to me. 'No Dutch treats today. What'll it be?'

Shamelessly I asked for a sweet wine (dry for late evenings), forgetting the Croatians do not make sweet wines. In fact, now I came to think of it, they didn't like anything sweet – and this included their desserts. Perhaps this was why they were all so lean and hungry-looking. In the end I settled for a gin and slim, though I realised my timing was not right. After the second sip, my other self stepped outside me and gave the warning, You should not drink on an empty stomach, but I was feeling so good, I ignored it and listened in a dreamy state of well-being to their conversation. I came to the conclusion that Petar's woman must do all the work of the café, for people came and went, and were attended to in due course.

The evening korzo was about to begin – the strolling about to admire and be admired. It was all very friendly and meant that the women who had been cooped up all day doing their chores had no need to feel buried under domesticities. Always, there was the evening and a gossip to which to look forward. In a nearby high tree, a thousand birds were settling for the night, their contented chirping quite deafening.

Eventually we were sailing back to Split in the Labud. Already the brilliance of the day was fading and there was a coolness on the water. Gareth tied up in the same place and we scuttled across the other two boats, whose owners were now aboard stowing their fishing gear. There were greetings all round and some rude remarks about Petar Vratmic and his mother's honour.

But it was all very good-natured. Gareth gave me a quick glance to see if I had translated freely; I suspected he knew far more of the language than he pretended.

'Quite a character, Petar,' I said. 'I notice he keeps his savings in gold.'

He laughed. 'That tooth! His ancestors were pirates. He can't help his nature.'

'Why should he? I've enjoyed meeting him. Thank you for taking me.'

He gave me a warm peck. 'Shall we meet later?'

'I'll think about it.' Still feeling rather dreamy, I went to my room, expecting to find Azalea there, resting, but she was not around, nor was Angelique. I decided they must be dining and went to the dining room where I bumped into Gareth.

'They haven't got back. I've just checked. Oh, well we might as well have dinner in case you have to leave in a hurry.'

A tiny pang of worry shot through me but I tried to shrug it off. 'She's with Colin. He'll look after her. You know Azalea – she's probably got mixed up in something.'

We enjoyed our dinner and were awaiting the dessert when a man in the uniform of the Militicja entered. 'Oh- ho,' Gareth muttered. 'Here come the police.'

Mark Dubci approached our table and drew up a chair after greeting us. Without any preamble, beyond a smile, he asked Gareth, 'Any news from Omis?'

Gareth had to smile. 'My friend tells me Wemys approached Ivo Bravo about a boat. Perhaps he intends to leave for Italy soon?'

Dubci stroked the small mustache he was encouraging to grow on his handsome top lip. 'I think not. But we will keep watch. You will be there when the time comes?'

'Try and stop me,' Gareth said blandly.

'We could do that,' Dubci said, waving a finger at him. 'But we shall not. You must do as you wish. It is most amazing to watch you, but do not blame us if you get hurt?'

'Of course not,' Gareth was saying as the waiter approached. 'A message for you, sir. Please go to the information desk.'

As Gareth went out, Dubci sank back contentedly. 'Ah, something is about to happen. Since Magic Carpet Tours came to Split, life has been so interesting – so rewarding.' In a few minutes Gareth returned. 'Telephone call from Petar Vratmic. Wemys called. No sign of Brovac. I asked Petar to have a boat ready for eleven o'clock tonight, fully fuelled for a long trip.'

'Let's go,' I said, jumping to my feet. Gareth's hand on my arm detained me and I subsided into my seat again.

'No hurry,' he pointed out. 'It's only 9.15. Besides, we haven't finished our dinner.'

'Azalea must be having dinner out. I wish she had thought to phone me.'

Dubci interrupted, deep interest in his eyes. 'Your friend with whom you travel? Miss Dunbar?'

'Yes, have you seen her?'

'Yes, we go in and out museums until I grow tired. I put my man to follow and come here. Your friend is an artist– so enthusiastic. But I think her friend is not so artistic, no.'

'Poor Colin.'

Dubci was amused. 'You think he suffer for love? It is true.' Almost immediately his expression sobered. 'I do not think it is suitable for you to come to Omis with Mr Findlatter tonight.'

'I can't be kept out of it. I wouldn't sleep a wink.'

Dubci rose, spreading out his hands in an attitude of resignation. 'Then I must leave you to make preparations of my own.' He saluted us and strode out, an impressive, handsome figure.

'He's right,' Gareth said. 'It's no place for a girl.'

'Come on – you get women on active service these days!'

'There may be trouble.'

'It's just something I have to do. Okay?'

He looked me straight in the eye, allowing his gaze to linger as if studying some impenetrable truth – seeing for himself the place in the past that still spooked me. Suddenly he seemed to understand. 'The thing you saw in the woodshed. Got it.'

Something strong and real had just passed between us. Understanding, knowing, whatever you call it. It was real. 'Th-thanks,' I faltered, unsteady.

'No, no need for thanks.' His voice was soft, caring. 'There is some mystery about you, Barbara.' My heart was beating. I wanted only him – and yet the longing scared me.

'I don't mean to be stubborn.'

This didn't even register a smile, the conversation silently going on between us was too loud. 'We'll need passports, of course.'

'Oh, we will,' I concurred.

'Yes. For the licence.'

'What licence? It's Petar's boat. We're just borrowing it.' He never answered the question. 'Suddenly very warm, isn't it,' he was saying. I made the appropriate comment in agreement, and suddenly the sun rose – just for me! – in his smile. He leaned toward me so closely I could feel his breath lightly caress my cheek. He said quietly, 'Are you ready?'

I closed my eyes, leaned in for that kiss, that special in the moonlight kiss, pursing my searching lips …

'I'm dead serious. Have you got your passport handy?' There it was, the cold water down my back. I sat back, cleared my throat and studiously ignored the satisfied smirk on his face.

Not skipping a beat, I answered, 'I've got Azalea's too. I'd better leave that behind. Also a note telling her where I'm headed for. Do you really think Wemys will go across to Italy? In a small boat?' I was trying desperately to get my head in gear.

'We'll soon know.'

For all his calm exterior, I guessed he was not able to sit still. Like Marko Dubci we needed action. Ignoring the dessert, we got ready for the trip to Omis, taking thick cardigans, waterproofs, chocolate – anything that seemed even remotely of use. More sensibly, Gareth stashed a torch in his back pocket. I forgot mine.

The boat was now tied up to the side of the jetty, the fishermen having gone – no doubt cursing us for the extra work. The water looked smooth and oily, reflecting the navigating lights and the illuminations of the town. A strong scent from some plant was overpowered by an unpleasant smell which could have been drains, dead fish or sewage. It was a relief to go beyond its tentacles.

But once on the water the magic returned; I felt I could have sped on forever over the black swell. It was over too soon.

As we ran into Omis and Gareth cut the motor, scarcely a sound broke the stillness. The moon had not yet risen. All was blackness.

Out of the darkness came Petar Vratmic's deep voice: 'Not bad time. We'll make a sailor out of you yet.'

'You're not fishing tonight?'

'No, I wouldn't care to miss the excitement.' As we walked closer we could see the gold tooth glinting, and as he turned, his eyes flashed in the lights from the sea front. We shook hands as if we had not parted little more than a few hours before. It was warm inside the cafe; inevitably we had to order drinks and I asked for a pot of black coffee, to keep me mentally alert. To my surprise, Peter would not accept payment.

'On the 'ouse,' he said grandly with a gesture that would have done credit to a tenor in Italian opera. I suspected he had more than a drop of Italian blood.

Talk was slow but interesting and I tried to keep my attention on it, but I couldn't help worrying about Azalea. No doubt she would be worrying about me too. Was I being an absolute fool, rushing off with Gareth on a crack-brained scheme to recover a picture for someone I'd never even met?

As the moon rose, silvering every detail of cliff and rock and tree to incredible beauty, I was made aware of my utter insignificance in the scheme of things.

For some strange reason I began to think of Angelique. Heavens, was Azalea's psychic psychology lark spreading to me?

'Asleep?' Gareth leaned forward to smile into my face.

'No, I was thinking about Angelique's liking for beer. Do you suppose she'll become an alcoholic?'

There was a hiss from Petar, motioning us to silence. 'Come,' he said and darted to the entrance. We waited, hearing a car pull in to the side of the road. A man got out and put the case he was carrying down for a moment as he paid his fare. The car turned and was gone. He stood uncertainly for a while, obviously trying to get his bearings. We recognised the hat, the old mac, and the artist's case.

'Wemys,' muttered Gareth. We watched Wemys walk forward to the edge of the water where he was joined by another man.

'Ivo,' said Petar grinning happily as he prepared to follow Gareth.

'Just a minute,' I whispered. 'There's something wrong.'

'What do you mean?' Gareth was impatient of the hand on my arm but I dug in, holding on.

'That's not Wemys.' I was sure of it. 'It looks like him – the same clothes – but it isn't Wemys.'

'We'll soon find out.'

'I'd know his walk anywhere. Azalea and I had a joke about it – said he walked like a stage comedian with one leg shorter than the other.'

'Another red herring.' Gareth swore.

Petar looked at him enquiringly. 'Not so good, eh? We'll have a closer look at what he carries, I think. Maybe I do this because you not wish to make the trouble. You are foreigners. I will go to see if this is the man Veems ...' His teeth flashed. 'I tell you my brother-in-law is a coastguard, yes? He left his uniform here for my wife to mend a little tear.' After a prodigious wink he dived inside the cafe and returned, struggling into the uniform. A few seconds later he approached the boat whose engine was only just now warming up. Somehow Ivo Brovac had not been able to start at once.

The man in the jacket proved to be a man from Mostar who knew nothing of boats or coastal officials, and was most awed by Petar's correct manner. From our cover we watched and waited, listening intently. Papers were examined and returned. The artist's case was opened, the contents examined. These proved to be the man's meal, a shirt and some socks. There were no false sides to conceal a painting. We heard Petar's knuckles rapping against the wood. When at last he allowed the man to leave, he was actually thanked.

Petar came jauntily across to us, holding in his laughter until the man was out of earshot. 'He is going to Dubrovnik. Ivo will see that he arrives safely. Also, I patted his back and his front most affectionately as he was going aboard. Believe me, he does not carry anything unusual on his person.' He laughed gustily. 'What do you do know? It is disappointing, yes? But an interesting evening. It is a long time since I enjoyed so much. Thank you.' He slapped Gareth on the back; he was like a boy enjoying a masquerade.

'We might as well go back to the hotel.' Gareth's voice was flat. 'Can you get us a taxi?'

'Why a taxi? Take the boat. It is yours. Tomorrow it may be of use – who knows? If you have other plans, do not worry. I fetch the boat. No trouble.'

'Thanks, Petar. You're a good friend.'

They clasped hands. Petar bowed with extravagant deference in my direction as we made our way back to the boat which floated gracefully as a swan in the moonlight. A stiffer breeze was blowing up; I snuggled down into my cardigan, not relishing the swell on the water. Petar shouted something after us but the wind snatched it away. With a roar we were away, headed for Split. Busy with our thoughts and our disappointment, we did not converse. As the night skyline of Split came glistening into view. Gareth slowed the motor, allowing the boat to barely judder in the water. The Adriatic sloshed against the Labud's sides and I joined Gareth at the helm. He dropped his arm around my waist, its warmth and heaviness as if it belonged. Had I really contemplated rushing over to Italy with a man I scarcely knew? Uncle Charles was right. I was stronger than I realised.

A faint sound drew my attention back to the receding shoreline. 'What's that? That noise.'

'I can't hear anything.' Gareth cut the motor completely, instantly putting us in silence. He shone the search light onto a lump of black on a dark road paralleling the coastline. I could hear it now. The shrill bark of a little dog barking. He adjusted the searchlight and it fell on the outline of several people moving about strangely against the silhouette of two cars – one of them, a beat-up taxi.

'There it is again. It's a dog howling. Someone's in trouble. Goodness, it sounds like Angelique.'

'Let's go into shore. Something's wrong there. Get that flare gun handy and if there's any trouble, use my mobile.' He tossed me his mobile and the Labud coughed eagerly back to life. Gareth sped toward shore, kicking up a strong wake onto the rocks as he spun sharply, bringing the boat to a stop.

Several of the shapes turned towards us we alighted from the Labud. As I went ashore, I wedged the boat anchor tightly between the big, sharp rocks that had been put up as an erosion barrier. As a result, I didn't get a good look at any of the group onshore until I had got onto the road. A short, round shape, which turned out to be the taxi driver, stood well off the other side of the road, about even with his taxi. A smaller shape stood bent over another lying in a heap, haloed by the edge of the taxi's dim, yellow headlamp. There were also two taller shapes standing threateningly over those. One of the bigger shapes, decidedly masculine, got in the black Citroen pulled in against the front fender of the beat-up taxi. The other went to get in but didn't make it.

Gareth tackled this second man to the asphalt, trying to get his arms behind his back. He flopped over and Gareth punched his face once before the first man jumped out of the car and grabbed me.

'All right. Ease up.' I could feel the cold, hard edge of what only could have been a gun barrel digging into my scalp, and the vice-grip of a big hand on the back of my neck. Gareth looked up, and seeing my predicament, went for the assailant. I literally couldn't breathe – I was so afraid for both of us.

'Uh-uh. None of that or she gets a new hole in her head.'

Gareth stepped back as the gunman threw me into his arms.

'Come on, mate!' a third called from the Citroen.

Freed, the partner quickly got up from the ground and climbed into the back saying, 'I'd have thought you would have known better than to let your playmates get into trouble.'

Gareth slipped on some loose scrabble at the shoulder and we fell.

'Let this be a lesson to you, Findlatter. Leave off it!' And with that he got in the back of the car and they took off, fiercely spinning gravel at us as the tyres went onto the pavement, and sped away back toward Split.

'Did you get a licence number?' Gareth cursed, looking into the dark after the car.

'No, I was too busy keeping the grit out of my eyes.' The shaking of my knees took my mind off the way they hurt from landing hard on the pavement. I had been turned to jelly so many times now I thought I might become one – it would save time.

'Babs? Gareth? It's you!' It was none other than Azalea. Followed by Angelique, still barking. Both ran out of the glare of the taxi's headlights. Gareth moved toward the heap on the ground. 'It's a miracle.' I could feel her shaking as she held onto me. 'I thought we were done for.'

'Barbara! Quickly! Get me the first-aid kit from the boat. Colin's been beaten up.'

'And that's about it,' Azalea explained as Gareth finished cleaning up Colin's cuts. We helped him lay Colin gently in the back seat of the taxi. Gareth said he felt at least two cracked ribs. The driver had said little, looking anxious.

'Better now,' Colin said. I had the taxi driver phone his manager for an ambulance. It was on its way. The driver sat in the front seat, taking a very long time to light a cigarette.

'Okay, now tell me this again. What happened when you arrived at the museum?' Holding my hand in his, Gareth gave his full attention to Azalea.

'Nothing. We were just walking around and Colin was terribly hot. We'd come out of there and were in the Marine Museum – I think it's called – further along the coast. Afterwards, we climbed up a lot of hairpin bends until I got quite dizzy. The views were terrific and I suddenly saw Wemys painting. At least he had his easel up. He was looking out to sea with a pair of glasses.'

'Watching us put out for Omis,' Gareth said gloomily,.

'I thought you said you'd doped his tea?'

'He can't have drunk it; he's a wily specimen. With us safely out of the way, my guess is, he'll move his picture. It looks as if he's continuing on the coach trip into Italy.

'Go on, Azalea,' I urged, ignoring him and his brooding.

'I don't think he had seen us – at least, not then – he just went back to the hotel – and then came out again. Colin was watching his balcony, and I watched along the corridor. When he came out of his room I signalled to Colin, who hid round a corner till Wemys was a good way ahead. It was quite exciting.'

Patiently, Gareth asked, 'Where did he go? Or did you lose him?'

'No. He went to a house in town. It was pretty dark by then and Colin was getting fed up but he insisted on being with me when I was following Wemys.'

'Good for him!' I said sarcastically.

'Can you remember the house in the town?' Gareth's voice was not quite so patient now.

'I think so. It was on Marjan Hill – the first terrace. There's a wrought-iron gate and a circular bed of red flowers which you can see from the entrance. Oh -and a birdcage made out of wicker in a doorway. I thought how cruel it was to keep a bird in sunlight without any shade. Have they got a RSPCA here?'

'I shouldn't think so – at least not with an 'R'. Society – politics, you know.'

Azalea looked vague. Gareth looked as if he were going to burst.

'No Queen. No 'royalty.' He blew out his lips and swallowed hard to contain his exasperation. 'Could you find this house again?'

'Of course.'

'Good for you. Your artist's eye is invaluable.'

'Wemys was in quite a while. We got awfully hungry. He came out with a man and a woman, and they all got into a car that had been parked nearby. Colin managed to find a taxi cruising on the prom and we told the driver to follow.

'We went way out into the countryside. It was almost completely dark by now and I was beginning to think we ought to give up the chase when the car we were following suddenly disappeared. Just like that.'

'They probably went down a side lane and turned off the lights,' Gareth said.

'We got out to investigate but not knowing the countryside, there didn't seem anything we could do and the driver was a fat help, I must say – just talked a lot of gibberish.'

'So you went back?' Gareth was trying to get her mental processes on a more helpful tack.

'No, we were just standing in the road when we were set on. Colin was splendid. He really was. I'd no idea he was so strong. He looks so thin. I never admired him more – particularly when he was trying to bash this man's brains out on the road.'

'You were attacked by two men?'

'No, there were three. Angelique went for one of them but he threw her off.'

'Was Wemys among them?' Gareth asked.

'No. At first I thought it was Wemys – the clothes were the same.'

'Yes, they nearly fooled us too,' I admitted. 'What about the taxi driver. Didn't he help?'

Azalea said, 'No. Perhaps he was in it as well?'

Gareth looked doubtful.

'And what were you doing during all this fighting?' I asked anxiously.

She looked blank. 'I'm not sure. I think I was screaming.'

'That'd help a lot.'

'It did. It made Angelique worried. You heard her barking.'

'That's true.'

'And I tripped one of them up. He came down with an awful crash! It was the one who kicked Angelique.' She kissed the pup's soft head. 'Poor darling.' Just then the ambulance arrived, and the engine on the taxi roared lustily to life. 'Someone's in a hurry!' Azalea shot the driver a look, cradling Angelique to her breast. 'Our little heroine!'

'Azalea!' It was Colin calling from the stretcher on his way into the back of the ambulance. They talked briefly and she walked back toward us. He waved and the doors were closed.

'Colin. Such a strong soul. He told me to go on back with you. I hope he'll be all right,' Azalea trailed off as we watched the ambulance follow in the direction the taxi took, back around the bay and into Split.

'Let's get you back,' I said protectively, patting Angelique on the head.

Gareth pushed off the boat and we started towards Split. I think I must have dozed off in my exhaustion; I came to as we docked, with Azalea's head against my shoulder.

The town was almost deserted, for the fishermen had not yet returned. Out at sea, a cruise ship, lighted from stem to stern, passed in majestic splendour, oblivious to drama that had unfolded and the turmoil in our minds.

The clerk at the reception desk looked alarmed at the sight of us, and stared in some disbelief at Angelique, who stared back with her usual complacency.

'Please, your name is Dunbar? There is a message for you from the hospital.'

Already white-faced, Azalea, managed to go even whiter. 'The hospital?'

'Yes, Mr Barnes. He say he stay there tonight. He returns to this hotel tomorrow at the time of midday. You understand?' The clerk smiled politely, pleased to have made us happy with his message.

'Oh. Is that all.' Her colour came flooding back. 'That's marvellous. He can't be too badly injured if he's coming back in the morning. I feel a whole lot better. In fact, I'm hungry.' She looked wistfully at the clerk. 'I missed dinner. Do you think I could have some food sent to my room?' Her accompanying gestures indicated that she needed a lot of food.

'I will bring it myself,' he promised and was true to his word, being no longer than half an hour over preparing the simple repast. We all helped Azalea with the rolls, the meat, and the cheese, and wished there had been twice as much coffee. We blessed him for the added can of beer, which we shared out scrupulously, including

Angelique, who fell asleep as if pole-axed after her drink. After a quick bath, Azalea crept between the sheets with a mere apology, leaving Gareth looking at me.

He said softly, 'I never thanked you adequately for letting me take you out this afternoon. I enjoyed it very much.'

'Then I have my thank you,' I retorted, pushing him through the doorway. I wasn't adroit enough for he had his foot in the door and pulled me until our faces were together in the opening.

The mischief in his eyes faded as I teased him, 'A good detective keeps his mind on his job.'

He released my hand. ''You're quite right. I'll get on to the Militicja about tonight's happenings. Night, then.'

As I closed the door and listened to his feet going along the corridor I could have kicked myself.

I'd just been kidding!

CHAPTER ELEVEN

VENICE

In which Barbara proves herself and Gareth saves the day

As I heard the rat-tat on the door for the second – or was it the third time – I roused myself and looked at my watch. A quarter past ten, and the sunshine was already hot against the shutters.

'Azalea,' I croaked. 'We've got company.'

'In the middle of the night? I'm not expecting anyone, are you?' She ordered Angelique to stop whirring, and surprisingly she did.

I slithered off my bed and shuffled through our small suite to the door. I felt as if every muscle were being pulled off my bones. Uncle Charles stood on the other side of the peep hole. I let him in, yawning widely.

'At last,' he said. 'Ran into Gareth downstairs. Said you had some trouble last night.'

'It's a long story. Come on in. Maybe you could make some coffee while I wake up?' I could hear him puttering around quietly in the little sink and cabinet area referred to generously on the hotel website as the kitchenette. I washed my face in cold water and cleaned my teeth, trying to will myself awake. The smell of coffee brewing had reached our bedroom by the time I had thrown on some jeans and t-shirt. Azalea's bed was empty of both girl and dog when I returned from the bathroom.

I walked through the suite to find Azalea and Uncle Charles petting Angelique, the latter seated contentedly on my uncle's lap. He was tickling behind her ears. Azalea gave me her chair. 'Here, Babs. I need to get dressed. Angelique will need to go out soon.' She went off quietly to dress and Angelique, taking one look at us, jumped down and padded after her. Chuckling, Uncle Charles got up and brought each of us a cup of coffee while I recounted the events of the night before.

'I've no doubt Gareth's the man for the job, Barbara. But it's getting dangerous. I can't accept my clients being attacked while on one of my tours. I'm worried about Colin. Have the hospital forward the bill to our office. But still –'

'He may have been killed. You're right, we could all have been killed. And so could you. Your mobile went missing because the low life that lifted mine was trying to find where I'd forwarded his picture. It's better to keep it …'

'… in the family? See your point.' But worry was still etched on his brow, a man protecting his clan and his livelihood. In this case the same thing, I thought.

'It's going to work out, Uncle Charles. I read your horoscope.' Azalea joined us with laptop, coffee and dog. 'See it says right here: Aquarius: Even independent souls like yourself need a little help now and again. You've helped others in the past, let them help you now. All will be well.'

Uncle Charles spluttered, 'Hardly something to trust, Azalea. Waste of time.'

'Oh no, Uncle Charles. You must believe. It's been right all along, hasn't it Babs?'

My uncle looked at me sceptically under arched brows.

'You're not helping, Azalea,' I said, redirecting her:

'Look, your dog seems to be interested in a spot on the bathroom floor.'

'Gotta go.' And Azalea and Angelique were gone. Angelique did come in handy, I must confess.

'Look, Uncle. I know you're right. But you can't just leave it like this. Now Mike's dead, maybe the blackmailing will stop. But what about Wemys? How long's been a client of yours? A few years. So how many times must he have used Madden's to facilitate his art smuggling business? If you turn it over to the local cops, they'll warn Gareth off and nothing will be done. And we'll never prove why someone wants Azalea and me dead.'

'Yes I see. You'd always feel at risk. And Azalea too. Well, all right. But I want to be included at every step!'

'You'll have to talk to Gareth about that. He never tells me much of anything.'

We took the lift down to street level, and followed our noses to the dining room from there.

We took a large table near the pavement so Azalea & Co. could spot us easily. The restaurant was open on one side to the street like most of the cafes and bars in Split. The effect was delightful; it could only happen in this sun-drenched coastline of the Adriatic. White streets, clean and bright, bounced the morning sunlight into the dining room.

Soon Azalea turned up, bringing Colin with her. Angelique, now a foregone conclusion, trotted along happily at her feet.

'Colin!' Uncle Charles greeted, shaking hands. 'How good of you to rescue Miss Dunbar, I must say. And I feel terrible you being put in this position. Please sit down.' He signalled to the waiter, and ordered more coffee, tea and some fresh lemonade.

'Really, Mr Madden,' Colin started by saying. 'It was nothing. I care very much about what happens to Azalea ... Miss Dunbar. It was my duty.'

He must be hooked, I thought yet again. I'd seen men gaze at Azalea in many stages of romantic stupefaction, but never from a washed-out face and over two cracked ribs. Average men would been put off by what he'd been through.

'I'm just so glad I was there,' Colin added.

Love had sobered him; there was sense of mature responsibility about him. Perhaps he really knew what he was letting himself in for with our little Azalea.

'Good man! Assured the hospital that insurance and stuff would be sorted out and so on,' said Uncle Charles. Colin stammered his thanks, and my uncle waved his hand deprecatingly: 'Not at all. Least I could do.' Each seemed as embarrassed as the other.

The waiter took our order when he served the drinks, and for a few brief moments we allowed ourselves to enjoy the holiday. Fresh sea breezes drenched in the sounds and smells of street vendors, cars, people on bikes and little scooters – all scurrying toward lunch and the daily siesta – wafted over us as we huddled together over the strong Croatian coffee, heavily sweetened, and lightened with real milk. We had lunched on baked calamari and potatoes, served with cheese, fruit, and the ubiquitous lettuce salad. The Greek influence was happily in evidence in Croatian cooking.

As usual, Gareth joined the meal as soon as we had finished ours, Police Inspector Dubci jogging along beside. The men got up from the table in a slight scramble to introduce Uncle Charles to the police inspector, and the waiter rushed over with two more of everything, and a bowl of cool water for Angelique, who looked quite wilted in the heat. Gareth grabbed a chair and plopped it next to mine, quickly ordering mlinci, a traditional pasta dish, for both him and the police inspector. 'No salad thanks,' Dubci added nonchalantly.

'Now, how is everyone today?' Gareth looked around at each of us, smiling brightly.

'You're obviously bursting with good news,' my uncle answered. 'Why don't you go first!'

'Dubci and I had a meeting of minds this morning. I told him about everything that happened last night. And he grabbed a copy of the statement Colin gave the police at the emergency.'

'I can identify them in a line-up. I'll never forget those faces as long as I live! Sorry – still a bit swollen …' He dribbled as bit as he sipped his coffee carefully.

'Oh poor thing,' Azalea murmured. Angelique even pawed at his knee, but only because she wanted a bit of roll.

Dubci started to speak but paused as the waiter brought plates of noodles, ham and peas in a light white sauce. 'Some wine, please,' he said in perfect English.

Azalea exclaimed indignantly, 'It's cruel to keep that bird confined in a place where there's no shade!'

Dubci was a little disconcerted. 'What bird?' he asked, naturally enough.

'The one outside the villa. It's in a cage in full sunlight. Of course, it may be in shade when they put it out, but later as the afternoon sun works round …!'

'Oh yes. Mr Barnes mentioned you following Wemys. Allow me, please.' Dubci took a folded sheaf of papers from his suit jacket pocket and studied the pages. 'Yes, here it is. We did go and take a look this morning.'

Gareth answered while Dubci took a bite. 'It was all shuttered up. There was even a cobweb across the back door, as if it hadn't been opened for months – a neat touch, that. I talked to a neighbour but she wasn't very helpful. She said the owner was away a lot. Anyway, we know who he is from Dubci – he's an artist.' For Azalea's benefit he added, 'The bird wasn't outside, but I recognised the place from your description.'

The police inspector kept his face perfectly straight, even sympathetic as he said gently, 'I will attend to the matter. It is probably an oversight. They may have other things to think about, yes? Now, as I was about to say,' he continued. 'I believe that the men who attacked Mr Barnes and Miss Dunbar here are part of the blackmail ring that has been victimising your clients, Mr Madden. It is my belief that Radnin was killed for being greedy. Some person had simply had enough and shot him. Then that same person planted the murder weapon at random. The case has been opened and is now shut. I would say that your worries are over.'

I sent a meaningful glance towards my uncle. Hadn't I just told him this would happen? Dubci would want to get the case solved quickly, then push the foreigners and their troubles off down the road to another police authority that might just be interested.

Uncle Charles asked, 'So how can you be so sure? If that's the case, then why did they attack Miss Dunbar and Mr Barnes yesterday evening?'

Dubci shrugged. 'We believe that is the end of it. Your tour is free to go.'

'But ...!' Uncle Charles's retort was interrupted.

'I thought you'd be pleased, Mr Madden,' said Dubci calmly.

Gareth swallowed a huge gulp of wine. His plate was already not just empty, but scraped clean.

'Your tour can go on to Italy today. In fact your new driver is pulling up now.' Dubci's composure was maddening.

Sure enough, the whiff of air brakes and the vision of our new huge chrome knight in shining armour breaking through the crowds blocked our view of all else.

I suddenly saw what Dubci was up to and whispered in Uncle Charles's ear that we should just get going.

'All right then, Dubci,' Charles conceded. 'I'll have my lot cleared out of here within the hour. Thank you so much for your help. Split is the truly the most lovely spot on the Adriatic!'

They shook hands in parting.

'Very good of you to say so,' Dubci answered, gulping down the last of his wine and grabbing a piece of melon. Gareth walked him to the pavement, chatting. I saw Dubci hand Gareth something which he slipped into his jeans pocket. A business card I guessed.

'That Dubci must be in on whatever Gareth has going. Dubci knows that man who threatened him last night. Doesn't sound like blackmailers to me!' I was caught thinking out loud.

'Certainly not,' Gareth said rejoining us. 'The thug that got at me didn't behave like your average blackmailer. They normally keep a low profile.'

'Like rats,' Uncle Charles added. We pushed through the crowd of our fellow passengers queued up at the desk to turn in keys and comment cards. The lift pinged and we all got in.

'I just don't know why our attacker spoke to me as if he knew me!' Gareth shrugged it off. 'Just playing the convincing thug, I suppose.'

We all exchanged glances; suddenly light dawned on me. 'Of course – he must have been the man who spied on us at Lake Bled. The man you said had been following us in Germany and Austria. You know – he replied to you in German and you told him to come off it – he was wearing a Marks and Spencer pullover!'

'So he might be working on the case too. He could even be from Interpol.'

'That's just stupid,' Colin said. 'Why would he nearly beat me to death?'

'To scare you off because we're getting too close?' Azalea always thought the best of people.

'Because he thought we were homing in on the art- smuggling scheme, probably,' Gareth concluded.

'I don't think so,' I said. 'Something doesn't add up.'

The door opened just then and we all spilled out into the corridor.

'Don't you have a suitcase, Uncle?' I asked.

'No. Came with a minimum. Been buying bits and bobs as we go along. Don't worry. We'll put it on the expense account.'

'As a new partner in the firm, I must say I find that fiscally irresponsible!' I teased.

Gareth plopped on the couch to wait while Azalea and I threw our things together. 'It's nice to think I might have a pal. But we could be assuming far too much here!' He thought a bit. 'Dubci did tell me the man in Wemys' clothes was picked up in Dubrovnik but wasn't much use to them as he had merely been paid to make the trip. He didn't know any more than that.'

'Better hurry!' Colin shouted from the balcony. ' Wemys just got on. Looks as though they're pulling out.'

'Where's your baggage, Colin?' I asked.

'Right here,' Azalea said. 'I packed for him this morning.'

Colin beamed brightly under his bruises.

We went out to the coach. George Lonsties strolled past us and we regarded him with scant friendliness and some suspicion. Made aware of our concentrated gaze, his step faltered and he came to a halt. 'I say,' he began, looking at Gareth. 'I'm glad to have a word with you. About that gun ...'

'Yes, about that gun,' Gareth answered levelly.

'I'm sorry if I embarrassed you. It was just ...Well, you do realise I had to mention it to the police? After all, when a man is murdered right under our noses ...'

'But you didn't see me handling a gun.'

'I just thought I had. And remember, one was found in your room.'

His look of triumph faded as Gareth asked, 'What were you paid to make the statement – perhaps even put the gun there yourself?'

'I say, that's not very nice. I've apologised. We all make mistakes. You don't need to be offensive.' A red tide surged up his neck. 'Anyway, it doesn't seem to have harmed you.'

'No. It must be infuriating.'

'I don't understand you.' A mulish look crept over Lonsties' face. 'I'd better move on. You're in a bad mood. For the benefit of the rest of the party, I hope you'll let bygones be bygones.'

Gareth made no reply. Lonsties swept a glance round the group and continued his way, even his back looking self-conscious. No doubt Pansy and Daisy would take his part and glower at us too, even though Azalea and I had felt sorry for him. She had essayed a smile, guileless and pleading, to which – for once – Lonsties had not responded. It was incredible to think we were only halfway through the tour and so much had happened.

It was just about our turn to get on. Pansy had dropped her handbag, and the Frasers were helping her collect all her belongings.

'So where are we off to?' Uncle Charles asked me quietly.

Overhearing him, Mimi leaned in quietly to answer: 'As a matter of fact I've just met the new driver, sir. It seems a tour to

Solin is planned. You know, the Roman ruins. I'd rather hoped you would educate us.'

'Delighted,' Uncle Charles answered, looking anything but. The coach began to move and soon we would be in Italy. The mystery needed to be solved by the end of the tour. We had no excuse to hang around forever.

The new driver, Klaus Dujas, was as smarmy as Radnin. This did nothing to improve my mood. Although he drove well and kept his comments pretty much to the minimum, he was making Mimi a little uncomfortable the way he glanced at her every few minutes. I was gaining a new respect for our little redhead. Being a couch courier was obviously fraught with many dangers, and she'd seemed up to the challenge.

Gareth and I sat together facing Colin and Azalea. Uncle Charles and Angelique had seated themselves in the back near the kitchen in case the pup needed a snack. She was perched on his shoulder looking out of the window for all the world like a parrot on a pirate's shoulder. I made a mental note to take him shopping for some ordinary shirts. 'So, what now?' I whispered. 'And what will Wemys do without his mac and hat?'

Wemys had taken his usual seat behind Call-Me-Daisy and Lonsties.

'That's something I'm not going to worry about. I can't think Wemys would let his precious painting out of his control for long. Perhaps just long enough for it to be authenticated.'

We rode along, drinking in the dramatic mountain and coastline, until we took a turning onto the ridge road to Trogir, a medieval town laid out in the classical style. Mimi announced on the microphone that we were to take this little unexpected stop to see some perfect specimens of villas built during the Venetian Occupation. Very handsome they were too, with their many-storeyed buildings, balconies to upper windows, and heavy doors bearing the arms of the proud families who had lived in them. The city was set like a jewel on a narrow island, made accessible by a bridge from the mainland. Here, time seemed to have stood still; even the old crones in their black garb looked much as their ancestors must have looked.

A look from Uncle assured me this had been okayed in advance.

From her little book Mimi read: 'There was a city founded here by the Greeks three centuries before Christ and it suffered each successive invader, until the twentieth century. It's all here in the stones for those who can read. ' The locals were politely incurious about us – being used to visitors – and appeared neither friendly nor unfriendly. But when I tried out a tentative smile on an old lady, her dark face lit up, and she returned the smile in full measure. 'Divan!' I murmured. (Wonderful, beautiful.) She heard me and a fierce look of pride came into her fine-featured face before she bowed with innate dignity and went into her beautiful house.

Sometimes Klaus was with us – sometimes he was not – for he glided everywhere like a ballet dancer, seemingly tireless, his camera at the ready, hanging round his neck. That can get you into all kinds of trouble, I thought silently.

We were soon to learn just how much of a camera fiend he was, for we stopped in the most unlikely places, Klaus evidently finding inspiration there. We followed anxiously, willing him to get on to Italy so we could nail Wemys for the criminal he was.

After a bit we retraced our steps through the narrow streets leading us back to the square, which was dominated by the town-hall tower. All was incredibly solid and most of it beautiful, with its manorial carvings. We looked at palaces, churches, cathedral, convent and abbey, with their priceless treasures of painting and works of art, until we were dizzy. Only the Reverend Burnett and his wife seemed indefatigable, so we left them to Mimi's care and wandered back to the coach, where we found an extraordinary scene in progress.

At first we thought the coach was empty until we saw Pansy and Daisy Watford crawling about the seats and along the aisle on their hands and knees. Daisy looked vexed, almost as if she might indulge in a tantrum at any moment. We heard her say explosively, 'It's got be somewhere. It can't just disappear.'

The reply from Pansy was a grunt; she was too busy searching.

After a quick glance at me, Lea sang out, 'Can we help you?'

Their heads came up, flushed and angry. Pansy heaved herself stiffly to her feet and for a minute it looked as if she might say something rude, but then her expression became guarded. 'We're looking for ..."

'A coin,' interrupted Daisy. 'It rolled away down the coach.'

'We'll help you look,' I offered, curious that they should be so upset about a coin, unless it held sentimental value.

'Please don't bother,' Daisy said before the most extraordinary expression crossed her face. She was still on her knees; her groping fingers had pulled loose some studs holding down the leather of the seats.

'Be careful,' Pansy snapped. 'We don't want to have to pay for repairs as well.' Grumbling, she stood up to dust off her knees with a paper hanky. Aware of the interested silence surrounding Daisy, she looked at her younger sister as the latter pulled a stiff piece of painted canvas from under the seat.

Azalea gripped my hand. We waited tensely as Daisy examined the painting with every degree of surprise. At least, if it wasn't a surprise, she must have been a very good actress. After a while she passed the canvas across to her sister, who took it, frowning.

'Could it be valuable?' she asked doubtfully. We craned to see the painting, which was dark with dulled varnish, and depicted a man wearing a loose robe in purple material. 'Not very,' a male voice said and we all turned to see Wemys entering the coach. He looked completely unperturbed. 'So you found my little cache?' Gareth stepped up right behind, craning over his shoulder to see what Daisy held in her hand.

'How do we know it's yours?' queried Daisy, holding the painting tightly as if he might snatch it from her.

'You'll find my initials on the back – with a recent date. I purchased it from my friends in Marjam Hill. I didn't want any trouble getting it out of the country so I decided to conceal it. It was very naughty of me. I was going to make a copy of it and then sell the original in Venice.' He laughed quietly. 'One has to have money on these trips. This way I can make a little extra. I hope you won't expose my wicked plan to the authorities.' This last directed at Gareth.

The Misses Watford still looked dubious. 'I wouldn't know who the authorities were,' Daisy said, visibly recovering from her first excitement.

Gareth pushed forward. 'May I see?'

'Certainly.' Wemys gestured to Daisy, who grudgingly handed over the painting, having satisfied that Wemys' initials were indeed on the back of the canvas.

'Do you know the artist?' asked Gareth, relaxing now that he had seen the subject matter. I surmised it was not the one he had hoped to see.

Wemys hesitated. 'No. After Bellini, I suspect. It might have a little value in Venice, Bellini being a Venetian and having his school there. I'm hoping to make some cash on it – perhaps enough to buy a canvas I really want. This is interesting because of the man's hands. They are extraordinarily well painted.'

He looked with fondness at the picture which he had recovered from Gareth and which he now handled carelessly. I felt sure Gareth was feeling totally frustrated with Wemys and his games.

Wemys smiled pleasantly round at us, as if trying to get us to acknowledge his crafty business acumen. 'Now that you all know about it, I might as well carry it in my case.' He lifted it down and placed the picture inside, carelessly replacing it on the shelf.

Even when we arrived in Solin he left the artist's case in the coach as we surged outside for a brief look at the Roman ruins. Mimi had arranged for a learned professor, a man of charm and distinction who luckily could speak good, if hesitant, English, to give us little background history. Uncle Charles was relieved, and blended happily into the back of the crowd to avoid Mimi's eye.

'Two centuries before Christ, the Illyrians had built the city, which flourished even after the Romans occupied it, until it was destroyed by the Avars.' All this, and more, the professor explained painlessly, drawing to our attention a score of details we would otherwise have missed in the clearly visible layout of theatre, arena and baths. He insisted that we visit the museum before it closed for the night. When we realised we had perhaps been keeping him from his own plans, Mimi gave him a charming vote of thanks on our behalf, to which he responded graciously.

As I was at his elbow I added, 'We love your country. Everything except the biting flies.'

He looked me over in some amusement and said in his precise English, 'They must find you very sweet.'

An appreciative chuckle came from Klaus our driver, who shook the professor by the hand before we returned to the coach. The professor waved as we moved off.

Once everyone was settled, we were assuredly on our way to Venice. I asked Gareth about the painting the Watfords had discovered. Cautiously he admitted, 'It wasn't the same subject matter. The size was right. I was given a photograph of the lost painting to study. That one was a Madonna and Child, by an unknown artist and it covered the original one by Rembrandt.'

'What was the original,' asked Azalea with an absorbed air. 'Do you know?'

'Not exactly. My client was told by Astell that the X Ray indicated a boy with some round object in his hand.'

'Just one figure?'

'No. There was a small animal – perhaps a dog – as well, stretching up to the boy's hand.'

'As if he might be about to throw a ball?' I felt extraordinarily interested. 'You don't suppose Wemys has painted over the painting, which in turn was painted over the original?

'Could be. I wonder…'Gareth stroked his chin thoughtfully. 'I suppose he wouldn't be above faking some of the copies he makes to give an appearance of age. These would show up in a thorough examination, of course, but might be good enough to fool a more casual buyer. But he didn't seem particularly bothered about leaving it in the coach.'

'Once we'd seen it. That might be to pull the wool over our eyes. Remember, he'd thought enough of it to hide it under a seat.'

'It might also be just another of his red herrings.'

We stopped that night in Rijeke, a coastal town on the northern Croatian coast. From there we were to take the train to Venice, and hopefully, to the end of the trail for Wemys.

When Azalea and I reached the hotel corridor that led to our bedroom, a thought suddenly occurred to me. 'I wonder what Pansy and Daisy were really looking for?'

Azalea went into the bedroom but, as I made to follow her, I saw Wemys enter the corridor at the far end with his artist's case, which he took to his room, closing the door with an air of relief. For our benefit?

The door to the room behind me swung open. Oblivious to my presence, George Lonsties stormed out, shouting back, 'Good grief, you can't have lost it. Do you know what it cost?' This was obviously to Daisy. Embarrassed, I slipped quickly into our room before he could become aware of me, and watched the rest out of the peep hole.

It sounded as if Call-Me-Daisy had burst into tears. Lonsties made more of an effort to placate her. 'It's not the money, it's the sentimental value. You can't be such a little nit as to have mislaid it already.'

Pansy swept her sister out of the room George Lonsties followed them uneasily down the corridor.

'Daisy's lost her engagement ring,' I said to Azalea who was brushing Angelique.

'Ah. They're engaged!'

'She's lost it and he's as mad as … well, he's livid! She must have taken it off in the coach, and they must have been searching for it when we walked in on them.'

'When she said she was looking for a coin! Poor Daisy. But at least she found the picture.' She paused. 'I always said Wemys was sitting on it – that is, if it's the one Gareth is after.'

'Gareth, doesn't seem to think so,' I said. Although with Gareth it was hard to tell.

'Yes, but I needn't stop thinking about it.' She gave me a sunny smile. 'Let's go and help Daisy in her search for the ring. They're practically taking the coach apart.'

'Let's stop and ask Gareth and Uncle Charles if they would like to help.'

It was quite a search party by the time we all trooped on. Daisy was saying, 'I was going to put it, and I was a bit shy about wearing it. Then Pansy jogged my elbow and it flew out of my hand.'

'Did you see it roll?' enquired Azalea.

Daisy looked thoughtful. 'I assumed...'

'It might have flown over into the seat in front,' Azalea offered. As we watched, Daisy scrabbled beneath the arms of the chair ahead of her and suddenly gave a screech of joy. 'It's here. I've found it! Isn't it wonderful! Oh thank you, all of you.' She held up the ring and we admired its sparkle.

Looking both pleased and embarrassed, George Lonsties said gruffly, 'Sorry, I made a fuss, old girl.'

'It's just as well you're sorry,' Daisy said, the skin round her nose whitening. 'You can have your ring back. I'm sure I don't want it.'

'Here, steady on ...'

But with a superb gesture, Daisy slammed the ring into his hand and sailed off down the coach, leaving us all staring after her. After a moment, Pansy followed, not even glancing in George's direction. We couldn't help but feel rather sad. By now we were almost a family – what affected one, affected all.

Gareth and I passed Klaus the new driver as we stepped back inside the hotel. He was nursing a very red scratch on his cheek.

'It is nothing,' Klaus protested happily. 'A cat scratched me, is all.'

Mimi met us at the lift and set the record straight. 'Can't keep his hands to himself. No don't bother – I've already spoken to your uncle, Barbara. He's going to arrange a replacement driver from another firm.'

'I do hope you won't abandon us, Mimi. In fact, I've been wondering about this for a while. How would you and your husband like to work together for a change? I'll speak to Uncle Charles if you like.'

'Oh, Barbara, that would be brilliant. I'll call him tonight.'

We parted from her company, Gareth following me back to my suite. 'That was a very nice gesture, Miss Wills. You're a very nice boss.' He was leaning against the door blocking me from slipping my key in the lock. I leaned into him and he kissed me sweetly. Of course I dropped my key. He unlocked the door, still holding me; the door closed softly behind us. We were holding each other tightly now, just making those first tentative explorations of bodies, when ...

'Oh, I thought I'd heard someone!' Azalea came out of the bathroom, obviously in the middle of a mopping-up operation. 'Where did you two go?'

We disengaged hastily. 'You'll have to put that pup into nappies!' I suggested wryly.

Gareth opened the door. 'Goodnight, Azalea. Goodnight Barbara,' he said, winking at me.

We slept well.

In the morning, everyone in the coach seemed anxious to get to the train on time. Except Wemys whom we watched warily, despite his mild, friendly manner. It was hard to erase from our minds the thought that he might be a murderer, and capable of striking again.

The train journey went smoothly, and we arrived in Venice. Once out of the station we stopped at an open-air restaurant, where we were upset and angry to see a waiter kicking a hungry dog out of the precincts of his dining room. To placate Azalea, who would have started a minor riot, we bought some slices of meat, and enticed the animal to eat. Not that it needed much enticing! Its appetite partly satisfied, it became interested in the bag Angelique travelled in, and we had to break up what might have developed into a beautiful friendship. More food followed to placate our consciences.

We spent the day sightseeing, struggling to keep an eye on Wemys, who seemed determined to explore every square inch of the city. We took countless pictures of the villas and the people, trying desperately to capture that cosmopolitan air you associate with Venice.

It was after midnight when we returned to the hotel, the Gran Palazzio just off the Grand Canal. We followed the others to the reception desk, admiring the black marble floor, the tessellated pavements, with here and there a handsome rug thrown down before couches which might have won the approval of a fashionable courtesan. We hovered in the background, particularly when Angelique threatened to make her debut performance. It was with relief that we followed a maid into the room allocated to us. As always, we first went to the windows, which in this case opened on to a small balcony, giving us a view up and down the narrow canal, and affording a glimpse of the Grande Canal. Our room was on the sixth floor, and we had a wonderful view out over the city and its twinkling lights.

The next morning, on a guided boat tour, Mimi read to us from her guide book: Peeling paint, the water-fretted woodwork – one recognises instantly that Venice is unique – a living port of quite fantastic beauty almost beyond description. The city is built on a hundred and eighteen islands, and the hundred and seventeen canals are crossed by four hundred bridges.'

Our minds boggled with such detail; we were too intent on looking at each palace as we passed – and they all seemed palaces to us. They were a feast of colour even where they had faded in the brilliant light, and the sinister black of the gondolas looked exactly right by contrast. We were entranced when a voluble gondolier got his craft in the way of a vaporetto, one of the quick motor-boats which ply up the main canals, and driven by men equally voluble. The exchange was impressive!

Azalea gave a squeal as she recognised the bridge we were approaching, and began reciting 'What news on the Rialto?' so dramatically that heads were turned, including those in a passing flat, barge-type boat. The captain looked at us as if we were quite mad.

We felt a little mad too. The people on the bridge waved to us and we found ourselves loving Venice. We thought we were going to sail past the Duomo of San Marco, but the engine of the motor changed to a lower note and stopped, and we floated into a side canal, up to the marble steps of our hotel. A tiny man in a smart uniform bowed so low to us that his magnificent hat almost touched his knees. A flood of Italian poured over us as he helped us to alight.

'Angelique is wiggling your all-purpose bag,' I hissed at Azalea.

'She does that when she wants to spend a penny.'

'Or twenty!' I groaned.

'We can always pretend she doesn't belong to us.'

'It won't work every time. I saw the look in the eye of the hall porter. It was mean. He suspects us already. He's going to watch us. I bet he's had a word with our maid already. She'll haunt us – ready to report anything at all.'

'Anyway, we're only here two days. Let's take every minute as it comes. If we're found out, we'll play the 'my Uncle owns the tour business' card. I'll hint he would take his trade elsewhere.'

Her expression became pitying. 'Then they're the ones who should look out!' She asked, 'Are you going to take notes about everything that goes on?'

'Every blessed thing, starting with the old goat at the door. I feel like a proper Pepys.'

'I will say this for your Uncle Charles. He doesn't stint on the hotels. Apart from the 'authentic olde worlde' ones that I'm not sure about.'

'Nice of you to notice, my dear,' Charles said joining us.

'Thank you again for allowing me to come along.'

'Nonsense Miss Dunbar, You've earned your keep. Wouldn't mind having you around to help out all the time.' This statement produced a condition rarely associated with Azalea: she was at a loss for words.

Gareth had disappeared, and as we looked around, we realized Wemys had too. Funny, we hadn't seen much of my uncle either during the trip. I was just about to ask him about that when I turned around to find him gone too. 'Well, I like that,' I muttered. 'Where have they all gone?' Colin joined us, fresh from the gift shop. 'Where's Gareth?' I asked.

'He'll be following Wemys, won't he?' Colin beamed. 'Oh, I've a good idea, by the way! I could have my meals at different times and look after the pup while you eat in peace.'

'Oh Colin, how thoughtful you are! Perhaps we can do that sometime when she's restless. But perhaps she'll be tired by dinner time, and no problem.'

Angelique tired? We all felt worn down to our ankles within two hours. Venetian pavements are hard and there are (cunningly) no seats, except those temptingly displayed outside cafes. Prices are high – especially those in the vicinity of San Marco which seems to be the biggest tourist attraction, despite the other magnificent churches.

'It's too much,' groaned Azalea as we collapsed onto the steps of a bridge and the pup tactfully retired behind a brimming dustbin, one of three which stood in an untidy row awaiting the attentions of the men who emptied them. By boat? Everything and everyone seemed to be carried by boat.

Even coffins?

I watched Azalea make a lightning sketch of a fat tourist who was bargaining furiously over the price of a canal trip with a pirate out of Gilbert and Sullivan. The pirate won: surely she could not expect him to reduce his fare when she was equal to two women, two magnificent creatures – here he kissed his fingers explosively – who would be the crowning glory of any man's life? Grinning happily, she plunged aboard, making the boat rock alarmingly, but with a few deft strokes, he avoided the other craft and shot out into the main stream. I heard Azalea sigh with pleasure, her aching feet forgotten for the moment.

As two policemen strolled in our direction, Colin said out of the side of his mouth, 'Police.' Angelique disappeared abruptly into the bag.

'Better move,' I directed. 'I saw a gorgeous, mandarin silk dress in a shop window. Do you think we could find it again? Might as well keep moving if we're to find Gareth and Wemys.'

'And Uncle Charles,' Colin added.

Azalea piped up, 'Going to squander all your commission?'

As we wended our way, we presently discovered we had mislaid Colin, who had stayed behind to look in the window of a camera shop. The crowds milled past us, gradually forcing us to continue or our way, and after half an hour we found the dress shop in which I was interested. I went in – and came out almost in one movement...

'You look stunned!' Azalea observed in fascination. When I told her the price of the dress she looked as stunned as I felt. 'You could make one for a tenth of that!' she added. 'I saw some marvellous brocade back there.'

Feeling excited, we hared back across the bridge into the market and spent some blissful minutes choosing the silk – a length for Azalea and a length for myself. The price was so reasonable that we also bought ourselves a printed silk blouse each. Thrilled with our bargains, we made our way back across the Rialto to a cafe on the pavement, where we ordered some ice cream – mainly for Angelique's benefit, though it was heavenly to take the weight off our twitching leg muscles. We chose a table well under the striped canvas awning and gave the pup her freedom, also taking the opportunity to write a few postcards.

'I seem to remember passing a post box near here.' I said.

'Can I stay here,' Azalea begged. 'I'll watch your parcels for you. And watch for Colin too.'

I had just dispatched my post cards when I spotted Wemys dressed as a waiter, ducking out of a doorway into a side alley. I moved through the crowds and watched as he darted down another alley. Naturally I followed him.

He was dressed as a waiter in rusty black and carried a tray with a covered dish on one hand. Deftly he skimmed in and out of the crowds milling about the narrow thoroughfares, showing no hesitation in his choice of direction.

I blinked my eyes against the sunshine. Was it someone who looked like Wemys? And yet that walk ... No two men, however much alike, could have an identical gait. I felt my head grow hot and my mouth run dry. Where was Gareth? Had he lost him? Was this the crucial moment when Wemys hoped to disappear so that he might hand over the painting, a new Rembrandt to be given to a marvelling world?

Almost without volition, I started to follow him, keeping the trolley of goods between us until it turned off at a tangent, and then dodging from doorway to doorway, managing to keep him in sight. I was soon out of breath for his speed was unusual, and he glanced back only before he turned a corner. Anticipating this I stepped out of sight, guessing that if Gareth had lost him, he would be in despair – the whole object of his chase lost. Once, having left Wemys' hands, the picture's ownership could never be proved. As I realised the crowds were thinning out, I began to feel scared. Was Wemys aware of me and leading me into a trap? He seemed very, sure of himself as he darted down the labyrinthine passageways.

Some children stared at me; I smiled at them as I edged round their pitch, hoping I'd be able to find my way back again to where I'd started. Though I knew I was becoming confused. I tried to imprint landmarks on my brain.

Distracted, I lost Wemys. I entered a kind of courtyard and there was no sign of him. What to do now? Lungs labouring, I considered the prospects. The buildings, which were several storeys high, and which closed out much of the sunlight, were on three sides, the canal making the fourth boundary of the yard. Unless Wemys had a boat waiting, he must surely have gone into one of the houses. Two of the three doors proved to be locked or bolted. The third, larger door, which had a smaller aperture cut into its massive timber, also seemed immovable. I imagined Wemys watching me from a window, laughing.

Pausing to consider my options, I was startled by a lean, grey cat which slithered, flattened, under the larger door. Seeing me, it shot up the tree, mewing plaintively. As I walked to the edge of the canal I saw what had been concealed – a narrow, walled path which led to another path serving the front of the villas. A burst of music came from somewhere along the canal but the houses themselves seemed deserted, and many of the shutters were closed, giving the whole area a feeling of dereliction.

If Wemys had crossed the bridge he could be anywhere by now. This part of Venice was not new to him; he had proved that by the speed of his progress. My best plan was to retrace my steps and find Gareth. By now, Azalea would have given me up for lost and returned to the hotel. I had almost reached the place where the children were playing when I was almost swept off my feet by Gareth.

He looked physically dishevelled, fed-up and utterly furious.

'Thank heavens!' he said but I knew his concern was not for me. 'Have you seen Wemys?'

'Yes, I was following. I lost him. Sorry, but he went too fast.'

'I've lost him myself, damn him!' He released my arm, which I felt might be bruised for some time. 'Can you show me the last place you saw him?'

'I'll try.' As we walked hurriedly along I asked, 'What happened to you?''

'A couple of thugs set on me in a café. In the excitement, Wemys faded out. Luckily I met Pansy and Daisy Watford and they said they'd seen Wemys darting down a street with a tray.'

'There are so many of us about it's a wonder if he wasn't seen by someone. Are you hurt?'

'No. At least, not as much as they are.' I assumed he meant the thugs, not the Watfords.

After a couple of mistakes, I found the courtyard with the tree, and pointed out the passage along the embankment. 'He could have reached the bridge but I feel he's in one of the houses. He disappeared so quickly, he must have gone through one of the gates.' An idea shook me. 'Of course – the cat.'

'What cat?'

'Wemys disturbed the cat in crossing the inner yard – it came out from under the big gate nearest the canal. I suppose the main entrance faces the canal. What are you going to do?'

'I don't know.' He looked as abstracted as he sounded; I forbore asking questions.

As we waited, a figure loomed up against the light from the canal side and we were as astonished to see George Lonsties as he was obviously disturbed to see us.

His bulky figure came to an abrupt halt. 'Fancy seeing you,' he said feebly and then, deciding to play it cool, gave a playful leer – Father Christmas at his most ingratiating. 'Have I interrupted something?'

'Did you notice which way Wemys went?' Gareth asked, almost disinterestedly. A shuttered look closed Lonsties' jovial features. 'No. Still sleuthing? He must be fed to the back teeth now. What's he done that you can't let him out of your sight? He's a right to make a little on the side with that talent of his. Clever bloke, Wemys.'

'Very. Are you sure you don't know what he's up to?' Gareth's compelling gaze made Lonsties shift uneasily. 'He's in there.'

Lonsties shrugged. 'If you know, why ask me?'

'I think we'll call on him. It should be interesting seeing inside a Venetian house.'

'Looks like a warehouse to me,' Lonsties said, not giving way as Gareth approached, indicating that he wished to reach the front entrance via the bridge.

'Do you mind?' Gareth said and was preparing to shove past when Lonsties' arm shot out and they glared at each other close range.

'I've had about enough of you,' Lonsties began, breathing hard. 'Some of us are trying to enjoy our holiday.'

'Then why don't you go off and enjoy it?' Gareth said pleasantly. 'Do you mind removing your arm? It's bothering me.'

I heard the cat mewing again and glanced in the direction of the tree. A second later, as I looked back, I saw George Lonsties flying towards the canal where he arrived with a terrific splash.

'Oh no!' I ran down the stone steps near the bridge to see if I could reach Lonsties. He came up spluttering and cursing, and threshing about so wildly that he went under again immediately. Wildly I looked about; a motor boat was coming, driven by a man who had taken in the situation at a glance. Somehow he did not appear to think it was serious, for he was grinning widely. He made me think of Petar Vratmic and the fortune in his tooth. As he reached Lonsties, who was flapping his arms, he dragged him aboard, a moment later steering the boat into the side and carrying his burden to the handsome entrance of the nearest house. When I saw the sacks of cement in the boat, I realised why Lonsties' weight caused him such little concern.

'We must get him into the house,' I said in Italian, indicating the building which had intrigued us so much. If it were a mistake, and Wemys was not there, apologies would be in order to the inhabitants. One could expect some aid to be given to the stricken. And Lonsties looked very stricken as he floundered and gasped and retched on the marble steps.

The man with the boat pounded on the great door until it opened a few inches; there was a rapid exchange in Italian, with much shrugging and gesticulating, until the boatman, losing patience, almost pushed the dripping Lonsties inside. The door was slammed almost before I could assemble my wits.

Seeing my dismay, the boatman shrugged apologetically. 'Scusi. I am ashamed.'

'No, I'm very grateful. It was an unfortunate accident but this man is not my friend.'

He smiled winningly. 'I see. Then which way do you wish to go? My boat is at your disposal. I am going up to San Marco. A little job there at a cafe.'

I told him I must stay and look for some other members of my party (Where had Gareth got to? I wondered). Still grinning, the man steered his boat expertly into the canal and began to sing in ballad-style, fixing me with his admiring gaze. The song appeared to afford the man great enjoyment. I understood the gist of it and felt flattered, despite the gravity of my situation. As I ran to the rear of the house, Gareth was nowhere to be seen so I returned to the front and pounded on the door in the heavy manner which had been so successful with the boatman.

Presently I heard the slither of slippered feet along the passage and when I judged the owner to be listening behind the door I seized the knocker and made such a shattering noise that I imagined the inmate must be wincing with shock. It brought results. Slowly the door opened a few inches and an incredibly old man without a tooth in his head mumbled at me.

'I wish to see my friend who has just been brought in after falling in the canal,' I said clearly.

The old man gave several reasons why I couldn't come in. Ignoring him I focused past his skinny shoulder and he turned to see what had alarmed me. In that instant I slipped past him and into a corridor which smelled of damp and mice. Or perhaps they were rats?

After a few pungent remarks the old man spread his hands in resignation and pointed to a door at the end of the corridor. I took a step in its direction, was about to thank him when I saw he was shuffling away to the handsome stairs which led upwards

– presumably to tell someone in authority of my arrival. It was too late now to ponder the wisdom of my behaviour; I could only rely on my wits to help me.

Dashing down the corridor, I pushed open the door indicated and saw it was sparsely furnished with a bed, a table, a chair and a stove, all of which promised scant comfort. Lying on the bed, covered with a blanket which once might have been brightly-coloured there was a bulky form.

'Mr Lonsties,' I began, starting forward in relief. 'I can't tell you how sorry I was about your accident.'

When he didn't stir I thought he might have drifted into unconsciousness and lifted the blanket from his head. And was met by a disagreeable and all too familiar feral smile. It was Hyena Face.

'My little love!' he said in Italian. 'How thoughtful of you to call. Do you truly love me so much?' And with that he was off the bed and had both my arms behind my back. 'But you are so nice, and I know you are about to be even nicer.'

I started to panic, wanting only to wrench free. But I knew instinctively I had to think. This time I must not allow myself to freeze! He pushed me back on the bed and I fell, drawing my knees up protectively before me. I caught him in the stomach, knocking the breath out of him. Then he slapped me hard across the face. Dazed but still fighting him, I felt my right wrist coming free. So did he. He slapped me again, and that's when everything went black.

I woke up a few minutes later, for he was just finishing tying my hands together and my ankles to the bed posts. I pulled against the rope on my ankles to free myself and he lunged at me. Squeezing my face hard in one claw-like hand, he threatened me: 'You make one noise and I will kill your boyfriend.' He registered the fear in my eyes. 'A lucky man, no?' This last was said in English, and he found it very funny.

'You have only an hour at the most to wait. They've rented the place for a time only. And I'm to have a cut of the profits too. Won't that be pleasant? When they've gone I'll come back and we'll have fun.'

He threw himself on me, and I bashed his front teeth with the top of my head. His hand flew to his mouth to dab the blood from a cut lip. He looked up. Someone was calling him. I drew in my breath to scream when suddenly everything went black the second time.

When I came to I was alone. Like any sensible girl I gnawed on the knot tied around my wrists, trying very hard not to think about the rats I saw scurrying past the door to this room. Once my hands were free it was nothing to free my legs as well. I saw a pile of junk laying on the beat-up dresser in the corner and looked for a weapon – a bottle opener maybe. Anything!

But what I did find was my mobile and a snub-nose revolver. I turned on the mobile, selected SILENT, and prayed that the revolver held bullets and that I would be able to figure out how to use it.

'Got my weapon, and my mobile still holds a charge. Time to even up the score,' I whispered under my breath.

I crept quietly over to the door, revolver in hand. The weight of the thing was lighter than I expected, but honestly, I couldn't wait to put it down once I got out of here. Holding it frightened me, but being mauled by Hyena Face frightened me even more. No more little victim me.

I was just turning the door knob to take a peak and see if the coast was clear when a heavy pair of boots scraped softly, and stopped just outside the door. The revolver wavered in my hand. I flattened myself against the wall as the door opened, hiding me.

'You in here, love?' a man with an Australian accent, whispered. Washed-out brown eyes in a strong, tanned face, topped by a thick mop of brown hair, peeked at me around the door. I held the revolver in front of me.

'There now. Want me to take that for you, Miss?' I shook my head.

'Interpol, Miss. Sandy O'Rourke. Would you mind lowering that? There, that's the ticket. I followed two men here earlier. Perhaps you've seen them? Older gent. Short. Funny walk. Another – dark hair, good-looking – following him.'

I was trying to place Mr O'Rourke. He looked like the man in Hellbrunn, at St. Michael's. But I never really got a good look at that one.

I decided to answer. 'Wemys. The one with the funny walk.' My voice cracked as I whispered back. My throat was dry, and I tried swallowing. 'The younger man was my friend. He's trying to catch Wemys. Wemys stole a painting.'

'I see. Well, you want to get outa here?'

I shook my head.

'I think you ought to get to safety, Miss. Things here are about to get quite messy.'

'No, I want to help my friend!' I insisted.

'Look, I really don't have the time to argue! Come on then. But when I tell you to get down, get down. Got that?' I nodded.

'Then we've got to get upstairs without being seen. The man who tied you up is in the basement with the old man. They're biding their time until they can get their money and lock up, and then ...'

'Yes, I heard him.'

'Let's go then!' he urged.

I followed him, creeping quietly along the corridor, and then up the stairs.

As we gained the next floor O'Rourke quietly opened doors and peered inside, finding them mostly empty except for a candle or two, and in one room a pile of timber to effect repairs to the floor.

He halted suddenly and indicated that I should listen. Faintly, we heard voices coming, from a room nearby. We traced it to double doors which were close to the front staircase. He opened one of them a crack and we were able to see into what was an anteroom. The voices were louder but their owners were not visible. As we stepped into the anteroom I recognised Wemys' voice. He was answering the older man. There was something about the timbre that suggested age and authority. They were speaking in English, arguing. Wemys was wheedling. The older man sounded impatient.

'So many people involved! It is dangerous.'

'I told you, he is nothing. I had to make use of him to keep that private detective off my back. That guy thinks he's helping me avoid export taxes. He has no idea what we're doing.'

'Get rid of him as soon as you can. I do not like strangers in my affairs.'

Wemys chuckled. 'He's been paid and gone already – glad to. He was soaking wet. He's certainly earned his money today, getting the other fellow off my tail.'

Lonsties! No wonder he'd defended Wemys to Gareth and kept hanging around. He must have been eavesdropping for Wemys.

'You are sure you were unobserved?'

'Do you know what it has been like for me? Smuggling it out with umpteen people breathing down my neck all the time? You're sitting pretty,' grumbled Wemys.

'You've done well. I have no quarrel with you. I am grateful. You will also be paid.'

'Less than a quarter what it's worth.'

'There is a certain risk to me,' said the other man.

'It's a genuine Rembrandt,' Wemys pointed out.

'I'm not disputing that! I have had the report from our mutual friends in Split. Believe me, if you had tried to trick me over this deal you would not live long to enjoy it.'

'Pretty tough for an art dealer!'

'I appreciate your reputation for copying old masters. But I am satisfied this is genuine. I referred a moment ago to the risk of removing the top painting. It must look like a cleaning job. This alone will be a delicate operation and expensive. The person I employ is no fool – I shall have to buy his silence. It is not a matter of killing him after he has done the job – he is too useful to me. Besides, we are old comrades. We live for our art.' There was a thin sneer of laughter. 'Money is not everything when you are old. You wish to gaze upon and handle beautiful objects. It has always been an obsession with me. In my way, I have given much beauty to the world. My galleries are famous.'

Listening from the adjoining room, I wondered impatiently where Gareth was.

'And how will you find another Rembrandt when they are catalogued in every gallery in the world?' asked Wemys.

'Ah, it is simple. At my place in Florence I have many objects spoiled by the terrible floods. I am still cleaning and repairing. It will take me to the rest of my life. When I clean this old picture, I will discover that it is concealing something precious. I will find the original painting. When news reporters call, I will tell them the whole romantic story – of how I purchased it from a poor man many years ago – to help him. Oh, I shall enjoy telling such a story – and in a way it is true. I am helping you. What will you do with such a large sum of money?'

'I haven't got it yet,' Wemys answered pointedly. 'When I do, it will go to an off-shore bank account and I shall live off the interest, while I indulge myself in painting.'

'That is good. In time, I hope you will produce a masterpiece yourself. Who knows...?'

Wemys laughed. 'How did you manage to get so much cash?'

Ignoring the question, the other man went on: 'Here it is! You will please to put the picture on the table and I will place the money – so! We must trust each other for a little while. You have it with you?'

I was astonished at this last question. The other man was obviously acting purely on the word of his friends in Split. I couldn't resist peering through the curtains where they draped against the wall, and I found a hole through which I could see Wemys slide down his baggy trousers and unroll the canvas from around his right leg. Truly ingenious!

Wemys grabbed the money off the table in one hand, the other hand fumbling as he pulled up his trousers. The art dealer caressed the painting.

I made an involuntary sound and the art dealer turned in my direction.

The curtain was flung back before I could move, and I realized O'Rourke was gone.

Wemys dragged me into the larger room. 'Really, Miss Wills! You're very tiresome,' he began. 'What am I to do with you?'

I could have made several suggestions but I was too fascinated with the art dealer as he scampered out of the other door.

'He's going!' I said to Wemys indignantly.

'And good luck to him.' He pushed me, none too gently, into a chair. 'How did you get in? Who's with you?'

'Never mind about me. What about me asking you a few questions, Wemys! Did you kill Mike Radnin?'

'I'm not a killer! I'm not the violent type.'

'Really!'

'But whoever it was who killed that blackmailing snake did me a good turn,' he insisted.

'So he'd found where you had hidden the painting. And where was the hiding place?'

'Behind the metal luggage compartment.' He confirmed our earlier suspicions.

'How would you explain the money?' I asked.

'What money?'

'Putting the money in an off-shore bank! That should be easy to trace.'

He smiled benignly. 'Look, Miss Wills. You'll have to stay here for a few hours. It's your own fault. I must have time to make my getaway – isn't that the phrase? I'll tell someone to release you later.'

'Thank you very much. If it's any interest to you, there's a hyena downstairs who isn't to be trusted with women. He still thinks I am tied up and awaiting his attention.' I had let it slip; it was too late to recover it.

Wemys grabbed me by the arm threateningly. 'How did you get loose? Who's with you?'

'I freed myself. Your hyena friend was in a bit of hurry and didn't check his knots. I didn't realise George Lonsties was in your pay – or I wouldn't have been so concerned for him.'

'How much did you manage to overhear?'

I pulled my arms away from him, and was heading for the door when the revolver clattered to the ground. Neither of us was sure what to do. Then Wemys laughed, reaching for a bell push.

Suddenly I could hear feet racing up the front stairs, and Hyena Face burst into the room. I grabbed for the gun. It was his turn to be afraid. It was his gun.

Wemys said curtly, 'You're a fool to let her in. This is no part of our arrangement. Tie her up. You can do what you like with her when I've gone.'

'No, I don't think so, Wemys. If he tries for me, I'll shoot you first.' I could just see Hyena Face circling me out of the corner of my eye. I pointed the revolver directly at Wemys. When Hyena Face reached me, he went to knock the gun from my hand. But he was too late, and I was too close to miss; I winged Wemys in the wrist just before the gun fell. Wemys screamed.

Hyena Face was on me, his thumbs and fingers digging into me. He reached the bell pull, snatching it from the hook to tie my arms behind me. He leered in my face, his eyes boring into mine, drinking in my fear. Then I snapped. The top of my head broke one of his teeth, and I followed with a knee to his groin. He fell, tugging me after him. I landed a foot in his stomach and he released his grip. Shaking, adrenalin burning through me, I scrambled on the floor for the revolver. And when I found where it had been kicked under a musty window drape, it did not tremble in my hand. I held if very steady as I pointed it at Hyena Face's crotch.

'Move! I dare you.'

'You are too scared. A little girl.'

I fired a round into his thigh, exploding the bones through the skin and jeans. He stared at me, as if he couldn't believe it. I remember the smoke curling up from the burned denim fibres around the entry wound. 'Seem scared to you now?' But he didn't hear me. He had passed out.

Wemys screamed once more and ran for the door.

'Get a hold, mate,' O'Rourke said, blocking his escape. 'What's going on in here, Miss? You beat up all these men?' 'O'Rourke, you angel. Wemys here stole the painting and sold it to an old man, an art dealer. Did you hear that part? Anyway, Wemys found me listening and you'd disappeared. Where did you go by the way? This other guy is the one who tried to attack me. It's all right now. I guess I'm talking too much. I'm excited. Oh, I'm just dying to call my uncle.' Putting the gun down in front of me, I pulled the mobile out of my back pocket and started to dial. 'I wouldn't do that if I were you,' O'Rourke said soberly.

'Why not?' I asked innocently.

I looked up to find his pistol aimed at my temple. 'Well, well,' Gareth entered the room.

Finally! I wished he had been there to see me take out Hyena Face, and Wemys. He saw my pistol and picked it up. 'What's going on? A party? How nice! I've a few more guests.' He gestured to someone out in the hallway and Wemys came in, leaning heavily on the old art dealer.

'Drop it or the girl gets it,' snarled O'Rourke.

'Isn't that a bit of a cliché?' But Gareth obeyed, placing the gun carefully on the floor again.

'Shut up, both of you.' O'Rourke went towards the table and kicked out a chair. 'Sit down. You, art dealer! Tie up the girl and her boyfriend.' He kicked out the other chair from the table but the old man suddenly dived for the window.

At that point, the door burst open. 'Hey Babs! You in here?' It was Azalea.

The distraction was all Gareth and I needed. Gareth went for O'Rourke, and I dived for the disputed pistol on the floor. Wemys started to run out the other door.

'No you don't.' I shouted, pointing the barrel into his chest.

The art dealer looked back for Wemys, and, seeing his predicament, simply said, 'Adieu,' and dropped out the window. There was a soft splash, followed by a lot of cursing.

Azalea stood shocked, hands on her cheeks, too stunned to take it all in. Her eyes moved about the room. Angelique barked fiercely at the man sprawled on the floor as he tried to stand up. 'Hyena Face!' Azalea gasped with recognition, and kicked him back down onto the floor where Angelique bit his trouser leg and wouldn't let go. 'That's for Babs,' she said and kicked him again.

O'Rourke's gun fell to the floor and Gareth made a dive for it. O'Rourke tackled him. I fired a warning shot into the air. 'That's enough.'

Both men froze. Gareth saw that the revolver in my hand was trained on O'Rourke and he smiled, panting.

He took a business card out of his shirt pocket and handed it to me. 'Call Dubci. This is his mobile. And I'll take that.'

I reluctantly handed the Hyena's revolver over to him.

EPILOGUE

Future Bound

We soon realized that our hotel in Venice didn't approve of Angelique. Yet really, she had been partly responsible for the capture of the thieves that had stolen the last Rembrandt canvas. And that had happened in their city no less, making them famous! Now all they could think about were rules and regulations. Some people can be so stuffy. We ignored them.

Reporters came from all over the world awaiting news of the outcome of the criminals and the future of the canvas. Several art museums had already shown interest in acquiring it. For now, it was to be held in the gallery's royal vaults until its provenance could be traced.

We sat on the promenade of St. Mark's eating sandwiches and drinking warm Italian beer from the can. None of us minded, least of all Angelique. Uncle Charles sat beside me, feeding her bits of bread and cheese followed by beer trickling slowly, drip by drip, into her mouth. He looked up at me sheepishly. 'Well, she is a heroine after all.'

'Here, here!' we chimed in – Colin, Azalea, Gareth and I. Funny how things end up.

'So, what happens now?' I asked Gareth.

'The Italian government will take over and work with Scotland Yard to determine the extent of international involvement. Wemys still isn't saying much, except that he'll never paint again.'

'That is sad,' I said. 'But he would have left me for Hyena Face with no compunction whatsoever. Who was that creepy guy anyway?'

'He was Wemys' second. He's in hospital and will be taken to jail once his leg has been operated on. He and Wemys will both stand trial here. There were other charges against them. They'll be in prison a long time.'

I didn't feel guilty. I was proud of myself. I'd defended myself against a thug, and I'd won. Too bad for him.

'Good.' Uncle Charles was now carefully wiping Angelique's chin. 'All I want to know is how many times those two used my tours to conduct their smuggling business. Any word on that from the police or your people, Gareth?'

'None as yet. Of course he'd be stupid to own up. This wasn't a first offence.'

'True enough,' Colin added. 'Now who was that Australian man, O'Rourke. Rival gang or something?'

'Something. You see, he was in on Radnin's blackmail scheme. And when he heard Radnin had landed Wemys and Hyena Face as clients, so to speak, he didn't just want the hush money. He wanted the whole package. He killed Radnin to keep him off his back, and was going to steal the painting and the art dealer's money too.'

'I suppose the art dealer was lucky, even though he was arrested for hiring Wemys and receiving the canvas. At least he wasn't killed. Chances are he would have been if he hadn't got out when he did. But what was Wemys waiting for, talking and talking up in that room?'

'Me,' Gareth answered simply. 'No, it's true, Barbara. Hyena Face was to kill me or bring me to Wemys and then kill me. O'Rourke just happened to be there to steal the painting and the money too. All in all, I'm glad you showed up when you did.'

'Are you?' I was being coy.

'Yes, I am. You saved my life.'

'Hmmm.'

Lea who had been very quiet, and studying her toes, said sadly, 'Tour 78HOE' has gone on without us. And I'm a little sad. I wanted to go to Mr Lonsties' and Miss Daisy's engagement supper tonight at the Avogoria.'

'No thanks,' I retorted 'He lied for that Wemys. And I'd bet my Prada sandals he planted that gun in Gareth's room. He's lucky I don't throw him in that canal myself.'

Gareth winked at me. 'She could do it too. But I appreciate the effort.'

I punched him in the arm for laughing at me.

'Ow!'

'Well,' said Uncle Charles. 'We'll have to catch up the coach tour home after the police are finished questioning us. We'll have to fly back for the trial anyway.'

We stood, brushing crumbs from our laps. Uncle Charles turned to Colin. 'What are your plans for the future?'

'I have lots of studying and training and I'm starting work in a new upmarket restaurant this autumn. I m hoping I will still be able to see Azalea though – if she wants to.' He smiled wistfully in her direction.

'Azalea!' Uncle Charles turned to her. 'What if I offered you a position at my firm? The pay won't be much at first, but it'll earn you your bread and butter while you're waiting for your painting career to establish itself, as I'm sure it will one day.'

Azalea looked enigmatic but accepted the offer with alacrity and a wonderful smile. It gave her options and a way out with Colin when the time came. She would be based in London and he would be in Manchester so distance would work its course on them. Still, that was a way off yet so she basked in his adoration throwing him a lovely look.

Uncle Charles suddenly caught the eye of an elegantly-dressed Italian woman at a nearby table. He sauntered over to engage her in conversation

Gareth drew me aside. The morning sky cast a rosy glow over the carved steps of St. Mark's. He took my hand.

'Now then Mr Findlatter – don't get too many ideas!' I said. 'You're dealing with a fully-fledged member of Maddens Magic Carpet Tours now. Got my responsibilities!' I tried to sound serious. 'A bit of fun, though – I'm up for that. Even a lot of fun!'

'Suits us both then. Why don't we just take a few days to relax and see what develops?'

'No promises. Okay?'

'Okay by me!'

'Babs?' Uncle Charles called over to us, holding up his mobile. 'Just received a call. Problems on the Spanish tour. Need someone there very soon. You and Azalea up for it? Means packing up and setting off soon! I'll take care of my new best four-legged friend till you get back!' He winked at the Italian woman and bent down to give Angelique a tickle. 'All right with you, Lea?' He gave her one of his most charming grins. Azalea smiled back coyly.

I turned to Gareth and said, 'That still leaves tonight.'